A Farewell to Legs

AN AARON TUCKER MYSTERY

Jeffrey Cohen

bancroft
press

Published by Bancroft Press ("Books that enlighten")
P.O. Box 65360, Baltimore, MD 21209
800-637-7377
410-764-1967 (fax)
www.bancroftpress.com

Cover and interior design: Tammy Sneath Grimes, Crescent Communications
www.tsgcrescent.com • 814.941.7447

Author photo: Frank Dougherty

ISBN 1-890862-29-0 (cloth)
ISBN 1-890862-34-7 (paper)
LCCN 2003108324

Printed in the United States of America

First Edition

1 3 5 7 9 10 8 6 4 2

To
The Brotherhood
of the Tray

PROLOGUE

Cheri (pronounced "She-REE") Braxton got out of bed and walked to the bathroom door, not bothering to cover her naked body with a sheet, the way they do in the movies. She'd never understood that: two people have just spent the night going at it like sex has just been invented, and the next morning, they're always covering up, as if they hadn't just spent ten hours looking at each other's good parts.

The guy in her bed, Louis (pronounced "Louis") Gibson, pushed back the few strands of hair left on his head and admired the view as Cheri walked to the bathroom. He smiled as he always did, and it was convincing, ingratiating, and emotionless.

"Baby," he said, "I like nothing better than watching you walk away."

She stopped, turned, and modeled her form, giving him a good long look. "What's the matter, Louie?" she asked, her voice a disgusting drawl she thought sounded cute. "You don't like seeing me walk toward you?"

"Of course I do," he said flatly, dismissing her. "I was trying to be romantic, and you spoiled it."

She harrumphed, and walked into the bathroom. Cheri had intended to splash some cold water on her face and pee, but if that was the kind of attitude he was going to have, Louie could just lie there and wait while she took a long hot shower. She turned on the water in the tub and opened the medicine cabinet. Might as well brush her teeth, too.

Louis put his hands behind his head and lay back on the pillow. This thing with Cheri was already starting to get old, he thought. Six weeks, and she was pissing him off as often as his wife. At least his wife had waited until they were married a couple of years before she started complaining that he wasn't romantic enough. So he'd gotten her pregnant again, and then she had so much to do watching the boys that she didn't have time to nag about his ignoring goddamn Valentine's Day.

Cheri, though, was another story. She'd broken the land speed record for annoying Louis. A nice ass—he'd certainly admit she had that—but she had a mouth on her, too, and who needed that in a mistress? Mistresses were for sex, for chrissakes. If he wanted backtalk, he could stay home. It was a good thing this relationship would be over soon.

Louis smiled as he lay there. If he wanted, he could find six or seven other girls within a week—exotic ones, too. Not white bread bores like Cheri Braxton. Life was good these days. The right people were getting elected, and that meant contributions were pouring in. He had his pick of the women he knew, and he had plenty of money. More than anyone knew. What else did a man need?

Louis closed his eyes and smiled contentedly.

Cheri stayed in the shower as long as she could, until she couldn't think of any other body parts that needed cleaning. And the longer she stayed under the hot water, the more steamed she got.

Who the hell did this joker think she was? A $40 whore he could call whenever he felt like it, screw however many times he could that night (which was usually once), then turn and leave and not call until he got horny again? Why not leave money on the dresser when he left? She had a college degree, after all! She worked for a government agency, and had the potential to move up into a managerial position. She didn't have to put up with this from a guy 15 years older than she was!

She got out of the shower and put on a terrycloth robe hanging from a hook on the back of the bathroom door. Screw him! It wasn't like she loved the little jerk. She didn't even like him. But he had powerful friends, and she had ambition. Still, no job she could get in this government was worth having to put up with him. She could find somebody else to screw, and maybe even enjoy it.

Cheri opened the robe and looked at herself in the full-length mirror on the back of the door. Not bad at all for 27. Everything was still where Nature had put it. Gravity hadn't started its inevitable pull to the ground. She looked damn good, if she did say so herself. Better than she'd been giving herself credit for. Better than anybody old Louie out there would see again, for a long, long time.

That was that, then. It didn't even take much courage to decide. She'd just go out there right now and tell Louis this was the last time they'd see each other. Let him find somebody else to watch walking away from the bed.

She tossed back her damp hair in a defiant gesture, left the robe open (so he could see what he'd be missing), and marched out to give Louis his marching orders.

The only thing that stopped her was the stunned, amazed expression on his face. That, and the kitchen knife sticking out of his chest.

Part I:
The
Lizard

Chapter One

In retrospect, it all started with the lizard.

"A gecko?" I said. "You want to give an eight-year-old girl a gecko?"

I stared into my bedroom closet with what I'm sure was the same expression Dr. Livingstone had assessing the Nile for the first time, a combination of absolute wonderment and complete confusion. My wife Abby stood behind me, doing her very best not to snicker.

"They make very low-maintenance pets," she said in a soothing tone, as if she were addressing a potentially dangerous mental patient. "You don't have to walk them, you very rarely have to clean the aquarium and they never make any noise. Try the blue one."

She indicated a royal blue Gap t-shirt I'd been avoiding. I turned to her, surprised, and pointed at it. Yes, Abby nodded, that one.

"I can wear a t-shirt to a high school reunion? And why, exactly, does our daughter even *need* a pet that looks like it escaped from The Land That Time Forgot?"

Abby smiled tolerantly, once again secure in the knowledge that I would, indeed, collapse into a heap of quivering jelly without her. On her way to the bedroom closet door, she pressed by me (and I did very little to get out of her way, thus necessitating as much pressing as possible).

"Leah loves animals. I want to encourage her to develop

that interest, and this is the easiest way to start her on her way. Don't worry—you won't have to do anything."

"Famous last words."

My wife, befitting a woman of her dignity and accomplishment, stuck her tongue out at me. She leaned into the closet (we have a lean-in closet in our bedroom, meaning that it's roughly the size of a small refrigerator, so all you can do is lean in) and came out with the blue T-shirt, a pair of black jeans I actually fit into, and my black sport jacket, which is made of something that approximates suede without actually harming any animals to produce it. Abby laid the clothes out on the bed. "There," she said.

"My Hollywood scriptwriter disguise," I said, nodding. On the rare occasions that one of my screenplays has generated enough interest for me to actually meet with a producer (and that is upwards of once), I have worn this exact ensemble. I began to take off my hideous flannel shirt (with only two holes in it) and my worn-to-the-white jeans (three holes, but two are in the knees).

"Certainly," Abby said. "Show your old classmates how cool you are."

"Cool, my love, is something I've never been able to pull off successfully."

"Fake it," she said. I grunted at that, and considered the question of the lizard again.

"So let's suppose—and I want to stress that *suppose*—that I agree to this lizard thing. What does Jurassic Junior eat?"

It's so rare I get to see my wife blush. As with everything else, it becomes her, but it's unusual that she'd be flustered enough to let it show. I braced myself. She mumbled something.

"What?"

"WORMS!" she shouted, unintentionally, I presume. "It eats…worms. And they have to be…live."

"Live? As in alive? We're asking our eight-year-old to feed one living thing to another living thing as a character-building experience?" During this exchange, I had managed to don my entire screenwriter disguise, minus the jacket (which would make me sweat no matter what the weather, and so was best left for later).

"Well, she's perfectly okay with it," Abby said as I sat down again to put on my classy sneakers. "Melissa has one..."

That's all I needed to know—the discussion was over. Leah and her friend Melissa are actually the same person, but you need two bodies to harness all their combined energy. They're constantly in motion, constantly talking, and constantly *together*, so whatever one does, the other must certainly do. There's no arguing with Melissa. Ever.

"Where do we get these worms?" I sighed. "Do we have to dig in the back yard? Remember, we have no, um, soil in the back yard."

"The pet store. Then we keep them in the refrigerator."

"The same refrigerator where we keep *our* food?" She nodded, and I think actually looked a little nauseated.

I stood up and put an arm over my wife's shoulder. "Is there any power on heaven or earth that can stop this?"

"No."

"Any chance I can get some sex out of saying yes?" I figured it was worth a shot.

"Not tonight. I'll be asleep long before you get home."

From downstairs, I could hear the doorbell ring, followed by Leah's shrill shriek. "It's Uncle Mahoney!" Abby and I started wearily toward the stairs.

"All in all," I told her, "this night is not starting out terribly well."

Chapter Two

"Remind me why we're going to this thing."

Jeff Mahoney, all six-foot-whatever of him, was scrunched into the passenger seat of my 1997 Saturn four-door. He had pushed the seat back as far as it went, and still his knees were threatening to hit his chin.

"It'll be fun," I said unconvincingly. "We haven't seen these people in twenty-five years."

"And we didn't like them *then*," he reminded me.

"You're not going in with a terrific attitude," I pointed out.

"And you expected... what?"

I grumbled something under my breath and shoved a cassette into the car radio. John Mayer. *Room for Squares*. He grimaced, but didn't say anything. To him, any music recorded after 1979 is suspect.

He was right, of course, although not about the music. There was no reason for me to have anticipated anything but a sour attitude from him, since it had been my idea for us to go to our 25th year high school reunion. Overcome by a sudden, inexplicable wave of nostalgia, I had responded to the invitation in my mail (along with the inevitable bills) by convincing him that we would spend the evening drinking and making fun of our former classmates. Well, *he* could drink, anyway. I'd appointed myself designated driver. The major effect of alcohol on my system is to make me sleepy.

I don't know what it was that convinced *me* to go. At

Bloomfield, NJ's prime example of a high school in the mid-1970s, students divided themselves into the usual cliques: the jocks, the cheerleaders (who existed mostly to sleep with the jocks, thus serving to doubly tweak the rest of us), the brains (this was years before nerds were invented, and decades before computer geeks), and the remedial students.

And then there was Us. Myself, Mahoney, Friedman, Wharton, and McGregor. We were a group because we didn't fit in with any of the other groups—we fell between the cracks. And we got along because we expected nothing of each other, and got exactly that. Besides Mahoney, who was still my closest friend, I hadn't seen the others in at least 10 years.

So maybe it was that kind of reunion I had been trying to manufacture. I'd blackmailed Mahoney into going by telling him I wouldn't go without him, and had emailed Bobby Fox, who was coordinating the reunion (and who was still, at 43, calling himself "Bobby"), to be sure Friedman, Wharton, and McGregor would be there. But I hadn't told Mahoney, and I didn't know why.

Now, he listened thoughtfully to the music, wrinkled his brow, and turned it down a notch. "This guy's not bad," he said. "But he's never going to replace Jim Croce."

"I'm sorry. I left my Bad Company tape back home in my white double-knit leisure suit."

Mahoney grinned. "Somebody get up on the wrong side of the bed this morning?"

"I can't remember why I wanted to go to this thing, either," I admitted.

"It's because Stephanie Jacobs is going to be there," he said matter-of-factly. "You've had the hots for her since Gerald Ford was president."

Stephanie Jacobs! I hadn't even thought of her. Would she be at this miserable wing ding?

"*Everybody* had the hots for Stephanie Jacobs," I reminded him. "And when I say 'everybody...'"

When Mahoney and I were seventeen, all of us considered Stephanie Jacobs the ideal woman. Built so that she looked naked even in a down parka, Stephanie was rumored to have caused cardiac arrest in middle-aged men of, say, 30 or so.

"Not everybody," said Mahoney.

"Your memory fails you," I told him. "I remember a time you gave Stephanie Jacobs a ride home in the Mustang, and you talked about nothing else for six weeks."

"Bullshit," he said. "It was only four weeks."

"Nonetheless. You had just as many hots for Stephanie Jacobs as everybody else."

His eyes got a little dreamy. "That Mustang was a great car," he said.

I decided to pretend he hadn't spoken. "Anyway, she's not the reason I wanted to go tonight," I protested as I pulled into the parking lot of the luxurious Vacation Inn of Carteret, New Jersey. "I hadn't thought once of her before you mentioned her name right now."

"Sure," said Mahoney. "You just knew she liked me better, anyway."

"Uh-huh."

We got out of the car after I parked, which made sense. If we'd gotten out before I'd parked, the car might very well have run over our feet and hurt us, and possibly destroyed property at the Inn. It's important to follow certain procedures.

I led the way toward the door marked "Banquet Room," which was sure to be an overstatement. And about 20 feet from the door, I stopped dead in my tracks.

Mahoney, who came close to barreling into me and causing permanent damage, slammed on his heels. "What the hell is wrong with you?" he yelped.

"I can't go in. Let's go to the movies or something. This was a bad idea."

He laughed. "It'll be *fun*! We haven't seen these people in *twenty-five years*!" he said.

"Yeah, and we didn't..."

"Why, Aaron Tucker," purred a voice behind me that was laced with sex and nostalgia. "I hear you solve mysteries."

Mahoney and I both spun around and muttered something in the tradition of Jackie Gleason's classic "homina, homina, homina."

Stephanie Jacobs, in a dress covering considerably less than a down parka would, stood maybe five feet away.

She smiled a satisfied smile that indicated she knew exactly what effect her voice would have on us. On *me*, really, since she wasn't looking at Mahoney at all. Her deep blue eyes bored into me, and I'm pretty sure left a hole in the back of my head. Stephanie looked just as good as she had at 18, which was entirely unfair of her.

Maybe I hadn't come just to see Friedman, Wharton and... what's-their-names, after all.

Chapter
Three

It took me a few moments to regain the power of speech, and a few more to look Stephanie in the eye, something her plunging neckline wasn't helping me achieve.

"I don't solve mysteries," I said when English once again became my primary language. "I'm a soldier on the bottom rung of the literary battleground." It sounded good at the time. I have no idea what it meant, since battlegrounds don't generally have rungs, but there was no time to think of that.

"That's not what I heard," she said, still not taking her eyes off me. I thought Mahoney might begin doing the tarantella behind my back just to get her attention. "I heard you found out who killed some woman in your town a while back."

Well, therein lies a tale. And one I have told elsewhere, so I'll spare you the details. I decided, in this case, to be modest.

"Oh, I was just working on a story and got lucky," I said.

"You were lucky I was backing you up," grumbled Mahoney, "or you might not be here today."

His booming voice finally penetrated Stephanie's radar screen, and she turned to him. "I'm sorry," she said. "You don't have a name tag, and I'm embarrassed, but I can't remember..."

"Come on inside," I said, gesturing toward the door. "Let's see who we can remember without name tags."

I didn't hold out my arm, but she took it anyway, and as we walked inside, Mahoney gave me the same look arsenic would give you if it had eyes.

Inside was a table with "Hello My Name Is" name tags, next to which was tastefully arranged an array of pictures from the football highlights of Bloomfield High School's team for my graduation year (meaning three pictures, one for each of our victories against nine losses). Mahoney and I walked past the table, having decided ahead of time to forego the stupid tags and let people guess who we were. Stephanie stopped and carefully found hers, then tried to find an artful place to attach it to her dress. It took a while, but she managed.

I was across the room by the time she had assembled herself, but I did take some amusement in the looks our male classmates gave Stephanie as she made her way around the dining room. The nametag gave them a legitimate excuse to look where they wanted to look, which I believe was exactly the effect Stephanie had desired. But before I could make my way back to her, I felt a hand grab my upper arm, and turned.

Mark Friedman, looking every bit his age at 43, was smiling, tall, trim, and healthy-looking. I fought the urge the choke him.

"Hey, Tucker!" he yelled. "I saw you come in with the Goddess. How'd you manage that?"

"It's nice to see you, too, Mark," I attempted. "Are the other guys here?"

"I saw Wharton earlier," he said. "He's trying to get everybody to vote for him for something. But what about the Goddess? You banging her?"

"I'm married to a goddess," I told him, "and it's not Stephanie Jacobs. Before the parking lot five minutes ago, I hadn't seen her in twenty years."

"Could have fooled me, the way she was hanging onto your arm," he said, doing his best to leer but coming up with a lopsided grin instead. Friedman could never really transcend his original image, that of a cute little boy. But he was constantly trying.

After showing off pictures of our respective children (they throw you out of the Father's Union if you're caught not carrying), Friedman and I caught up on professional accomplishments. His took longer than mine. He owned three carpet stores. I made a mental note to change professions.

We headed for the bar, where I got a Diet Coke (they never listen when you tell them to forget the lemon) and Friedman opted for a Chivas Regal with water on the side. I knew what I had paid for the Diet Coke, so, if Friedman could afford a Chivas at the cash bar, I figured there must be money in selling carpet in Central New Jersey.

The problem was, we weren't making eye contact very much. And when we did, it was that kind of tentative, accidental eye contact that's really just a way of finding out if the other guy is looking at you, or if he's just checking out some woman he went on a date with 27 years ago.

"Where'd you say you saw Wharton?" I asked.

He looked relieved, pointed, and we walked across the room more or less together, waving at people we thought we recognized and avoiding the glances of people we were certain we recognized.

Halfway there, Stephanie grabbed my arm again. I thought Friedman was going to have a hemorrhage right then, and he found himself caught in one of those awkward situations where you don't know if you should continue on the path you've begun or stop to ogle a woman's cleavage. He was clearly leaning toward the latter, but I pushed him in Wharton's direction and stayed to talk to Stephanie.

"You didn't show me pictures of your children," she said. "You have some, don't you?"

"Two," I admitted, reaching for the evidence. "Ethan is twelve, and Leah's eight."

She made the usual noises you make when you see someone else's children. "So what do you do when you're not solving murders?" she asked.

"I freelance." Stephanie gave me the same confused look everybody gives me when I say that, and yet I persist. "Writing. Magazines and newspapers." I actually pulled a business card out of my wallet and gave it to her.

"No kidding. My husband knows a lot of editors. Maybe he can help you get..."

Mahoney loomed up behind her. "Do you remember me yet?" he asked Stephanie. Clearly, the man was trying way too hard.

"I do. You drove me home once in the rain, didn't you?" Damn, she was good. Mahoney's grin got so wide I was afraid it would meet at the back of his head and his brain would fall out. While they were reliving this fascinating episode in their lives, I followed Friedman from the bar (where he'd replenished his Chivas) toward our resident politician.

Greg Wharton, New Jersey state assemblyman (and osteopath), brushed the forelock out of his eyes as we approached. Wharton was a little heavier than I remembered him, but then, I was a little heavier than I remembered me, too. His suit was nicely enough tailored that it was hard to tell exactly how much heavier he was than his early-30's self, the last version of Wharton I had seen.

He smiled when he saw Friedman and me approaching, but as with all politicians or would-be politicians, it was hard to know if he meant it. I guess it doesn't really matter. Wharton shook my hand heartily, as if he were campaigning outside a Stop & Shop and had just asked for my support.

Out of the corner of my eye, I saw Stephanie Jacobs talking to Mahoney, but she was looking past his left shoulder toward Michael Andersen, Bloomfield's one-time quarterback, with whom she had performed all sorts of delectable acts in the back seat of a 1968 Ford Fairlane, at least according to rumor.

"So, what are you running for this time?" Friedman asked Wharton. "Board of Chosen Freeloaders?"

"That's *Freeholders*," said Wharton, his sense of humor sharp as ever. "And no, this time it's State Senate. There are too many issues…"

"Spare me the campaign rhetoric," I suggested. "I can always look it up on your web site, Whart. Besides, I don't even live in your district."

"You could move."

Friedman rolled his eyes. "Nothing ever changes," he said. "You still expect us to get you elected." Wharton's eyes narrowed. That one stung. It's a long story, involving a stuffed ballot box in a student council election. And even though the statute of limitations has in all probability run out, it's probably better left untold.

Before a fistfight could break out, I gestured to Mahoney. Stephanie was walking away. Mahoney bit his lower lip, but walked over to us anyway.

"Well, look who it is," said Wharton. "Jerry Mahogany."

"Knucklehead Smiff," Mahoney answered, completing the ritual. The reference to the *Paul Winchell Show* was a long-standing bit between the two of them. They didn't shake hands, but nodded at each other.

I recognized about twenty percent of the people in the room, and discounting for spouses, that still gave me a woefully low batting average. No one approached us—and I almost gave a long-lost-friend greeting to a man who turned out to be the bartender.

Still, the four of us—Mahoney, Friedman, Wharton and Tucker (that's me)—managed to create a mini-reunion in our corner of the room. Old jokes, half-forgotten, were dragged out and given one more road test. Stories that were three-quarters forgotten (at least by me) were retold and embellished. Facts were disputed, opinions dismissed, and current lives and families, not to mention the past quarter century, completely ignored. And when Alan McGregor was spotted walking through the door, our mini-group was complete.

Mahoney, who had jump-started his sense of humor and assumed his customary court jester role, bellowed from across the room: "McGregor!" Heads turned. No one cared. McGregor reddened a bit, but walked over to us, smiling.

McGregor is about the same height as Mahoney, but not as muscular. He looks more like Clark Kent, and less like Superman.

In our group, no one member was more important than the rest, but it wouldn't have been "Us" without McGregor. He provided the humanity in a gang of four who would have gone for the throat for the sake of a joke had he not been present. He also held his own, providing puns that would send lesser men running from the room.

He had barely caught up with the rest of the group (wife, three kids, some sort of financial job I didn't understand) when I spotted a short, trim woman with casually coiffed brown hair standing by herself in a corner, nursing a ginger ale. I must have gasped audibly, because Mahoney turned in her direction, and broke into the nastiest grin I'd seen on his face in six months.

"Gail Rayburn," he said, and the whole group turned first to her, then to me. I felt like my face was giving off heat beams. And they were enjoying my discomfort immensely.

Gail Rayburn, who had been considered something of a hot number during our tenure at Bloomfield High, had inexplicably decided one week during our senior year to make me her pet project. She found me at a party at Bobby Fox's house, seduced me in some subtle way the beer wouldn't allow me to remember (like saying "come here"), and then given me my first—and to date, last—hickey, a 24-karat beauty that I'd worn proudly for close to a week. She had, of course, then moved on to someone else, leaving me to look foolish, which was not unusual for me in high school, and continues to be not unusual for me to this day.

"You ought to go over and say hello," said Wharton.

"Too bad you're not wearing a turtleneck," Friedman added. "Your wife might find out."

"Don't go over," McGregor chimed in. "You don't want to stick your neck out."

I looked at Mahoney. "Why'd we come to this thing, again?" I asked.

"*I'm* having a good time," he said. It occurred to me that he'd started having a good time when I started being the object of ridicule, but hey, what are best friends for?

I assessed them carefully. "I can do better than this group," I said, and walked to where Gail was standing.

On my way, I noticed Stephanie standing among five or six ex-jocks desperately trying to suck in their guts. If you squinted, it was like a football huddle in *Playboy*. Except that Stephanie was dressed. Mostly.

Gail Rayburn, on the other hand, was completely dressed, and, at 43, gave the appearance of someone who was less a hot number (although still attractive) and more a moderately successful entrepreneur. She still had a figure she could show off, but had chosen not to do so, and was wearing her nametag on the lapel of a suit jacket. The tag read, "Gail Armstrong (Rayburn)."

"Gail," I said, and she smiled, somewhat gratefully. I hoped I also noticed a flicker of recognition in her eye.

"Aaron Tucker," she said after a moment. "It's good to see you."

She reached over and hugged me. Yes, the figure was still there. But it was a friendly hug, and I appreciated it as that.

"I'm glad you remember me," I told her.

"Of course I do," Gail said. "You were the nicest guy in the class."

"In high school," I told her, "that generally means you're the one who gets the least…"

"Hickeys?" she asked, and we both laughed. I glanced over at the guys I'd left, and they were all looking at us, with adolescent grins on their faces. Gail raised her ginger ale to them in a toast. McGregor reddened and looked away.

"It's twenty-five years later, and I still haven't lived that down," I said.

"Do you want to?" she asked.

"Not really." Out of the corner of my ear, I heard a cell phone ring. Stephanie, at the center of the huddle, reached into her purse (she couldn't possibly have had pockets in that outfit) and pulled out a phone.

"You looked so cute with that thing on your neck," Gail continued. "You should have been fighting girls off after that."

"Was that why you did it?" I asked. "I've often wondered. You just picked me out of the crowd. Were you trying to see if you could change my reputation?"

She laughed. "I just did it because I felt like it," she said. "I was cementing *my* reputation. Your reputation didn't need any help. You were always the one with the most integrity, the one who never compromised his principles."

It was my turn to laugh. "It's easy not to betray your ideals," I said, "if nobody ever asks you to."

"Don't sell yourself short. You believed in things, and you stuck to them. You never did anything you thought was wrong. You had integrity."

"Where's my tape recorder when I need it?"

It was then that Stephanie made a sound that can't actually be described accurately. A cross between a cough and a groan, it was something primal, and every head in the room turned toward her, wondering if a wild animal had been let loose in the room.

She was standing, holding the cell phone, but not next to her ear. She was staring at it in her hand, as if the phone itself, and not someone on the other end, had just told her something she couldn't comprehend. Stephanie dropped the phone, then picked it up. One of the jocks tried to say something to her, but she waved him off and started toward the door.

The way to the door was right past where Gail and I were standing. Stephanie started to barrel past us, but I grabbed her arm. "Steph…" I said.

She didn't look at me. I'm not sure she was actually talking to me.

"My husband," she said. "My husband is… somebody killed him."

Gail gasped. A couple nearby turned their heads away, asking each other if either knew what she meant. I maneuvered myself into Stephanie's line of sight.

"Somebody killed your husband? As in…"

"Murder," she said. "That's what the police said."

"Are they sure it was him? Maybe…"

She laughed, not a merry laugh. "It was him, all right," she said, avoiding my gaze again. "Everybody in Washington knows Louis Gibson." And she just kept walking, right out the door.

I looked at Gail. "Should I go after her?"

"Why? Are you guys really good friends?"

I thought about that. "No," I said. "Before tonight, I hadn't seen her in years."

Mahoney beckoned me from across the room. He was pointing into the bar, which was adjacent to the banquet hall. There was a television over the bar, which normally this time of year might be showing a baseball playoff game. This time, a news report seemed to be on, and Mahoney was pointing to it.

"Is that her husband? Is that…?"

I looked at the face on the screen, which was identified as that of Louis Gibson. I was too far away to hear what was being said, but the inevitable crawl underneath the face indicated that this Gibson guy was the head of some political lobbying group in D.C. Mahoney walked to my side.

"Look at him," he said. "He lost his hair, put on some pounds, but he's the same asshole."

Louis Gibson. It took me a while, because we had never used that name.

We always called him "Crazy Legs."

Chapter
Four

"**C**razy Legs?" Abby was on the floor in my office/our family room, doing stretching exercises. After the brouhaha at the reunion, Mahoney and I had left early, so I actually made it home before my wife had gone to bed, and filled her in on the melodrama.

"It's a long story," I said. "I'm not really sure who gave him the nickname. I think it was Friedman, but he denies it."

"You guys never actually use each other's first names, do you?" She lay down on the floor and began doing pelvic thrusts toward the ceiling. Wearing a pair of running shorts and a light blue T-shirt, she was making it difficult for me to concentrate on the evening's bizarre events.

"It would be considered disrespectful," I said. "Anyway, I think we ended up calling him 'Crazy Legs' because he was the least 'Crazy Legs' person we'd ever met, and besides, it pissed him off."

"Always a... plus in your... social circles," said my wife, thrusting harder now.

"You have no idea what you're doing to me right now," I told her.

"What makes... you think... I don't?"

"You know, I did get home earlier than expected," I pointed out. No sense wasting a perfectly good opportunity.

She got up and immediately bent at the waist, touching the floor in front of her with her palms, stretching her hamstrings. "A friend's husband, a guy you actually know, is murdered, and you're spending all your energy trying to proposition your own wife. That's sad and flattering at the same time."

"I can't help it. Your legs can take my mind off of anything, except your..."

We both started, and looked up, when the doorbell rang. It was after eleven, and our doorbell *never* rings after eleven. It hardly ever rings *before* eleven. And at this hour, you could almost certainly rule out the Jehovah's Witnesses. Abby stood up, and pointed to the door, as if I didn't know what that bell going off in our living room might have meant.

I went to the door, cursing the fact that we have neither a peephole nor a door chain. For all I knew, Hannibal Lecter was standing on my doorstep, but a strange fear of insulting my guest would keep me from checking on his intention to eat my liver with some fava beans and a nice Chianti. Being civil has its costs.

On the way, I tried to see through the divide between the drapes on our front window, but the BMW parked in front of our house was unfamiliar. I wondered what Hannibal was driving these days.

Turned out, it didn't matter. I opened the door, and Stephanie Jacobs Gibson was standing there, still in the gasp-inducing clothes she had worn at the reunion. Her face, however, was a little wan, and seemed freshly damp on both cheeks.

"Steph," I said, more loudly than was necessary. Across the room, Abby was already sizing up the competition. As if anyone could compete with Abby.

"I'm sorry it's so late," Stephanie said. "I wanted to call, but I didn't know if that would wake the kids, or if you'd be awake, and then I needed to go somewhere, so I got out your business card..."

"Come on in," said Abby. I stepped aside to let that happen, then closed the door behind Stephanie. Abby walked to her, took her hand, and introduced herself. My wife has roughly seventeen times the social skills that I have.

I got Stephanie a beer, at her request, and we sat in the living room, Steph and Abby on the sofa, and me on the floor facing them, backed up to the entertainment center, an imposing piece of furniture Abby and I have dubbed "The Monolith."

"I'm so sorry to hear what happened," Abigail started. "You must be…"

"Shocked," Stephanie cut her off. "I'm shocked. But I'm not heartbroken. I'm not even sure I'm sorry."

Abby and I took a minute to pretend we weren't looking at each other, but Stephanie noticed.

"Don't get me wrong, I never wished him dead," she said. "But things hadn't been good between Louis and me for a long time. He had affairs. A lot of them."

I coughed, because it gave me time to think. Stephanie offered me a sip of her beer, but I shook my head. If I drink anything after nine o'clock, it'll be followed by a Maalox chaser before bed. "I never knew you were married to Cra… to Louis."

Stephanie grinned. "It's okay, Aaron," she said. "I know you called him Crazy Legs. Even though I never knew why."

Abby stood up and walked to me, put a hand on top of my head, the way you would with a little boy who'd just done something precocious. "Aaron never knew why, either," she told Steph. "He explained it to me, and I still don't know why." They shared an "oh, those men" look.

"How'd you end up married to Legs, anyway?" I asked, trying to shift the conversation away from me as the stereotypical man.

Stephanie stopped grinning and stared into the neck of her beer bottle for a moment. "Well, we dated a couple of times senior year after I broke up with Michael. I didn't think much of it, but Louis... well, Louis was persistent. Anyway, after graduation, I went to Montclair State, back before it was a university, and Louis went to NYU. So he'd come over, or I'd go into the city, and after a while, it got to be a regular thing."

I decided to ignore Abby's look and ask a question. Hey, I'm a reporter. We do that. "I think what I meant was, what did you see in the guy? I mean, we always thought he was kind of..." I quickly remembered that Legs was dead, and that stopped me.

"... an asshole? Well, that's because you were guys."

"We still are. Kind of."

"Louis was always nicer to a girl he wanted to impress than he was to anybody else," Stephanie said. "You didn't get to see what he was really like until he had gotten what he wanted out of you."

Abby sat down next to me. "I assume you mean he wanted sex," she said. Stephanie nodded. I gave Abigail an "I-thought-you-said-to-shut-up-and-let-her-talk" look, and she gave me a look with language you can't print in a family newspaper.

"But it was more than that," Steph went on. "He decided he wanted me to marry him, even after I slept with him. He thought I'd look good on his arm, so he kept up the charming act. God, this is an awful way to talk about the recently murdered, isn't it?" She stood up. "Where do I throw out the beer bottle?" she asked, sniffling a bit.

"Don't worry about it," Abby said. "Do you want another one?"

Stephanie shook her head. "I drank at the reunion, and I still have to drive back to the hotel tonight."

"You could stay here," Abby answered. "We have a sofa bed."

"No. I've already taken up enough of your evening. I should go," said Stephanie. "I have to drive back in the morning. Fact is, I would be driving back now, but both my sons are out of town, so I don't have to be there for them until tomorrow."

"Back to D.C.?" I asked, and she nodded. "Was Legs in the government?"

"He is… was, the head of a big political foundation, People For American Values," said Stephanie. "He actually became pretty important. Not as important as he *thought* he was, but important."

People for American Values. Somewhere in the back of my knee-jerk liberal mind I remembered something, but couldn't classify it. I probably grimaced, and stored that bit of confusion away until I could ask Abby, who knows everything.

Stephanie picked up her jacket from the banister hook and put it on. "Isn't there anything we can do to help you?" I asked, but she shook her head.

"You've already done it," she said. "You were here when I needed you."

"We live here," I said.

She laughed, and kissed me on the lips, gently. It wasn't a sexual thing, but it got Abigail's attention. Nobody who isn't me would have noticed, but she did narrow her eyes a millimeter or two.

"What bothers me more than anything else," Stephanie said, "is *why*. I know Louis wasn't the most lovable man on the planet, and he had political enemies, but everybody in D.C. has enemies. Why kill him?"

"The police will find out," I said. "Legs was important enough that they can't just forget about it."

I opened the front door for her, and as she was about to walk out, she stopped. "Aaron," she said.

I waited, but she didn't say anything else. "What?"

"Aaron, *you*. . . you found out who killed that woman here, right? You could find out about Louis."

I almost closed the door on her foot. "Oh, no. Steph, no. The

Madlyn Beckwirth story, that was…" I looked to Abby for help, but after the kiss, my wife was not in a charitable mood. "That was a fluke, a mistake. I'm just a magazine writer. Honestly."

But Stephanie hadn't changed much since high school. She knew how to get what she wanted, and her wheels were already spinning fast. "One of the journalists Louis and I got to know is a features editor at *Snapdragon*. And besides the music stuff, you know they cover politics."

Stephanie stepped back inside, and I closed the door, so the neighbors wouldn't be distracted by my terrified screams so late at night. I felt the trap being sprung around me.

"I know, Steph, but really. I don't know anything about politics. I write mostly about home entertainment equipment."

Steph was having none of it. "You know about murder investigations, and you knew Louis. You could write it, Aaron. Don't turn me down now. I can get Lydia from *Snapdragon* to call you tomorrow morning. Please."

In times of crisis, my wife is always my strength. I looked at her for help, and as usual, she came through with flying colors.

"How much does *Snapdragon* pay per word?" she asked.

Chapter
Five

"**W**ell, what did you *want* me to say?" asked Abby. I considered going downstairs for some butter, to see if it would melt in her mouth, but I was too tired. Stephanie had left, and we were in our bedroom, getting ready for bed a good two hours later than we'd expected.

"I was hoping you'd come up with a reason I can't write a story about something I can't possibly know about for a editor I don't know, whose arm is getting twisted to hire me, at a magazine I've never worked for before. That's all." We start getting ready for bed most nights by making the bed, since we almost never do that when we get up in the morning.

"I thought you'd want to write it," Abby said. She pulled the sheet smooth on her side, and started straightening out the blanket. "For crying out loud, Aaron, they pay two dollars a word, and you've got to figure this is at least a 3,000-word piece. That's a nice chunk of change." She had me there, but she couldn't stop, which is always a fatal error. "Besides, I figured you'd want to do anything you could to help Ms. Cleavage."

I pulled the blanket up on my side and started to take off my jeans. "So that's it," I said. "You know, it's funny. I've never actually seen you jealous before. I wouldn't have expected it. I'd have quicker expected it of me." I hung the jeans on a hook sticking out of the closet door. We live in a very classy house.

Abby satisfied herself that the bed was now acceptable, and slid off the gym shorts she had on, then started looking around the room for her pajamas. "I'm not jealous," she said casually. "I just find it amusing how easily you can be played."

"Played?" I stopped looking for a T-shirt disgusting enough to sleep in, and walked to her side of the bed. "What do you mean, played?"

"Oh, come on," my wife chuckled. "She bats her eyes, hikes up her boobs, and does that, 'oh Aaron, you're the only one who can help me' thing, and you go right for it."

"She has no reason to 'play me,' as you so endearingly put it."

"She wants you to investigate her husband's death," Abby said. "She wants you because she knows she can supervise the investigation as long as you're watching her bust line instead of the facts." Abby knelt down to look under the bed.

"Her bust line is a fact. Well, two facts actually. Besides, why does Steph need to supervise the investigation?"

"*Steph* is from D.C. All those people are control freaks."

I sighed, which I don't do often. "She's not from D.C.—she's from Bloomfield, New Jersey."

"And you've wanted to hump her ever since she lived there."

There are few things my wife does that seriously annoy me, but when she talks the way she thinks men talk, she can piss me off with the best of them. Mostly because *I* don't talk like that, and I'm pretty sure I'm a man. She found her pajama bottoms under the bed, and when she stood up, holding them, I was standing within a foot of her, looking right into her eyes. Abby was a little startled, but she grinned, thinking she'd scored a withering blow.

"I'd like to point out that I was looking for a way *not* to help her when you volunteered me," I told her, my breathing getting a little heavy. "Now, you listen to me. There is no one more beautiful, no one smarter, no one sexier, no one funnier, no one I'd rather be with on this planet, than you. You are the absolute center of my life, and I would gladly devote all my time on this earth to convincing you that nobody has ever loved anyone as much as I love you, but unfortunately, we need to sleep, eat, and pay the mortgage. So stop being a moron."

She took a moment, smiled, and dropped her pajama bottoms on the floor.

"Come on," Abby said. "Let's mess up the bed again."

And somehow, I forgot to ask whether she was familiar with People for American Values.

Chapter
Six

Lydia Soriano, *Snapdragon*'s features editor, called me at ten the next morning. Impressive, especially considering it was a Sunday. Stephanie, or Crazy Legs, must have had more clout than I'd estimated.

"Mr. Tucker, we're interested in a 5,000-word piece on the murder of Louis Gibson. I understand you have some background on the subject." Lydia had a very businesslike voice, but you could tell there was a human being in there somewhere.

"Call me Aaron. Please." I started. "And actually, no. I don't have any background at all. What I have is a knowledge of… Louis from his high school days and a very loose friendship with his wife from around the same time."

"I understand that you're reluctant," she said without missing a beat. "But I'm told that you have investigated some murders before."

Stephanie must have been very persuasive. "I've investigated exactly one murder, and I managed to solve it by annoying the murderers enough that they came after me. I wouldn't exactly call that a stellar record." I wanted *Snapdragon* to know exactly what it was getting, if it was getting anything.

"You know, Aaron, you keep this up, and I'm going to feel like you don't *want* to work for us." Well, what do you know? There *was* a sense of humor there after all.

"I've always wanted to work for *Snapdragon*. In fact, I've queried you guys maybe fifty times in the past five years. I just want you to have an accurate picture," I told Lydia. "If you hire me, you're paying, um…"

"Ten thousand dollars."

I took a cleansing breath, the only useful thing I got from being a Lamaze coach twice. "… Ten thousand dollars, for someone who is not an investigative reporter, a crime reporter or a political reporter, and you'll be hiring him to investigate a crime that is, in all likelihood, politically motivated. Don't do it just because Stephanie Jacobs told you to."

"I'm not going to pretend I didn't call because of Stephanie's reputation," said Lydia. "But I do the assigning around here, not her. And it's my ass on the line if you turn out to be a screw-up."

"Don't mince words, Lydia. Come right out and say it."

She chuckled. "Aaron, have you ever been a magazine editor?"

"Not on your level, no."

"One of the things you have to rely on is your own instinct. I called you because Stephanie recommended you. I did it because she's a friend, and because her cooperation is going to be central to a story that everybody who covers politics is going to want. We're tired of being thought of as *Rolling Stone*'s slow-witted cousin, and we want to make a big splash. She's giving you exclusive access to her, and 'exclusive' means *exclusive*. She isn't talking to anybody else. Also, I read as many of your clips as I could get off the Web. But still, I wouldn't offer you the story if I called you and you sounded like you were going to read through the police reports on the Internet and write a story about the extinguishing of a strong voice for the fundamentalist right on Capitol Hill. Frankly, I thought Louis Gibson was…"

"… An asshole?"

"Pretty much."

"He certainly was one in high school, and I haven't seen him since then, but I'm willing to bet he got worse. Am I allowed to write that he was an asshole?"

Lydia didn't miss a beat. "If you can back it up with facts, sure."

"Well, stop beating around the bush," I said. "Ask me if I want the ten grand."

Chapter
Seven

Monday morning was the usual blur of sandwiches made and bagged, drink boxes, water bottles, snacks and apples placed in lunch bags and boxes, clothing located, teeth brushed, cereal poured, medication dispensed (Ethan gets 15 milligrams of Ritalin every morning), hugs, kisses, hair brushed, shoes lost, shoes found, more hugs, and pushing the kids out the front door. All before eight in the morning.

I had an assignment from the *Newark Star-Ledger* about new video products sold in New Jersey. I work quite frequently for the *Star-Ledger*'s "Today" section, which concerns itself with lighter, feature material. Travel, parenting, consumer issues, that sort of thing. In this case, the section was about advances in video technology (there hadn't been any lately, so I was making it up), and I'd been given a list of four people the paper would like me to interview. I had reached two, and needed to make a visible effort at the other two before writing. The deadline was Wednesday, today was Monday, so I assumed this would be no problem.

Still, it was only eight in the morning, and you can't count on anyone being in their office before nine, so I started my day, as I usually do, with the *New York Times* crossword puzzle. I make a big show, when asked, about how it helps me to think about words and increases my vocabulary, but the fact is the puzzle is a good way to kill time and postpone having to do anything that approaches work. Does it improve my vocabulary and get me thinking about words? Sure. Does that make even a one-percent difference in what I would write about video technology for "Today"? Get real.

So, I was attempting to find a six-letter word for "dummies," and failing miserably, when the phone rang. Our newly installed Caller ID box informed me that the incoming call was from the Buzbee School main office, and at 8:30 a.m., that is never good news.

I'm used to getting calls from the school. Ethan suffers from Asperger's Syndrome, a neurological disorder like a high-functioning form of autism, which manifests itself in many ways, almost all of them socially unacceptable, or at least odd. The school calls often, if just to let me know when he's having a rough day. A paraprofessional named Wilma Coogan follows him around all day, and will frequently call me with a question, or when a situation arises she hasn't seen before. So I breathed a long sigh to gird myself for what was clearly going to be a rough day.

"Hi, Aaron, it's Anne Mignano." Uh-oh. The principal herself. Now I was *really* in trouble.

"Who did he set on fire, Anne?"

"Don't worry," Anne said. "Ethan's fine."

That stumped me. If Ethan was fine, what did Anne want to talk about? "Is Leah okay?"

"Yes. In fact, this doesn't have anything to do with either one of your children."

Well, that made sense. If it doesn't have anything to do with my kids, clearly the principal should get on the phone to me immediately. "What's going on?" I asked.

"Can you come over here for a few minutes?" she said. "I have something I need to ask you about." I was surprised, but didn't say anything to indicate it. It was a short walk to school.

Five minutes later, having given up on "_od__s," I found

myself seated in a chair in front of Anne Mignano's desk. And our principal, who takes great pains to be unflappable, looked very flapped. Not that the casual observer could tell, but I was an old hand: Anne's dark blond hair was just a bit mussed. Her left hand was playing with a paper clip on a desk that rarely, if ever, saw a paper clip out of place. And she was leaning forward in her chair just a little more than she should, giving me the intimation of urgency.

"Is something wrong, Mrs. Mignano?"

"No, not really," she said, her voice brittle. "Well, maybe. It's something I need some help with."

Whoa. If Anne Mignano, who can stare down five hundred seven-to-twelve year-olds on a rainy day with no movie, is admitting she needs help, there must be a catastrophe of biblical proportions on the way. I gave passing thought to whether Home Depot carries Do-It-Yourself Ark kits.

"You know I'll do what I can."

"Good." She stood, and closed her office door. There was so much silence in the room, Harpo Marx and Marcel Marceau would have screamed to break the tension. Anne sat back down, and leaned forward again. "I need you to investigate something for me."

"Anne, you know I'm not..."

"This has to be done discreetly, Aaron, and can't be seen as an official inquiry. I need someone who knows how to ask questions without giving away too much information, or drawing attention to himself."

It occurred to me that a guy who practically dares murderers to a duel usually draws some attention, but I held my tongue. Turned out my tongue was slippery and disgusting, so I let go.

"What is it that needs investigation?" I asked.

"You understand, then, that what I'm about to tell you can't leave this room?"

"Anne, stop talking like The Spy Who Came in from the Cloakroom. You know you can trust me—now, what are you trusting me *with*?"

She searched my eyes for a few seconds, then drew in a breath. "Aaron. We have had a problem with stink bombs."

Surely, I'd heard her wrong. Maybe she meant "sink bombs." Perhaps a sink in the boy's room had blown up, and she wanted me to find out who the culprit might be. Or Anne might have said she had a problem with Simba, which would mean a vicious tiger loose in the halls of the school.

"Stink bombs?"

"Yes."

Okay, so I'd heard right. "Stink bombs." You can never be too sure.

"Someone threw a stink bomb into the girls' locker room during soccer practice on Friday. It was the third one this month—there was one in the boy's bathroom on the second floor and one in the gymnasium. I'm surprised you haven't heard about it." Anne seemed disappointed, already, in my investigative abilities. "We spent the whole weekend fumigating in there, and the other two still haven't been entirely eradicated."

"So you want me to... what? Go around sniffing kids to see who smells bad?"

She smiled, but not sincerely. And Anne isn't as good at insincerity as a real politician. "I know it doesn't sound like much," she said.

"It doesn't sound like much? We have schools in this state where kids walk in every morning through metal detectors, and we're getting all bent out of shape over a few stink bombs?"

"I'm afraid so," she said softly. "One of the boys in the bathroom when the bomb went off has a mother on the Board of Education. A girl in the locker room's father is on the Board of Assessors, and, well, the science teacher was quite angry himself." I knew Mr. Marlton—he wore a lab coat wherever he went and was last pleased with something around the time Madame Curie discovered radium.

"…And they're putting pressure on you to bring the culprit, or culprits, to justice? Is that it?"

In Midland Heights, where New Age parents keep their kids away from red meat and the lack of organic tomatoes at the supermarket is a major scandal, three unanswered stink bombs could be enough to put a principal's job on the line, if—as seemed to be the case here—the wrong people's children were somehow involved. Put enough children with enough connections in the line of fire, and anything could happen. Word had it that a former health inspector was once fired for getting annoyed by a resident's constant calls about spiders in her neighbor's apartment because he told her to "teach them to tap dance and get them on Letterman." Anne could investigate, but her hands were tied. An independent observer (like a freelance writer, for example) could, in theory, use methods that weren't exactly in the Marquis of Queensberry's rulebook, and if I were caught or killed, the principal could disavow all knowledge of my actions. Clever.

"Something like that," she said. "Can you help? *Will* you help?"

"How much time do I have?" I asked.

"I don't know. I mean, I don't seriously believe the board would act against an administrator on something like this, but…" Anne let her voice trail off.

"I assume I'm not on the school's payroll," I said.

"No. I'm asking for a favor," said Anne.

"That's my going rate," I said. "Tell me what you know."

Chapter
Eight

It turned out the six-letter word for "dummies"—the cross-word puzzle item that had so stymied me—was "dodoes." That crazy, whimsical *New York Times.*

I spent the rest of that morning on the two phone calls for the *Star-Ledger* story and trying to absorb my other two current assignments. For one, I was being asked to find out who killed a relatively major political figure, and write about it because I knew him and his now-widow in high school. I had just about no experience doing such things, but was being paid $10,000 for my on-the-job training.

On the other hand, I had plenty of experience in finding out which little kid has been mischievous, because I have been a parent for twelve years. So discovering who had chucked the stink bombs into various rooms in the Buzbee School was considerably better suited to my talents. Of course, for this I was being paid nothing. The fact that I'd been asked to do it at all (or that *any-one* had been asked) was the hardest part to believe.

I decided to start on the paying job first, and put in a call to my friend Mitch Davis, who works for *USA Today* in the Washington, D.C. area. But Mitch was out, so I settled for his voice mail, and sat down to ponder.

Pondering is what I'm best at in the morning. Before two in the afternoon, I'm useless as a writer unless there's a deadline to meet. So I thought, and I put music on (since I'm not allowed to play what I like while the kids are home), and I had a Healthy

Choice frozen lunch while watching a rerun of *Hill Street Blues* on Bravo. Then, I reread the scene I'd written yesterday on my latest screenplay.

Screenwriting isn't the kind of thing you do because you want to—it's the kind of thing you do because if you don't, the story will leak out through your ears. I've been writing screenplays for upwards of 20 years in the increasingly vain hope that some maniac producer will read one, decide I'm worth throwing some money at, and eventually make a movie. So far, I've been given money exactly three times for options—a kind of rental agreement producers use to keep you from selling your script to someone else for a year or so—and come close to snagging a couple of other options. I've made so much money screenwriting that we were actually able to send Ethan to a day camp for kids with neurological problems last summer. Prorated over time, my screenwriting wages are just a couple of cents an hour below what slaves generally get.

What all this means is: don't expect rationality when discussing the "art" of writing for the movies. It comes from a deep, abiding love for the form that began roughly at age three, when my parents took me to see *Pinocchio*, and was cemented into place when I realized someone actually *wrote* this stuff, around the time I first saw *North by Northwest*. Cary Grant could be charming as all get-out, but without Ernest Lehman to tell him what to say, he'd never have made it out of that auction in Chicago alive. If you haven't seen it, go rent the DVD. NOW!

I read over the previous day's work, and it was actually better than I'd expected. After the Madlyn Beckwirth mess, I'd tossed the romantic comedy I'd been laboring with, and started a murder mystery. That was easier, since the true story was so bizarre, I only had to change some details and move a few characters around to avoid being sued. The writing was going well.

Today's task involved a tricky scene that included a lot of exposition. The problem with exposition, or plot points, in a script is that the last thing you want an audience to feel is that they're being told, and not *shown*, a story. You don't want your characters explaining everything in dialogue. The best way to convey the story point is in a visual, but that's not always possible. So, you have to hide your exposition in jokes or create a diversion, a task for the characters to perform while they're talking. An interesting setting or a subplot for the scene can disguise exposition, too, but it all has to be worked out ahead of time. And in this case, I was having trouble coming up with the proper diversion.

I'd settled on one—having the characters perform a piece of home improvement while discussing the plot—and started writing when, true to form, Ethan pushed the front door open and stomped into the house. My son doesn't walk, he stomps. It doesn't mean anything—it's not indicative of his mood. Asperger's kids aren't as in touch with their bodies as the rest of us, and Ethan is probably unaware that he's making enough noise to be heard three blocks away.

Sure enough, all the stomping hadn't meant a thing—Ethan breezed in the door with a sunny, "hi, Dad," and immediately set out to do his homework, which he announced was "the easiest thing since they started giving out homework." For math class, he had to write a poem about his favorite number. When I was in school, you had to do *math* for math, but that was a long time ago.

It was just as well that this was Ethan's assignment and not mine, anyway. I can't compose a decent rhyme about anything, let alone my favorite number. My few pitiful attempts at song-writing in college were enough to convince me to stick to prose.

Ethan, however, is blessed with a mind that can toss off complex, interesting metaphors as easily as… um, something easy. Okay, if I'd finished that simile, you'd get the idea.

He had just about finished his "Ode to Thirteen" when Leah pushed the door open and dragged her tiny, weary self into the living room, then flopped down on the bottom stair. My daughter, who wants to be an actress, has yet to master the art of subtlety.

"How was your day, Squishy-Face?" I asked. It's best to start with an endearing nickname. It sets up a good barometer for the child's mood. And with children, mood is everything.

"Good." Okay, at least I knew *something*. Of course, Leah always says her day was "good," even when something truly horrific—like a substitute teacher—has befallen her. Once, on a day when her beloved Mrs. Antonioni was absent, Leah actually had to spend five minutes in detention, something she considers an unpardonable shame that will tarnish her life until that fateful day one of her great-grandchildren ferrets out the truth. And the whole class had been detained—Leah hadn't been singled out.

"Anything happen that I need to know about?" She shook her head, and started to dig through her backpack, which was hanging on the lowest protrusion of our cast-iron banister. She sighed, evidently with great meaning.

"What's the matter, Puss?" She knows I almost never call her "Leah" unless I'm annoyed with her, which I am roughly every three months. But she didn't answer, got out her math book, and headed toward the kitchen, so as to stay out of Ethan's way. The two of them doing homework in the same room is not a pretty picture.

I was about to follow her and get a more detailed explanation of her mood when the phone rang. The caller ID box indicated the caller was "Out of Area," which is really helpful. But luckily, when I picked the phone up, Mitch Davis was at the other end.

"I don't care if I am your class correspondent, I haven't heard from any Rutgers people," he began, by way of a greeting. Mitch is a classic, old-style newspaperman—unkempt, hard drinking, and outwardly gruff. If he put on a seersucker suit and a porkpie hat, he'd be Carl Kolchak, the Night Stalker.

"I'm not calling about alumni," I assured him. "I'm calling to pick your brain on Washington, D.C. police activity."

"This for a story?"

"No. I've developed an overwhelming interest in cities that once busted their own mayor for drug use, and I thought I'd start at the top."

"I'm not going to help you on a story," said Davis. "Why should I give my sources to the competition? Besides, I thought you wrote about Palm Pilots and what's great about New Jersey. What are you doing talking to cops?"

I filled him in on my *Snapdragon* assignment, leaving out my ties to Stephanie and Crazy Legs. His voice rose about an octave when I suggested he let me know who was conducting the Gibson investigation.

"The biggest cop story to hit D.C. in ten years, and you want me to hand you the sources? Why don't you act like a reporter and get your own, you slacker?" Davis always was one for flattery.

"I'm not the competition, you *Daily Planet* reject. I'm writing for a monthly that's not going to publish until you've already moved on to the next scandal inside your Belt Buckle."

"Belt*way*."

"Whatever. You're not covering the story yourself, anyway. Besides, you know as well as I do that I could get all this information off the Internet in about 20 minutes if I wanted to. But you're faster, and more fun to annoy." College friends were just made to needle. You didn't know them in years that were as embarrassing as your high school friends, but you still have plenty of blackmail material that their present employers, spouses, or children would find interesting.

Davis sighed. "Oh, all right. It's nothing you wouldn't get from reading *USA Today* tomorrow."

"Make up your mind."

"Funny. When you grow up, maybe you can write comedy. Okay. The chief investigator for the D.C. cops is Francis Xavier McCloskey, known in these parts as Fax McCloskey because nobody ever actually sees him—they just get his messages from their fax machines. Fax works out of the Capitol area headquarters, and I'll give you the number once I dig it out. But you won't get Fax on the line, anyway." Once you get Davis going, you don't have to work very hard. He does it all for you.

"Who will I get on the line?"

"Sergeant Mason Abrams. You're better off with him, anyway. He's the administrative sergeant in the homicide division, and he'll know what's going on, even if Fax is the one doing the actual investigation."

"So, why don't I just go to Abrams first?" I asked.

I could hear the condescension in Davis' voice. "Because then Fax won't be able to show you what a busy guy he is by passing you off to Abrams. Besides, this way you'll get on his fax list, and you'll be getting messages from him when we're at our 50-year college reunion."

"Which should be a couple of weeks from now."

"Awwwwwwwww. Feelin' kinda down, Aaron?" Davis had as much tolerance for self-pity as he did for sloppy lead paragraphs or unattributed quotes.

"Just tired. Thanks for the help, Mitch."

"We live to serve."

He gave me the phone numbers I needed, grumbled again about the state of journalism in America today, and got off the phone. I hung up and looked in on my children. Ethan had written his poem, in his barely readable scrawl, and had moved on to the most important thing in his world, his Play Station. He would be totally devoted to Play Station 2, but we insist on his paying for such things himself, and $200 is hard to come by when your allowance is $5 a week, especially if your parents frequently forget to pay up.

Leah was bent over the kitchen table, which was covered with papers. A pencil she had sharpened almost to the point of a surgical instrument was in her hand. Tears were splashing down her cheeks, but she was silent.

"What's the matter, Puss?"

"I CAN'T DO IT!" she screamed, and put her head down amid the papers. I've seen this particular soap opera before, so I adopted my best Robert Young "Father Knows Best" manner (although I didn't have time to change into a sweater with patches on the elbows or learn to smoke a pipe).

"Can't do what?" I asked, sitting down next to her.

"THIS!!!!" She waved a worksheet at me. From this distance, and with the violent shaking she was giving it, I would have found it easier to read a sheet in ancient Aramaic. But I was willing to believe it was related to mathematics in some way.

"What are you supposed to do?"

"I DON'T KNOW!" Oh, *that.* I snatched the sheet out of her hand when it came by my face again. It contained all of three word problems.

"Have you read this?"

"YES!" she screamed, and flung her head back in what she thought was a melodramatic gesture. It looked more like a supermodel tossing her hair back.

"I'll bet you didn't. Look, what do the instructions say?" I admit it, my teeth were pressed together pretty hard. It's easier to maintain my calm with Leah than with Ethan, but a temper's a temper. And I have one.

Surprisingly, she decided to give up the soap opera act and actually do what I'd suggested. "Each of these problems has a fraction in it," she read in a singsong voice. "Decide which number is the denominator and write it in the space below." Leah's eyes widened and she pointed an accusing finger at the paper. "See? They want me to do fractions!"

"No, they don't," I said. "You could if you had to, but that's not what they're asking. They just want to know which number in the fraction is the denominator."

"What's a denominator?"

I sighed. "What did you talk about in class today?"

"The top number and bottom number."

"What's the bottom number called?" I said. I'd have drawn her a diagram, but my artistic skills are roughly on the stick-figure level.

"The denominator!" she shouted happily, then stopped. Her eyes narrowed. "So what do I do?"

"Oh, come on," I grumbled, walking out of the kitchen to my office. She followed me, waving the paper. "Daddy! How do I do this?"

It took me a few more minutes to convince her that this was the easiest homework assignment in history, and she went happily to work. So did I, only not as happily.

I started by calling Lt. Francis Xavier McCloskey, and, sure enough, was told by an actual human police department employee that Lt. McCloskey was "in a situational meeting about a case," but that I could talk to Sgt. Abrams. I asked him to transfer me, and what do you know, he did. After taking my fax number.

"Sgt. Abrams."

"Sergeant, my name is Aaron Tucker. I'm working on an article for *Snapdragon* Magazine about the Louis Gibson case, and I was wondering..."

"Everybody's wondering. Talk to the public information officer." Abrams' voice belied his tough talk. It was light, even cheerful. And there was no hesitation in his answers—he wasn't thinking about what the truth was going to sound like before he told it to you.

"Come on, Sergeant. I've already been blown off by Lt. McCloskey, and the P.I. officer is just going to tell me it's an ongoing investigation. I need to get my feet wet, and I'm behind everybody else on the story by two and a half days. So how 'bout just giving me what every other reporter in the whole world already knows."

There was a long pause, and I got the distinct impression that I could hear Abrams grinning. Straight-talkers generally appreciate talking to one of their own kind.

"Oh, okay." The grin broke through his voice again. "You got a pencil?"

"That's very amusing. Remind me to include it in my series on the Wit and Wisdom of the Capital Police."

"I was going to do you a favor, Tucker. Try and keep that in mind."

He was right. "Okay. I'm an idiot. So what were you going to say back when I was just an annoying reporter?"

Abrams chuckled. "Louis Gibson was killed with a six-inch kitchen knife to the chest while, um, relaxing in the apartment of one Ms. Cheri—that's C-H-E-R-I—Braxton, an administrative assistant in the human resources office of the Department of Housing and Urban Development."

"She's a secretary for the personnel department at HUD."

"Don't tell *her* that," Abrams replied. "Ms. Braxton is very adamant about being an administrative assistant in the human resources office of the Department of Housing and Urban Development."

"I'll try to keep that in mind. I'm also willing to speculate that Mr. Gibson was not, um, *relaxing* in Ms. Braxton's spacious living room. And I'll bet my last dollar she's a blonde."

"You would be correct, both times. He was in the bed, and the only thing he was wearing was an appalling comb-over."

"And a six-inch kitchen knife," I reminded him. "Which, I'll go out on another limb, did not have any fingerprints on it."

Abrams voice reflected his admiration. "Your instincts are amazing, Tucker," he said. "How have the police managed to get by without your penetrating insights?"

"Please," I said. "I'm blushing."

"Thank god I don't have videophone. Now. Ms. Braxton did not hear or see the attack, she says, because she was in the shower when it happened."

"Could the cops confirm that?" I asked.

"Well, the *officers* on the scene couldn't pinpoint the time of death that closely, but they did confirm that she was wearing a bathrobe when they got there, and she was unquestionably naked and wet underneath it," said Abrams.

My eyebrows shot up, giving Abrams another reason to be glad he didn't have videophone. "They checked?"

"They didn't have to. She hadn't bothered to close the robe when they arrived."

"Wow."

"That's what they tell me. There are no suspects at this time, and yes, this is an ongoing investigation, so there's a limit to the amount of information I can give you. Any other questions?"

"Just one. Is Ms. Braxton a real blonde?"

"Funny," Abrams said, "it isn't in the reports."

Chapter
Nine

That night, we were experimenting with the idea of the whole family eating dinner together, and it was going swimmingly, except for Ethan's palpable anxiety that he would miss the opening credits of *The Simpsons* rerun that started at seven. He practically broke a sweat shoveling food into his mouth with one eye on the digital microwave clock.

Leah, meanwhile, was giving us a sneak preview of what she'll be like as an adolescent, rolling her eyes every time we asked a question and *emphasizing every word she spoke* to us when she'd deign to grace the conversation with her chirpy little voice.

"May I please be excused?" Ethan asked, eyeballs nearly popping out of his head with anticipation. Problem was, his mouth was still full, so it came out "maya pease be estude?" Luckily, Abby speaks fluent gibberish. She's been living with me a long time.

"Not just yet," she said. "Chew and swallow your food first, wash it down with some water, and wipe your mouth with a napkin." Asperger's kids, generally speaking, don't like to watch people eat, and they don't see much point in sitting at the table after they've finished eating. Not to mention, Bart Simpson, Ethan's role model, was about to start writing on that blackboard to signal the seventeenth rerun of an episode Ethan still doesn't entirely understand.

He grumbled a little, but that was muffled by macaroni and

cheese, so it was easy to ignore. Ethan did follow his mother's instructions to the letter, though. As with many autism spectrum children, Asperger's kids tend to be very specific about doing what they're told, and do not vary in the least from instructions. He chewed, swallowed, drank, and wiped, an inch from hyperventilating.

"*Now* may I please be excused?"

Abigail nodded wearily. I try to stay away from such conversations whenever possible, and was staring down at my plate to avoid having to look at Leah, an adorable little girl who has the table manners of a rhinoceros. Ethan leapt up and started to run for the living room, before Abby reminded him to clear his plate from the table. With mere seconds to spare, he made it to the television, and Nirvana.

"So, did you have a lot of homework today?" Abby asked Leah, who was chewing so slowly it was impossible to tell if she was still alive.

"I *told* you!" she shouted. "I had *three pages!*"

"You didn't tell *me*," Abigail said with no outward trace of tension.

"I told *him!*" Leah pointed at me.

"Him?" I looked down at myself. "*Him*? I used to be 'Daddy.'"

She rolled her eyes and exhaled. Parents can be so inconvenient.

Abby's eyes had a faraway look, which meant she was trying not to scream. "All right, young lady, just exactly what has put you into such a mood that…"

The front door flung itself open, and Leah's best friend Melissa flung herself through it. Most of the people we know have given up on the formality of ringing the doorbell or knocking, and Melissa is through that door so many times a day I've been thinking of putting in a turnstile.

Leah's face brightened like a Hawaiian sky after a thunderstorm. "MELLIE!" she screamed, and ran toward her counterpart. They hugged like they hadn't seen each other two hours earlier, which they had. The remainder of Leah's dinner went untouched, and Abby sighed, scraped it into the garbage under the sink, and put the plate in the dishwasher.

It was just a little bit of a surprise when the front door opened again, and Melissa's mother Miriam Bonet walked in, with equal disregard for our doorbell. I made a mental note to test the button later to make sure it was still operating. Miriam and her husband Richard have become the closest friends we have in Midland Heights, and she was carrying a small box that looked like a mini-cooler, except that it had ventilation holes in its sides. Inside it was a lizard.

"Is that IT?" Leah squealed. She raced to Melissa's mother before Miriam even got a chance to take her jacket off. Miriam, normally a rational person, was beaming from ear to ear. She nodded.

"This is it, honey," she told my daughter. Abby walked to the dining room, where the females had converged. Leah was busy thanking Miriam so profusely it bordered on embarrassing. Ethan stayed in the living room, where the trials and tribulations of yellow people with blue hair who say "d'oh!" were far more real to him than anything going on in the next room.

"I didn't know you were bringing it tonight," Abby told our guest.

"I didn't know she was bringing it at *all*," I chimed in from the kitchen, where I was frantically loading dishes into the dishwasher, to better hide from "company" the fact that we load our sink with dirty dishes until someone makes us stop.

Miriam stopped and looked at my wife. "You didn't tell him?" she asked.

"I told him about the lizard," Abby stammered. "I didn't tell him you were bringing it."

"Why didn't you tell him?" Miriam asked.

"*He* is right here in the room," I reminded them.

"It's simple," said Abigail. "Miriam knew all about the whole gecko thing because Melissa already has one. So when we decided Leah could have one…"

"When *we* decided?"

Abby gave me her "the-child-is-watching-so-please-play-along" look. "Yes, when *we* decided, Miriam offered to buy it, and bring all the equipment, as an early birthday present for Leah."

"Her birthday's five months from now," I pointed out.

"A *very* early birthday present."

"It's so *cute!*" my daughter was gushing. "Is it a boy or a girl?"

I considered answering "yes," but more sensible heads prevailed. Miriam actually looked a little embarrassed. "Well, we're not really sure yet, Leah," she said. "We'll have to give it a few months, and then we can look, maybe with a magnifying glass, and find out."

"You know what they're looking for," giggled Melissa, and Leah laughed along with her. I finished loading the dishwasher and turned it on.

Leah walked in with the cage. "Look, Daddy," she said. "She's so cute!"

"I thought you didn't know if it was a boy or a girl," I reminded her.

"I've decided it's a girl," she said practically. "Look, Daddy, *look!*"

I have to admit to backing up just a tad. "It's really nice, honey," I said. "Why don't you take it up to your room and find a spot for it to live?"

Miriam had brought a small fish tank and other equipment for the tiny reptile, and she set it up on Leah's desk, with a heat lamp to keep the lizard, which the girls named E-*LIZ*-abeth, warm. I stayed in the kitchen, cleaning up, while the estrogen brigade set up E-*LIZ*-abeth with her new home. After a few minutes, Abby and Miriam walked downstairs and joined me at the kitchen table. Miriam put a small plastic container in the refrigerator.

"Is that the…"

"Worms," Miriam said. "And they have to be wriggling, or the lizard won't eat them."

"This is a lovely pet," I told my wife.

Abby started to make coffee, since she is the coffee drinker in the house. I tend to content myself with Diet Coke, but it was evening, and any caffeine at all would keep me up until roughly Thursday. So I abstained. Miriam sat down at the kitchen table with me.

"I'm actually glad you came," I said to Miriam. "Leah's been P.. P… P… PMS all afternoon."

Abigail turned the coffeemaker on and looked at me. "You still don't get it, do you?"

"Less and less, as I get older. Get what?"

"She was nervous because she knew Miriam was coming with the lizard, and she was afraid of you." Abby reached into the freezer and pulled out a box of Girl Scout cookies, which she started to arrange on a plate. Girl Scout cookies must be eaten frozen, or not at all.

"She's afraid of *me*?"

"You're the one who didn't want the gecko," Miriam said. "Leah knows that, and she thinks that if you say no, she can't have it."

"She's right. If I had said no, she couldn't have it. But I didn't say no. In fact, I don't remember being given a choice."

"Leah didn't know that," Abby said, putting the cookies

down. "She still thinks you're going to throw the lizard out of the house."

I groaned a little. "As long as I don't have to walk it or anything, I don't care. I take no responsibility for that animal. It lives or dies based on how well Leah takes care of it."

Miriam always knows how to change the subject—all she has to do is ask about me. "So, what are you working on these days?" she asked.

I told her about Legs and my conversation with Abrams. "You're a political science professor," I reminded her, in case she'd forgotten her profession since leaving work today. "Who would Louis Gibson's enemies be?"

"You'll notice the word 'science' in there, Aaron," she said, nibbling a tiny bite off a Thin Mint in the time it would take me to eat three cookies. "I don't deal in minute-to-minute politics—I'm teaching theory."

"Fine. Give me a theory about who Legs' enemies might be, based on his politics."

Abby frowned, but Miriam sat and thought for a moment. Abby got up to retrieve the coffeepot, which had filled.

"Anybody to the left of Mussolini would be an enemy of Louis Gibson," she said. "You remember that rumor about the Supreme Court nominee about five years ago?"

I resisted the impulse to smite myself in the forehead. "Of course! I *knew* I remembered that People for The Values We Decided Are American thing! Was he behind that rumor?"

"What rumor?" Abby asked, pouring a mug of coffee for herself and one for Miriam.

"Behind it?" Miriam said. "He leaked it himself."

"*Legs Gibson told the press about that?*" I was torn between pride that I knew someone that famous, and revulsion that I knew someone that Fascist.

"What rumor?" asked Abby, putting the mugs down and sitting with us at the table.

"Oh, you remember," Miriam said. "During the hearings for that woman the Democrats were trying to get on the Supreme Court. And all of a sudden this article appears in the *Washington Times* about how it was rumored she'd had an abortion when she was seventeen…"

"Oh my god, *that* rumor?!" said Abby. She turned to me. "You're telling me you went to high school with the sexist idiot who kept Madeline Crosby off the Supreme Court?"

"I didn't actually go to school with him," I defended myself. "He was one town over."

Miriam took a sip of coffee and nodded her head—apparently Abby had manipulated the brew properly. (You can't prove it by me, I think coffee tastes like hot, liquid dirt.) "Well, all you needed to hear was the words 'Supreme Court nominee' and 'abortion' in the same sentence, and you could forget that one," she said. "That's how Gibson made a name for himself, and the name, in many areas, was…"

"*Asshole?*"

"Pretty much. But I don't know how many people wanted to kill him because of it." Miriam thought thoroughly about that.

"Well, it only took one," I said.

"Yeah, that's what I mean," said Miriam. "How do you pick just one from so many?"

Chapter
Ten

The next morning, after getting the kids out the door, I worked out at the local YM/YWHA. I've been trying to do that more often these days, but things like work, children and a generally lazy attitude tend to get in the way.

After the workout, I walked into the Kwik'N EZ store on Edison Avenue, headed for the back, and selected a bottle of spring water. I tried not to stand too close to the guy behind the counter, since I figured I wasn't smelling my best at the moment.

Kwik 'N EZ, despite its appalling spelling, is the kind of convenience store you'd expect in Midland Heights—that is, it features fresh, unusual produce, it has lactose-free everything, and is so organic you can practically smell the manure. Still, the guy behind the counter could easily tell you where the Spam was, or direct you to the Tastykake area. There *is* a limit to how upscale a convenience store can go.

The cashier was maybe 30, thin and bored, but without the tattoos and body piercings you might expect. He leaned over the counter, waiting. At this time of the morning, there weren't many people in the store.

"Can I speak to the owner?" I asked.

Not a flicker. "You are," he said.

"You're the owner?"

He resisted the impulse to overstate the obvious and mock me. But he thought about it first. Being at least a decade younger than me and actually owning his own profit-making business gave him a certain advantage. "That's right. Something I can do for you?"

I put the water bottle on the counter and reached into my denim jacket for my wallet. But before he had time to ask why I needed the owner to buy a bottle of water, I pointed to a box on the counter.

"How long have you been selling these?" I asked. The box, open to make its contents more accessible, bore a logo that read "STINK BOMBS! The Ultimate Smell Weapon!"

"We just got them in a month or so ago," he said. "Why?"

I picked one up and looked at it. For something called a "bomb," it was small, and wrapped in brown paper that bore the same logo, with a line drawing of a kid holding his nose. "I remember when you had to make your own," I said.

"Thanks for the nostalgia. The water's a buck and a quarter." The wrapper even had instructions for how to use the stink bomb—kids can't even make a bad smell without reading about it first, it seems.

I reached into my wallet and gave him two singles. He started to make change. "You been getting complaints about these?" I asked about the little wonders. Anne Mignano had mentioned that parents thought the offending item had been purchased here.

"Yeah," he said, handing me three quarters. "But the kids buy them."

"You wouldn't be able to name any of the kids who buy them, would you?"

"Stink bombs don't require ID," he smirked. "Anybody can buy one."

"What do they do with them after they buy them from you?"

He shrugged. "That's their business."

"You know, three of these things have gone off in the elementary school in the past week. That's a bunch of eight-year-olds who couldn't use the boy's bathroom for three days." I thought maybe underlining the severity of the crime might soften the businessman's heart.

"Whatcha gonna do?" A wolfish grin broke out on his face.

In accordance with the instructions, I opened the wrapping on the stink bomb and twisted it. "This," I said, and threw it into the back of the store. Smoke started to emanate from it as the counter guy ran for the bomb. I left the seventy-five cents on the counter and walked out the front door.

Chapter
Eleven

"**A** *stink bomb?*" Chief Barry Dutton of the Midland Heights Police Department stood over me, eyes wide, his voice full of contempt. "You couldn't think of anything better to do today than throw a stink bomb into the Kwik'N EZ?"

"I paid the guy for it," I said.

I was sitting in the chair in front of the Chief's desk, and wasn't terribly frightened by his display of pique. I've known Barry for nine years, and even had dinner at his house a couple of times. I was a *little* frightened, though, because Barry is about six-four and looked like Arnold Schwarzenegger would if he were ten years younger and African-American.

"You think paying for the stink bomb makes it okay to use it in a convenience store?" Barry was James Earl Jones-ing his voice to full effect, and the chair vibrated a little, but I wasn't going for it.

"The owner of the place seemed to think that once such an item is purchased, its use is strictly the responsibility of the owner," I explained. "Besides, the name of his store breaks so many rules of grammar that, as a writer, it was a moral imperative for me to teach him a lesson."

Barry sat down heavily and sighed. He knew perfectly well that he wasn't going to get anywhere with me on this subject. It was either charge me or let me go.

"You didn't just go in there to teach this guy how to spell 'Quick,'" he said. "What were you doing there? Did this have something to do with the stink bombs at the school?"

"You knew about that?"

"Of course I knew about that—I'm the chief of police." Barry fixed an imposing stare at me. "You think the parents in this town would let something that heinous happen without notifying, and then badgering, the chief of police?"

"Well, what are you doing about it?"

"The question isn't what *I'm* doing about it—it's whether *you're* doing something about it, and if so, who asked you to do it."

I actually looked away from him. "I'm... not at liberty to say."

He snorted. It's rare you get to hear someone snort, but he did it well. "What is this, freelance writer-client privilege? You're not a private investigator, Aaron."

"No. I looked into becoming one, but the state regulations are that you have to have..."

"... Five years of experience as a police officer or investigator with an organized police department of a state, county or municipality or an investigative agency of the United States, or any state, county, or municipality." Barry said it all with what appeared to be enjoyable malice. "I've read the regs, and we've discussed them before."

I fixed him in my gaze. "So you also know that in order to become a police officer in this state, you have to be under 35 years of age. So my time to start getting five years in as an investigator..."

Barry grinned. "... Passed about ten years ago."

"Eight."

"Nevertheless. That doesn't explain what I'm going to tell Mr. Rebinow about his store. He's got fresh produce in there, for crissakes, and now he's going to have to close for two days." Barry closed his eyes and rubbed them with an enormous thumb and forefinger.

"That may be produce, but it sure as hell ain't fresh. Besides, the guy doesn't seem to care what happens to the stink bombs he sells unless they get used in his store. I don't see where I broke any laws. Doesn't he have anti-stink-bomb insurance?"

Barry's eyes opened wide again, and he started to point a finger at the sky, then gave it up. "Anti-stink-bomb insurance. What am I going to do with you?"

"You sound like me, talking to Ethan. Barry, while I'm here…"

"Oh god, you get pulled in for pulling a prank a nine-year-old would be ashamed of, and now you're doing to ask me to help you," Barry moaned. "Where do you get the nerve?"

"It's called *chutzpah*. My people are born with it."

"You must have been born a week late, because you've got twice as much as everybody else. What do you want?"

"Let's say I'm investigating a murder…" I began, but Barry put his head on his desk and began banging his forehead on the desktop. "You want to cut that out? It's distracting me."

"Didn't you learn anything from the last time? You damn near got yourself killed." Barry stopped the forehead move, but kept his head on the desk. His voice echoed from under the desk, around his feet.

"This is different," I told him. "I'm not anywhere near the killer this time. This murder took place in D.C."

"Washington, D.C.? Our nation's capital?"

"That was a question on the Police Chief exam, wasn't it, Barry? Yeah, that Washington, D.C. Now, the question is, how do you investigate a crime long-distance? I mean, I'm a good 250 miles away from the scene, and I don't want to move down there for however long it takes. What can I do?"

Barry sat back up and leaned back in his chair, thinking.

"Well, I assume you've already talked to the Washington cops."

"Yeah."

"What you want to do now is find out as much on the Internet about the victim as you can. Who he was… it was a man, right?" Barry asked.

"Louis Gibson."

"Oh, that People for Family Values, or whatever, guy? How'd you get on that one?"

I told him.

"I guess everybody you go to school with can't be as classy as you are," Barry said.

"Well, how many people are as classy as me?"

"I was thinking of it from Gibson's point of view, actually."

"You're funny. You should go into stand-up comedy. But wear the gun belt. If they don't laugh, you can shoot them."

Barry smiled a little. He'll deny it, but he did. "Well, a high-profile case like that will be all over the Net. Find out what you can, and talk to your friend with the chest about motive. You say she acknowledges he was cheating on her?"

"Yeah, but Stephanie had already driven up here by the time he was killed."

"She could have paid somebody to do it," Barry said. "That happens. We had a rabbi right here in Jersey convicted of just that."

"I remember something about that," I admitted.

Barry chuckled. "Now, *that's* chutzpah," he said.

Chapter
Twelve

Barry promised to smooth things over with Mr. Rebinow at the Kwik'N EZ, and let me go on my own recognizance, but not without threatening to kick me in the recognizance if I threw any more stink bombs near open food.

When I got home, sure enough, there was a fax from Lt. McCloskey of the Washington, D.C. Police Department, detailing how he had nothing to say in the Louis Gibson case. Also, on the answering machine was one of the sources for my *Star-Ledger* story, but when I called him back, he was out to lunch. It was going to be one of those days.

I called Stephanie at home in D.C., and she took the call right away. "Louis' funeral is tomorrow," she said. "They're actually talking about televising it on C-SPAN. Can you imagine?"

"Price of fame, Steph."

"I bet the President will show up. And here's me with nothing to wear."

"That'll make an impression," I said.

She chuckled. "You always could make me laugh, Aaron."

"That's not how I remember it, Steph. Not to change the subject, but we need to have a long talk about Legs. I need a lot of background before I go nosing around into what... happened."

"That shouldn't be a problem. I'm coming back up there over the weekend to deal with Louis' family. Maybe we can get together for lunch on Friday."

We made the date, and chatted for a few minutes before

Steph's larger task—planning a nationally televised funeral—intruded on her, and she called our conversation quits.

I spent a couple of hours after that on the Internet, which has completely replaced the library as the freelance writer's main site for research. One of the few luxuries I allow myself is a high-speed cable Internet connection, and it pays for itself in time spent waiting for pages to pop onto the screen. I'd sooner give up my thesaurus—I could always download one, after all.

Through various web sites, I gained the following information:

Louis Gibson was an attorney who founded People for American Values in 1992—

Louis Gibson once told an interviewer he was "appalled at the degradation of American values by the excesses and mistakes of the 1960's"—

Louis Gibson and his wife, Stephanie Jacobs Gibson, had been "happily married" for 23 years, and had two children, Louis Gibson, Jr., now 22 and a senior at Georgetown University, and Jason Gibson, now 17 and a junior at the Pringley School in Annapolis, MD—

Louis Gibson regularly appeared on such television programs as *Meet the Press, Sunday Morning, Larry King Live;* and *The O'Reilly Factor.* On his last TV appearance, on *Left of Center,* he had gotten into a shouting match with the host, Estéban Suarez.

I belong to an Internet bulletin board for writers called Writers United for Stage and Screen (WUSS), which was started by four disgruntled screenwriters about 10 years ago. Since the only kind of screenwriter is the disgruntled kind, WUSS is now populated by 250 professional and semi-professional screenwriters (like me), who leave messages for each other.

One of the great advantages of WUSS is the vast depth of

knowledge that members can tap. If you need to know about the migrating patterns of Canadian geese, the caliber of the most widely circulated gun in America, the lyricist of "Do Wah Ditty Ditty," or the perfect way to cook lamb chops, there's always somebody to ask.

I logged on that morning and read my messages for the day—there were two. One was from Margaret Fishman, a screenwriter and novelist who wanted to know if New Jersey really had more Mafia members per square mile than any other state. The other was from Gene Manelli, a comedy writer with some fringe credits, which put him a few rungs up the ladder from me. Gene was continuing a thread of conversation that between the two of us had degenerated into a war of puns. Don't ask me to detail it—you'd wake up screaming for weeks.

I left a message addressed to "ALL." It read: "Anyone with info about the recently deceased conservative lobbyist Louis Gibson, please get in touch privately. There's no money in it (for YOU), but it will be greatly appreciated."

Once that was done, I logged off the Net and made yet another follow-up phone call on the *Star-Ledger* story. This time, I actually got the person I needed, spent 25 minutes asking questions I didn't entirely understand, and wrote down answers I didn't understand at all. Hey, it's a living.

That left one more interview for the article, and I was awaiting a callback on that one. I decided to concentrate on the "Case of the Stinky Bomb."

Every year, the Parent Teacher Organization (PTO, not PTA, so they don't have to pay dues) of Midland Heights publishes what it calls "Find-A-Friend," the list of every child in the school district (who sends in a form at the beginning of the school year), with address, phone number, and parents' names. This year, it was rumored, email addresses (for the kids!) would be added, but since it was only October, the Find-A-Friend for this year hadn't come out yet. The book is a resource so central to a family's life it can often supplant the local phone book, and missing this year's edition would be a major handicap.

Luckily, there was last year's. I picked it up off the shelf on my desk (the Find-A-Friend is rarely far from my grasp) and started leafing through the pages, hoping to be hit on the head with the names of kids who might perpetrate such a dastardly crime.

I don't like to sound callous about it, but the fact is, if you live in a small community long enough, and your children go to the public schools, you pretty much know which kids are more likely to flout authority, and which ones are going to play by the rules or die. So, while I'll admit that this was a fishing expedition of the worst kind, it was not a witch hunt.

Besides, I had nothing to go on.

And after a good long look at pretty much every name in the Midland Heights school system, I had compiled a list of eight extreme long shots. In other words, I still had a grand total of nothing to go on. But I had killed an hour, and in freelance writing school, they teach that an hour killed is never a bad thing. Especially if you've avoided paying work.

I started in on the third act of the mystery screenplay. Screenwriting, for those of you sensible enough never to have tried it, is traditionally done in three acts. And the acts are defined in no better terms than those of Julius Epstein, who, with his brother Philip and Howard Koch, wrote a little picture called *Casablanca* that you might have seen, so he should know.

"In the first act," Epstein said, "your main character gets caught up a tree. In the second act, people come out and throw rocks at him. And in the third act, he gets down out of the tree."

So my bogus Aaron Tucker stand-in, Andy Trainor (I had to make the characters "less ethnic" to appeal to Hollywood), had already gotten himself up a tree by agreeing to investigate a crime. And various people had thrown rocks at him, mostly by threatening his life and cutting off his source of income. I'd even thrown in a chase scene to make producers happy. Now, in Act 3, it was time to get Andy out of the tree.

He'd started to climb down off his branch when my phone rang. As usual, the end of the screenplay was the easiest part for me to write, because I'd already gotten up a head of steam writing the first two acts, and because I'd been thinking about the ending all along. Of course, in this case, it was easier than ever, since I had reality to use as a template, so I was typing fast enough to elicit smoke from the keys. But I took a breath between sentences to reach for the phone.

The guttural voice on the other end spoke quickly, but clearly enough for me to understand. "Back off, man," it said. Then it hung up.

Stunned, it took me a minute. Then, I scrolled all the way up to the beginning of my second act, when Andy first runs into trouble from outside. And I changed the mysterious phone caller's dialogue from "stop your investigation," to "back off, man."

Chapter
Thirteen

Abby looked at me wearily. "A threatening phone call, Aaron? We're not starting *that* again, are we?"

"Beats me. I haven't done anything the other reporters writing about Legs didn't try. In fact, I'm sure I haven't done as much as most of them." I flipped over the chicken filet I was frying in the pan. "I wonder if Dan Rather is also getting terse, anonymous phone calls."

"I heard on NPR that Gibson's funeral is going to be covered live on CNN tomorrow," Abby said, taking out an earring. In a minute, she'd go upstairs to change out of her work clothes and into exercise clothes. "The President is showing up."

"Which begs the question of whether Stephanie will be naked or not."

She stopped. "Huh?"

"Don't worry about it," I told my wife. "Don't worry about anything."

"That's hard to do," she said, walking out of the kitchen, "when the phone calls are starting again."

"All he said was 'back off, man,'" I had to raise my voice to reach her. "It might have been Bart Simpson."

That cut through Ethan's perpetual haze. "Bart Simpson called?" he asked excitedly.

Abigail was not as talkative during dinner, even when Ethan made an awkward stab at dinner conversation and Leah actually used a fork on her mashed potatoes. Abby was seriously

unnerved by threatening phone calls we received during the Madlyn Beckwirth story, and was now clearly dealing with the possibility that they'd be starting up again. Maybe the ten grand was-
n't enough of an incentive to write about Legs.

After the kids beat a hasty retreat to the television, I started to
load the dishes into our dishwasher, an ancient model which, I
believe, simply made a lot of noise and spritzed a little water on
the dishes. They often had to be washed by hand after they came
out. Abby was clearing the table and leaving the dishes in the sink
for me to transfer when dishwasher space opened up.

Our kitchen isn't huge, so we often had to get out of each
other's way. And while I never mind bumping into my wife, I did
notice we weren't talking as much as we usually do.

"Do you want me to quit the *Snapdragon* story, because I will
if you do," I said.

"No," she answered in a heartbeat.

"You sure?"

"No," she admitted, wiping her hands on a dish towel. "But
we need the money, and there's no evidence there's any danger
from one phone call. It could even have been a wrong number."

"Maybe it was a telemarketer for a security service, doing the
set-up call." Abby smiled. As always, that was reward enough for
me.

"Where are you going to go with the story?" she asked, moving into professional-Abby mode. "You can't report it by reading
the other reporters' stuff."

I sat at the kitchen table. "Thanks for the vote of confidence,"
I told her. "Well, Friday I'll have lunch with Steph, and she'll give
me more details about their marriage, and what she knows about
the way Legs died."

"And where will that lead?"

I shrugged. "Where it leads. I don't intend to move down to

D.C. for months until something happens. I don't think you want me to do that, either."

"Of course not. Who'd take out the garbage?"

"Please, I'm overwhelmed with your sense of romance. Anyway, after I have some more to go on, I'll know where to go." I could hear the kids arguing in the living room about which side of the couch one or the other of them was inhabiting, so I stood up and headed in that direction.

"Sure, run from your problems," said my wife.

I turned back to face her. "Another crack like that," I said, "and you're going to have trouble getting me into bed tonight." I pivoted back toward the living room.

Abby chuckled. "Yeah, right," she said.

Chapter
Fourteen

Louis Gibson's funeral was a television event unparalleled since the last television event, and certain not to be eclipsed until the next television event. The President did, as advertised, show up, although he did not speak. Stephanie, to the disappointment of any heterosexual man over the age of 35 (and a good number of them under 35), was dressed, conservatively, in black. She dispensed with the traditional veil, and therefore managed to avoid looking like Lady Bird Johnson.

Standing next to Stephanie were her two sons, whom CNN identified as "Louis Jr., 22, and Jason, 17." Next to them was Legs' brother, and CNN was once again helping out, telling me his name was Lester Gibson, and that he was three years older than Louis.

From what I could tell, he was a couple of inches shorter than Stephanie, and shorter than Legs, too, and had opted to avoid the hideous comb-over Abrams had noted, in favor of a toupee that looked like someone had tossed a Caesar salad onto his head.

Stephanie did not appear to speak to Lester, her sons, or anyone else during the service. To her credit, she didn't weep openly, considering how little she seemed to be grieving for Legs when I had spoken to her. Lester looked a little shook up, and had to keep taking off his dark sunglasses to mop at his eyes.

Legs' mother, Louise Gibson, was doing more than just dabbing at her eyes. She was letting loose on national television. Her sobs could be heard over the commentator's whispered tones (to remind us that this was a funeral, and not the opening of trading at the New York Stock Exchange, but a tone which unfortunately sounded more like the play-by-play at a golf match). At one point, her knees almost buckled, but Jason held his grandmother steady.

He and his brother, lucky boys that they were, favored their mother. Junior had Stephanie's almond-shaped eyes and graceful chin, and Jason, the younger one, still hadn't lost all his baby fat, but did not, as best as I could tell from his infrequent close-ups, resemble his father, which is all either of Crazy Legs' sons could hope for, really. Maybe they'd both keep their hair, too. Rich kids have that kind of luck.

The eulogies were impressive, if your political bent was just to the right of Genghis Khan. Anti-abortionists, anti-civil rights activists, anti-just-about-everything-elses, all spoke of what a dear and valuable friend they had lost. I couldn't help thinking the country was in a considerably more positive condition now that Legs had bitten the big one, but rebuked myself that such thinking was cruel and insensitive. Besides, there were fifteen more just like him looking to take his place. No doubt the jockeying for position had already begun.

I discussed the funeral and its impact on my career with Mahoney as I drove us to racquetball that night. Mahoney and I had started playing racquetball when it was the hot new sport in the mid-eighties, and had been playing, on and (mostly) off, since then. We'd taken it up again recently, having separately despaired of our waistlines and inability to run up the stairs the way we imagined we used to. Of course, my waistline was more an issue than Mahoney's, since he gets some sort of exercise or another running around New Jersey fixing broken transmissions and other automotive ills for a large car rental agency based at Newark Liberty International Airport (EWR).

The racquetball itself was immaterial, anyway. Especially to me, since I always lost. What was important was the time I got to spend with my closest friend, letting him needle me until I wanted to jam a racquet down his throat, handle last. There are friendships, and there are friendships.

I was driving, so the cassette deck, and not Mahoney's ancient 8-track player, was ruling the musical choices. Mahoney was always interested in new music, but it never failed to compare unfavorably in his eyes to his Sixties and Seventies favorites. Still, he was willing to listen to the A.J. Croce album I had on, particularly after he heard A.J. is the late Jim's son.

"He's not bad, but he doesn't sound like his old man," he said, adjusting the volume from dominating to audible. "He's got that gravelly voice, like Rod Stewart."

"Not sounding like your old man can be a real plus," I said. "Think how it'll help Steph's kids if they don't talk like Legs."

Mahoney sat back and sighed. "I can see this is going to be a theme evening."

"I'm trying to work it out."

"So you're obsessing. That's how you work things out." Mahoney played with the fan button on the heater, then noticed the heater wasn't turned on, and forgot about it.

"If you've got a better method, I'd like to hear about it," I said. The guy in the BMW ahead of me had decided turn signals weren't necessary for those with upper six-figure incomes, and I'd nearly plowed into him, swerving at the last second. Mahoney hadn't batted an eye.

"It's whatever works for you," he said. "Me, I like to take stock. What do you know for sure?"

I was trying to remember which right turn I was supposed to make. "Almost nothing. I know Legs had become some kind of right wing lunatic and somebody stuck a big knife into him just when he was done playing Hide the Cocktail Frank with his latest in a series of blond secretarial school drop-outs."

"It's nice you're not taking this story personally," Mahoney said.

"You're not helping."

"And you're not trying. You're letting a 25-year-old crush on Stephanie Jacobs cloud your judgment."

I found the correct turn, but had to jam on the brakes to make it. Looking at Mahoney, you'd have thought he was watching an unusually slow-moving game of chess. "What judgment?" I asked. "I'm not letting any crush do anything, since I haven't got anything to go on yet."

"When a man gets himself killed in the apartment of his mistress, the first place to look is…"

"…With his wife, yes, but you and I both know Steph was two hundred and fifty miles away when it happened, because we were standing in the same room with her." I pulled into the parking lot at the Hillsborough Racquet and Fitness Club, and quickly found a space.

Mahoney got out of the car and pulled his gym bag from the back seat. "We know she was there when the cops called her, because we saw her take the call," he said. "How long had Crazy Legs been dead before they called her?"

"I don't know."

"Exactly. Were there fingerprints in the room other than Crazy Legs' and the blonde's?"

"I don't know."

"Even more exactly. Did Stephanie make a big withdrawal from her bank account recently, maybe to pay somebody who might like to stick a knife into her cheating husband?"

"I don't…"

We started up the stairs to the lobby door. "That's my point. If you weren't still living in 1977, you'd be asking these questions.

But it's Stephanie Jacobs and her unbelievable body, so you're giving her a pass."

He opened the door for me and we went into the club. "I hate it when you're right," I sighed.

"You ain't seen nothin' yet, pal. Wait'til you see the new serve I've developed." I groaned. It was going to be a long night.

Chapter
Fifteen

The faxes from McCloskey began arriving on a daily basis, each one less informative than its predecessor. After a few days, I started putting the same sheet of paper in the fax machine at night, and after a few days, it was completely black.

I'll spare you the gory details of my night of racquetball. Suffice it to say I got all the exercise I so richly desired. Still, after the usual pandemonium the next morning, I managed to drag my sorry butt to the car and drove to the local YM/YWHA, where I perform those tasks I laughingly refer to as a "workout."

The Y was once a very large residence, a brick structure parked in one corner of Midland Heights that overlooks the Raritan River and reminds us of the good old days, when Midland Heights actually had the room to include a home with 23 rooms, columns in the front, 20-foot ceilings, and four fireplaces.

About 30 years ago, it was determined that said residence was far too grand for a town like ours, and so it was bought by the YM/YWHA, converted into a public facility and, eventually, expanded to include an indoor, Olympic-sized pool, a Jewish pre-school, a basketball court, a couple of meeting rooms and, to my everlasting consternation, a "fitness center," where young and (especially) old alike could kill themselves on any number of torture devices.

My current device of choice was something called an "elliptical trainer," which presents itself as a sort of "Stairmaster-Meets-NordicTrack" contraption, requiring constant pedaling motion by its user, who is not allowed the luxury of sitting down, as with the old exercise bicycles. Level of incline and resistance can be regulated through a control panel, and the thing is actually sadistic enough to tick off the seconds you've spent and the calories you've burned on an LED screen right in front of your face.

Among the initiated, we call the elliptical trainer by its more appropriate name, "The Medieval Instrument of Torture," or "MIT," if you're an acronym fan.

I had my Walkman headphones on, and was playing a compilation cassette I'd made of fast-paced, inspirational songs by Paul McCartney, ELO, Santana, Sam Phillips, Matchbox 20, Barenaked Ladies, and Fastball, among others. If the beat is fast, you'll move your torso quickly to keep up with it. At least that's the theory.

I try to avoid looking at the other people in the room while I'm working out. For one thing, I wouldn't be too nuts about them looking at me. I've been meaning to talk to the Y management for years about their sadistic predisposition toward putting mirrors right in front of the MIT. But I also keep my eyes averted because the Y's fitness center is often populated with Jewish exercisers over the age of 70, and that's a preview of coming attractions I can live without, thank you. If I'm ever spotted on the MIT wearing corduroy pants, black, orthopedic shoes, and a button-down short-sleeve shirt, it'll be time to put me out of my misery.

So I usually close my eyes and let the tape motivate me as best it can. But today, I was on the lookout for the nosy type of parent who can be of help in any story involving the Midland Heights school district, and I got lucky. Faith Feldstein took the MIT right next to mine about five minutes after I got on.

Faith, a past president of the PTO at Buzbee School and present Board of Education member, is the queen of Midland Heights concerned parents, which is to say, she is never happy with the way the school system deals with anything, and is therefore a prime source of information and gripes on any school-related subject.

I had to admit, though, that working out had benefited her greatly. In the slinky unitard she was wearing, it was clear she'd lost a good 20 pounds in the past year, and was looking quite fit, for a woman in her early forties, or for that matter, any other age. I, on the other hand, was wearing a baggy pair of sweat pants from the Gap and a T-shirt announcing the upcoming video release of *Forrest Gump*, so you can imagine how swell my ensemble was making me look. I nodded in Faith's direction, and she smiled the vague smile you get when someone isn't exactly sure how they know you.

"How you doing, Faith?" I said. "Is Estella having a good school year?"

Her mind immediately compartmentalized me, and she knew how to respond. Faith rolled her eyes. "It's been a nightmare," she said. "She's not being challenged by the curriculum at all. Gifted children are totally ignored by this school district."

I knew Faith's daughter Estella from Leah's Brownie troop, and the only time she's actually "gifted" is on the first night of Chanukah. I let that go, however, and nodded at Faith in a sympathetic manner.

"Did you hear about this stink bomb thing?" I asked as casually as I could. But I did pump a little harder on the MIT.

Her eyes practically sprang out of her head, and since she only had the MIT on level 2 for resistance, I knew I'd struck a nerve. "It's a disgrace!" she said loudly enough that a 75-year-old codger on the treadmill halfway across the room took off his headphones and stared at her. "Some little hooligan thinks he can ruin three days for a bunch of girls who just want to play soccer, or close the gym for three whole days, and they're going to let him get away with it. Why, Karen Mystroft's little girl didn't even want to go to school the next day, she was so upset."

Hooligan?

For the moment, I shook the word out of my head and concentrated on the task at hand, ignoring the fact that Faith didn't care if boys couldn't use the bathroom, because she doesn't have a son. "Him? You know who did it?" I asked.

"Well, it was obviously a boy," she replied, with the air of someone explaining that the sky is, indeed, blue. She also said the word "boy" with the same inflection most people reserve for "slug." "A girl wouldn't have thrown such a projectile into her own locker room," she added.

"Why not? I would have been happy to throw a stink bomb into my high school locker room if I didn't have to shower with Harold Ramiriak for a week."

Holy mackerel, did I say that out loud? Worse, could Faith actually *know* Harold Ramiriak? The way she was looking at me, it was possible *she'd* actually showered with him, and believed it to be a more enjoyable experience than she was having now.

"Of course," I added, trying to cover my faux pas, "I *was* a boy."

Faith chose to ignore me, which is something I'm used to. "Any way you look at it, it's the administration's fault," she went on after a stunned pause. "Things just haven't been the same since Mr. Ramsey left."

Elliot Ramsey, the principal of Buzbee for seven years before Anne Mignano took over, was the type of self-help psychologist, crunchy-granola-bar principal that Midland Heights took to its bosom. I'd met him only once, since my children hadn't started yet at Buzbee when he left, but his sneaker-wearing, benignly smiling demeanor practically begged for New Age music to be played behind him as a soundtrack. By some parents in the school district, he was considered to be an appropriate candidate for sainthood. Thus, one didn't argue with Mr. Ramsey.

So I didn't. I nodded reverently, then adopted the most confidential tone I could muster, and leaned over toward her. She almost recoiled, thinking I had designs on her fabulous body, but then she realized I was going to speak quietly, and leaned toward me expectantly.

"Who do you think did it?" I asked, as if I had my own suspicions and wanted her to confirm them.

Faith looked profoundly disappointed, and went back to pumping away on the MIT. "I haven't the faintest idea," she said, looking away from me. She spotted another soccer mom walking in, and waved, doing her best to point herself in another direction. "Hi, Marcie!" she cried, and was soon involved in a heated discussion of Harry Potter vs. Lemony Snicket.

I put my headphones on and cranked up Fastball so I wouldn't have to hear the conversation taking place to my right. But no matter how loud the music was, it couldn't drown out one question left over from the last conversation: Did she actually say *hooligan*?

Chapter
Sixteen

After a shower at home (I wouldn't shower at the Y for fear of getting athlete's everything), I dressed for lunch with Stephanie, and headed to R.W. Muntbugger's, a New Brunswick restaurant so adorable you pretty much want to adopt it and take it home with you.

New Brunswick, NJ is the home of Rutgers, the state university. In the 1970s, when I was an undergraduate there, New Brunswick was a depressed little city with a glorious past (Benjamin Franklin and John Adams used to get drunk there) and a lot of porno theatres. But since then, the city has undergone something of a renaissance, mostly due to the continued presence of its number one benefactor, the Johnson & Johnson company.

These days, downtown New Brunswick still has a number of stores that sell cheap merchandise to the people who actually live in the city. But it also boasts any number of trendy restaurants, three separate live theatre venues, a wine store, and an Ethiopian boutique. Not a porno theatre (or, for that matter, a movie theatre) anywhere to be found. This, in New Jersey, is called "progress."

Muntbugger's is a prime example of what is right and wrong with New Brunswick. In an attempt to please people blatant enough to embarrass a cocker spaniel, the restaurant tries to be all things to all patrons. It boasts a homey atmosphere in a building that could accommodate a small warehouse, has "antiques" hanging from its walls and ceiling, calls its hamburgers "Muntburgers," which borders on the disgusting, and charges $4 for an imported beer like Molson, which is imported all the way from Canada. In a truck.

Naturally, such an establishment packs 'em in, as Rutgers professors and J&J execs alike have decided they "discovered" the place, so normally, one has to wait a good 20 to 45 minutes to get a table at lunchtime. This was apparently not the case for Mrs. Louis Gibson. I actually found Steph at a table the minute I walked in.

She was resplendent in black, but her widow's weeds were in this case a black Gap T-shirt and a pair of black jeans. No sense being uncomfortable just because somebody else was dead.

I sat down as she smiled at me, and apologized for being late, despite the fact that I was on time. Finding her waiting for me made it feel like I was late.

"Don't worry," she said. "I just sat down when you walked in." The fact that she already had a drink, and had consumed about half of it, gave away the lie, but I let it go.

I ordered a Diet Coke and we both ordered salads. I was pretending to be dieting, and she was just showing off. After the waiter left, I pulled my interview cassette recorder from my jacket and put it down on the table.

Steph looked a little surprised. "We're taping?" she asked.

"I'm on assignment. You wouldn't want me to misquote you."

"Wouldn't I? Anything you make up would probably sound better than the truth."

I gave her my famous half-grin, guaranteed to be ingratiating. "I'm forty-three," I told her. "You can't expect my memory to be what it once was. Who are you, again?"

She smiled. "An old friend."

"You don't really mind the tape recorder, do you?"

She thought about it, but shook her head. "It's okay," she said.

I hit the record button. "You didn't seem terribly upset when Louis was killed. Do you worry that makes you seem like a suspect?"

Stephanie's eyes widened. "Whoa!" she said. "You don't waste any time, do you?"

"Who's got time to waste?" I said. I looked at her for a few moments, letting her know I was waiting for her to answer the question. She exhaled grandly.

"Okay," she said. "I said you could have unlimited access. Well, you know Louis was not a model husband."

"He had affairs."

"He was rarely *not* having an affair," she said, her voice empty of emotion. She didn't seem upset, just reporting an unhappy fact. "Once he became well known in Washington, he could pretty much have his pick of the cute blondes, and there was a long succession of them."

"Anyone who thinks you're not enough is an idiot," I blurted. Sometimes, even I don't understand why I say some things.

She smiled. "You're not seeing me clearly. You look at me through a haze of twenty-five years."

"Not at all. I see you the way you are now. It was Legs who was trying to get back to being eighteen again."

"You're sweet," she said. "But Louis needed younger women. He didn't care who they were, or even if he liked them. He didn't care if he was embarrassing me by being seen with them. He didn't care if his children knew about it, either. After a while, I stopped caring, too."

"A lot of people would say that was reason enough to have him killed," I suggested. Strangely, she smiled.

"You have to care to be that angry," she said quietly. "You can't have a crime of passion if you don't have the passion."

"So how *did* you react?" I asked.

Stephanie hesitated. In fact, she came to a complete halt, and if the lighting at Muntbugger's hadn't been fashionably dim, I'd have sworn she was blushing. The waiter bailed her out by bringing our lunch, and she waited until he left, then tried, unsuccessfully, to express her thoughts again. She started her answer more than once, and never uttered a complete word. I decided to bail her out.

"You had affairs of your own," I said, and she looked down at her food, and nodded. "Why couldn't you tell me that?"

"I didn't want you to think badly of me." I had to strain to hear her.

"I never thought my opinion meant so much to you," I said.

"Well, it does." She spoke quickly, to get past this sticky point. "Anyway, I decided to match Louis embarrassment for embarrassment, but I couldn't do it. I had a couple of quick… episodes, and then I gave up. He didn't care, and I learned not to care, too. Finally, our marriage found its level of dysfunction, and we made it work for us."

"Functional dysfunction."

"Yeah," she chuckled. "Besides, if I was going to have Louis killed for having an affair, why wait for this particular one? He'd had more than I could count."

"Who do you think *did* have a reason to kill Legs?"

"That's what I've been agonizing over. Politically, there were lots of people who didn't like Louis. God knows, even I didn't agree with him politically much of the time. But to kill him? In Washington, if you don't like somebody, you make their life miserable. Killing him would just end the fun."

"How about personally? One of his ex-girlfriends?"

"Most of them were politically motivated—they wanted to move up, and sleeping with a connected guy helped them up the ladder. I can't imagine any of them being in love with him, certainly not enough to kill the next in line."

"Nonetheless," I said, "who was the one just before Ms. Cheri Braxton?" She winced at the name.

"Cheri?"

"I just report the facts—I don't make 'em up."

"Let's see. The most recent one I knew about was named… oh, come on… Robyn. With a 'y.' Robyn Ezterhaus." She spelled the last name, too.

"Did the affair with Robyn last an unusually long time? Was it especially intense?"

"They all tend to run together, but I don't think so. And after all, Aaron…"

"What?"

Stephanie frowned. "It doesn't make sense. If she wanted Louis so badly, she had to get rid of the competition. His being married was the problem. Why didn't she come after me?"

I stared down and speared a piece of grilled chicken, which was the only thing making the salad even marginally interesting. "Why, indeed?" I said.

Chapter
Seventeen

Stephanie gave me a few names and phone numbers, including some of Legs' political adversaries (of whom there was a large selection). Somewhere on the list was talk show host Estéban Suarez, with whom Legs had a very public argument not long before he died. Through Internet sources, I managed a few additional names. She promised to let me talk to her sons, and to Legs' mother. When I asked about his brother, she said, "I don't really know him very well. I can't make any predictions." Still, she promised to try.

When I got home from lunch, I changed back into my civilian clothes (which would have gotten me kicked out of even a classy McDonald's) and checked on the answering machine, which was unblinking, and the computer, where there was a message for me on WUSS.

Peter Arnowitz, a novelist, occasional screenwriter (no credits on anything you've ever seen), and overall conspiracy theorist, had read my post about Legs. Pete is the kind of guy who has mysterious "sources" in every branch of the government, the movie business, law enforcement, and for all I know, the local 7-Eleven. He never divulges a source, and he's never wrong. *Ever.*

Pete's reply read: "I can't confirm this, but I'm told through sources close to the investigation that the wife is the prime suspect. An arrest could happen within days. No physical evidence (that is, fingerprints) that I know of, but Gibson messed around so much they figure his wife *has* to be mad at him. What's puzzling is why they're looking to act so quickly. They don't have anything to go on, and a thin case could get tossed in minutes by the wrong judge. That's it for now. I'll let you know."

That's Peter. He never even asked why I needed to know about the investigation. He probably knew already. Arnowitz more than likely had sources inside *Snapdragon*, or a bug on my phone. If he did tap my phone, I hoped he didn't listen to the tapes. Pete is way too valuable a source to bore him to death.

I sent him back a message, private like his to me, thanking him for his effort, and moved on. I called Sgt. Abrams in D.C.

He actually answered the phone despite knowing it was me on the line. "What do you need now, Tucker, a free pass to the White House tour?" It's nice to know when people are happy to hear from you.

"I hear you guys expect to arrest Stephanie Gibson within the next few days," I told him. "Can you confirm or deny?"

There was a long pause. When somebody thinks you're a drooling idiot and you sucker punch him with competence, it creates a delicious moment. I savored this one.

"I have no comment."

"That's the best you can do? Despite being what you consider a bozo, I get this far this fast, and you can't do any better than 'no comment?' Geez, Abrams, I thought more of you than that."

Perhaps I laid it on a little thick, because Abrams did not take my comments in the jocular spirit with which they were intended. "Do you have anything else to ask, Tucker, or is this strictly a call to annoy me?"

"Let me ask you this: how can you possibly be thinking of charging Stephanie when all you have are hunches and circumstantial evidence?"

"No comment."

"You're no fun, Abrams."

He hung up. I suppose I deserved that. I made a mental note to make it up to him the next time we spoke, assuming he'd take the call.

Meanwhile, there wasn't much I could do today, so I got back to work on the third act of the mystery, and was in tantalizing proximity to the end when the door burst open and Ethan walked in, singing to himself.

"How's it going, pal?" I said.

"*Comme ci comme ça.*" In sixth grade, you get French lessons.

"Bon," I told him, and was about to attack the keyboard again when Leah came in, with a grump on her face, as had suddenly become usual.

Before I could ask her about it, I was saved by the phone. The voice on the other end was somewhat hushed, but I recognized it. I'd been talking to it three minutes earlier.

"This is Abrams."

"Yeah, listen, Sergeant, I didn't mean…"

He cut me off as my daughter hung up her book bag and slumped into the kitchen for a snack. "I'm on a cell phone outside the building. How did you know about the arrest?"

I stuttered for a second, trying to absorb what he said. "There really is going to be an arrest? You have enough to do that?"

"Soon. And I need to know your source."

"I can't do that, Abrams. You know I can't."

Abrams sighed. He *did* know I couldn't. "This is from the top, Tucker. *Nobody* knows about it. I'm not even sure *I* know about it. How do you?"

"The fact of the matter is, Lieutenant, I'm not even sure where I got the information from. It was from a friend of a friend, if you know what I mean, and that's all I'm going to say. But, how soon? And what do they have to use for…"

"Soon. And I can't tell you anything about evidence. You

know *I* can't." He was right about that, too.

"Thanks for the heads up," I told him. We both hung up.

Stunned, I tried to call Stephanie, but got no answer at her hotel. At least she hadn't checked out yet. I tried her cell phone, and got voice mail. I left a message telling her it was urgent she call me before she left town.

I'd like to say that Steph's plight dominated my every thought for the rest of the evening, but the truth is that my mind is far too egocentric to allow such a thing. I concerned myself with making sure Leah fed the gecko (something that had immediately become a chore after the first time she'd done it). I chose not to watch, since leaving live worms on a little dish and then watching something that must, to them, look like Godzilla show up to devour them was a little more than my delicate sensibility could handle.

After that, we had the daily tantrum over homework, followed by the making-up and post-tantrum hugs, then preparing dinner, celebrating the arrival of Abby, eating dinner, packing Leah off to her soccer game, talking to the other parents at the cold, damp high school field during said game (nobody there knew anything about the stink bombs, either), then back home, baths, showers, pajamas, brushed teeth, arguments about why one has to go to bed at the same time as the other despite the age difference, then a cuddle on the couch with my wife before she headed off to bed.

Through it all, my mind was occupied with something else. I had to get to "THE END" of that damn screenplay, so I sat down to complete my task at 11:30 p.m.

By 1:30 a.m it was pretty much done, and purged from my conscious mind. I'd pay for it in the morning, but I already felt better. The mystery had been solved, the wicked punished, the good rewarded, and most importantly, the words "FADE OUT" typed. I'd print out a copy in the morning and force Abby to read it the next night.

The computer went off about a quarter to two, and I headed for the stairs, with the lights out everywhere on the ground floor. Luckily, I know where everything is in my house, so I only stubbed my toe twice and tripped once.

But the moment my foot hit the first stair, I heard a jarring crash of glass and the sound of a car peeling away. Quick as a cat, I stood transfixed on the first stair, and gaped into my living room wondering what to do.

Amid the broken glass, a splinter of wood from the frame of what used to be our bow window and the usual clutter of remote controls, discarded socks, and forgotten toys, was a rock about the size of a softball, covered in a man's handkerchief.

I shook off my initial stupor and walked to the rock, careful to avoid the shards of glass. Passing the side table, I picked up a pair of gloves I'd left there the previous March after the final snowfall of the season. No sense rushing these things—we might have gotten one of those freak blizzards in July you're always hearing about.

I pulled on the gloves and bent down to pick up the rock. It was fairly heavy, and the handkerchief, it was now obvious, had been lashed to it with thick rubber bands. I eyeballed its trajectory from the street, and marveled at the thrower's arm. The Yankees could use a guy like that for middle relief.

Written in permanent marker on the handkerchief were the words, "YOU WERE WARNED."

Chapter
Eighteen

You don't often get a rock with a threatening message thrown through your front window at two in the morning, so I savored the moment. In other words, I stood there a long time with a knot in my stomach and a definite shimmy in my knees.

The knot in my stomach leapt to my throat when the light in the room suddenly came on. I spun, sending broken glass sliding to various corners of the room.

"Jesus!" said Abby, standing on the stairs and looking down at me. "What happened?"

To my eternal shame, I considered lying to her. Abby was already on edge about the phone call, and this would be about sixteen times worse than that. So what could I say—that I'd been walking across the room on my way to the stairs when the window inexplicably exploded?

I held out the rock, like a little boy explaining to his mother how he hadn't meant to break his fire engine, but displaying two, neatly snapped-apart pieces.

"Somebody threw this through our window."

"Holy shit," she said daintily. Abigail walked down the stairs and surveyed the wreckage that is our living room, layered with the wreckage that now was our front window. "Are you okay?"

"Yeah, I was on the stairs when it happened." She put on a pair of slippers that were on the stairs, came over and gave me a hug anyway, which I would have appreciated more thoroughly under different circumstances.

"Why would somebody throw a rock through our window?" she asked. Abby hadn't seen the words on the handkerchief, and I wasn't rushing to show them to her.

"I didn't have time to ask."

Her eyes narrowed. She knows when I'm being evasive. Apparently the only emotion she can't detect on my face immediately is lust, or all our conversations would begin with "okay," or "not now, for goodness sake!" "What aren't you telling me?" she asked.

My lips pursed with a "you just don't trust me" look, but she wasn't buying it. I showed her the note on the handkerchief.

Abby sat down on the bottom stair. She started to rub her temples with both index fingers. "It's starting again, Aaron," she said.

"Put your head between your legs."

I got a sharp look for my trouble. "You know what I mean. The threats. The worrying. The constant feeling that we'll be under attack at any moment. We swore we weren't going to have this again, didn't we?"

"I don't know why we're having it now. It doesn't make sense."

"Do rocks through a window usually make sense?"

I started picking up the larger pieces of glass and stacking them gingerly on the coffee table. "You like to think a message is being sent," I said. "But there's no message here."

"I think the message is pretty clear. They don't want you looking into Louis Gibson's murder."

"Who doesn't? Every reporter in a three hundred mile radius is looking into the murder. I don't have anything the others want. I'm not so close to the solution that whoever's responsible has to be worried. Driving from house to house and throwing a rock through every reporter's window would take months. I just don't understand why they're after me, and not anybody else."

Abby stood up and walked into the kitchen. I followed, because there's no point in trying to get her to stop going somewhere, and she generally has a good reason. Turned out she did this time, too, as she reached under the sink for the garbage bags. She was going to throw the glass and splintered wood away.

"Wait," I said, and went into the closet for the contractor garbage bags, which are heavier and less likely to be torn by broken glass. "Did you hear any of what I said?"

"Of course."

"So?"

She turned to me and did a perfect imitation of the face Leah puts on when she's in her "I'm-about-to-become-a-pre-teen-and-boy-are-you-annoying" mood. "I'm *thinking*!" Abby fussed, and we both chuckled.

This time, she followed me back into the living room, and we started the process of separating the wreckage the rock in our window had caused from the wreckage that normally makes up our living room. I was already thinking about how to cover the pane of glass that had been damaged until repairs could be made, and decided that cardboard and duct tape were the way to go.

Abby exhaled, which I took to be a sign the thinking was over and she had something to say. And sure enough, she said, "You're right. It doesn't make any sense that they'd come after you as opposed to any of the other reporters. So there's only one explanation."

Intrigued, I looked up, and came close to cutting off my left pinkie on jagged glass. "Really? What?"

Abigail frowned, and spoke quietly. "They must be coming after *me*."

Chapter
Nineteen

You have to understand, it was now after two in the morning, and my mind wasn't firing on all cylinders. So I gaped at her for a few seconds, and not in the way I usually do.

"I'm sorry," I said. "I must have heard you wrong. I thought you said they were coming after you."

"I did," she answered, and I noticed she hadn't met my eyes for a while. "That's the only logical explanation."

"We need a broom," I told her, and got up to get one. Abby stared at me as I left the room, went into the same closet where I had gotten the bag, and emerged with a broom and dustpan. I came back into the living room, and she was still staring.

"Don't you want me to explain?" she asked.

I began sweeping up the smaller pieces of glass. "I'd be willing to bet fifty bucks you can't," I said. "What the hell do you mean, the only logical explanation is that people are coming after you?"

Abby sat down on the stairs again and got a dreamy look on her face, as if she weren't actually there in the room with me. When she spoke, it was as if she were talking to herself.

"I had a case a couple of months ago, a guy who shot his girlfriend and left her in an alley," she began.

"I remember," I told her. "The pro bono case you were assigned. She was in the hospital for a couple of weeks, but she's okay now, right?"

She didn't appear to have heard me. "The girlfriend had to

have four separate surgeries, but she's mostly all right. But the client, the shooter, went to jail."

"You lost the case."

This time, Abigail heard me, and her face sharpened. She met my eyes for the first time in a number of minutes. "It had a lot to do with the fact that he was really, really guilty," she said. "When six people see you shoot somebody, it's hard to say you were actually at the Dairy Queen."

"Sorry." I dumped the last of the glass into the bag and put the broom down.

"It's okay," she said, dismissing my apology with a wave of her hand. "Anyway, he got six years. But he got himself another lawyer, and he's appealing the decision. The client—his name is Preston Burke—is out on bail."

It took me a second. "And you think he's out to get you for losing his case?"

"I got a letter at the office last week from him, and while the language wasn't direct enough for me to file a complaint, it was obvious he blamed me for his conviction."

"Yeah, clearly it was your fault he shot his girlfriend. You shouldn't have made him do that," I said. I sat down next to Abby on the stairs and put an arm around her. "Why didn't you tell me?"

"I don't know. You were all caught up in this thing with Ms. Cleavage, and I didn't... I don't know... lawyers get letters like that, but..." Abby looked at me, words failing her, and I held her close in my arms.

"It's okay, baby," I said. "We'll deal with it together."

Chapter
Twenty

The first order of business Saturday morning was to find someone who could repair what was left of our front window. It's tricky, since the bow window was made of nine separate panes of glass in a tic-tac-toe design, and two of them, plus a piece of the frame, had been destroyed by the rock. I called a few of the names under "glass" in the Yellow Pages, and finally got one guy who agreed to come out and take a look. I almost had to promise him my firstborn male child to get that, but I figured Ethan probably wouldn't notice the difference until it was time to pay for college.

Once that was out of the way, and I had patched up the window to keep some of the breeze out, I picked up the bag with the offending projectile in it and walked to police headquarters.

Barry Dutton wasn't in yet, but his only detective, Lt. Gerry Westbrook, was. Just my luck. Westbrook had gotten into the police academy on a scholarship for the mentally challenged, and had conducted his long, undistinguished career on the police force with such excellence that it had taken him more tries to become a detective than it took Susan Lucci to win an Emmy.

I'm no snappy dresser, but Westbrook was wearing an outfit that would make Emmett Kelly blush: his sports jacket had kept Polly and Esther weaving for a week, and was so loud a plaid people shouted at Westbrook to be heard over it. I can't describe his pants, because there are some things I make it a point never to look at, and the lower half of Gerry Westbrook is one of them.

He couldn't see his feet on his best day. But I know he was wearing shoes because I heard them squeak when he walked into Barry's office to talk to me,

"What is it now, Tucker?" he said by way of greeting.

"What's the matter, Gerry?" I asked. "Get up on the wrong side of the sty this morning?" His hand went to his left eye, as he misinterpreted the comment. Gerry is as quick-witted as he is stylish.

"What's in the bag?" he asked. "Someone's head?" Westbrook laughed, for reasons known only to him.

I dumped the rock onto Barry's desk, and Westbrook, who is built a little bit like Lou Costello, only heavier, jumped back for a moment.

"Those lightning-quick cop reflexes at work again, huh, Gerry?" I said. "Don't worry—it's not loaded."

"What the hell is that?"

"Where I come from, we call it a rock," I offered. "This one came flying through my window at a quarter of two this morning. And look, it's inscribed."

Westbrook stared at the rock for a moment as if it were the Rosetta Stone and he was in charge of decoding it. Then, sheepishly, he took a pair of reading glasses from his shirt pocket and put them on.

"It's hell getting old, isn't it, Gerry."

"What does it mean, 'you were warned'?"

"You're the detective, you tell me. All I know is I got a strange phone call the other day, and this came flying through my window as soon as I turned my lights out last night."

Westbrook actually ventured to touch the rock, and amazingly, it did not give off a strange radioactive glow, so he picked it up.

"I did my best not to get prints on it, but you go ahead,

Gerry," I told him.

"You think we're going to dust a rock that came through your window for prints?" he asked. "Probably some kids out on a joyride who wanted to scare somebody. Tucker, stop trying to be so important that the whole police department has to stop in its tracks every time you walk in."

"Put on a couple of pounds, and you could <u>be</u> the whole police department," I noted.

This witty banter threatened to go on for hours, but luckily, Barry Dutton chose that moment to reclaim his office. He walked in and looked at Westbrook, then at me, then at Westbrook, then at the rock. Barry stopped to read the nameplate on his office door.

"This is still my office, isn't it? I mean, I didn't get fired while I was out, did I?"

"The police are here. Thank god," I said.

"See?" said Barry. "And they say we're never around when you need us."

"Once again, I'm proven wrong," I said.

Barry sat down behind the desk, making it necessary for Westbrook to back up toward the window. "Chief," he said through clenched teeth.

"What's that you've got in your hand, Gerry?" he asked. "A geological specimen you brought in for show and tell?"

"It's Tucker's, sir," was Westbrook's hilarious reply.

I explained the situation to Barry, and he, in police chief mode, sat quietly and listened with complete concentration. I added Abby's theory about Preston Burke, which earned me a snarl from Westbrook.

"You could've told me that part," he said.

"I was waiting for someone who might be able to help," I countered. "No sense asking the piano tuner how Mozart composed the symphony."

Westbrook's eyes rolled back in his head as he tried to determine if that was an insult, but he didn't have enough time.

Barry, however, was deep in thought. "You think this guy is after Abby?" he asked. "Can I see the letter she got from him?"

"I asked her to fax it to you this morning," I told him. "Marsha might have it already."

Barry picked up his phone and pushed a couple of buttons. "Marsha, did we get a fax from... okay, okay. Thanks."

He found the fax at his left hand, where it had been sitting the whole time we were in the room. I'd have chided Westbrook on his keen powers of observation, but I hadn't noticed the damn thing, either. Barry read it over, and handed it to me. The letter read:

Dear Ms. Stein: (which right away I thought was odd—if you're threatening someone, do you address them with "Dear?" Maybe Burke was being sarcastic)

I'm writing to inform you that I have decided to hire another attorney to represent me in my case. While I'm sure that this is disappointing to a high-powered lawyer like you, it's necessary, since I don't believe you were always concentrating fully on my defense during the trial. We were both distracted. This was reflected in the jury's verdict, which, as you know, I consider entirely unfair and unjust.

I intend to proceed with my appeal under the advice of my new counsel, M. Robert Monroe of Hackensack, and will have no further need for your services. Still, don't be surprised if our paths cross again sometime soon. I look forward to seeing you.

Sincerely,
Preston Burke

"What do you think?" Barry asked. Westbrook had been try-ing to read over my shoulder, but his breath smelled too much of salami (even at this hour) to allow that, and I turned away. Now, he grabbed the fax out of my hand.

"I don't know," I replied honestly. "It doesn't exactly say he's coming to get her, but it does make that veiled threat at the end. What do you think?"

Before Barry could answer, Westbrook piped up. "It's noth-ing," he said. "The guy's blowing smoke."

A second or two went by. I looked at Barry Dutton. "That's good enough for me," I said.

"Me, too," he nodded. "I'll start making phone calls this morn-ing. I'll have patrols drive by your house at night, and alert the police in Roseland to stay near her office. Don't worry, Aaron. Abby's going to be just fine."

Chapter Twenty-One

The window guy, who showed up exactly when he said he would, took a look at the 35-year-old specimen that had been decimated by someone's pitching, and you could almost see the dollar signs roll up in his eyes, like in an old Warner Brothers cartoon.

"Before you quote a price," I advised him, "take a look at the rest of the house."

He did, and seeing the dilapidated surroundings, the laundry on every available piece of furniture, the socks on every square inch of floor and the water damage in the living room ceiling, the dollar signs were replaced by cents symbols. His face fell.

"Don't feel bad," I said, "I know some people who have money. Maybe I can recommend you."

Window Guy brightened a bit, made a show of measuring everything in sight, and then delivered the knockout punch: an estimate of $2,000. After I came to, I told him we'd give him a call and sat down to think.

In the meantime, I decided I couldn't interview the parents of possible stink bomb offenders on the basis of a guess, so I put off that task, although I knew I'd have to do something to help Anne Mignano, and soon. The previous night's Board of Education meeting, according to the local paper, had been "tumultuous," with "residents asking for explanations as to the discipline problem in the Buzbee School." One mother was quoted as saying she was "afraid to let my son go to school anymore."

In other towns, where the lack of discipline in a school leads to shootings, stabbings, and beatings, that quote would have been understandable. In Midland Heights, where there hasn't been a serious injury in a school since the janitor slipped on a wet floor and broke his arm in 1995, the pressure building on Anne was just plain silly.

Problem was, I had no idea who might have thrown a stink bomb into the girls' locker room, the gym, or the boy's restroom, nor did I know why bringing the culprit(s) to justice would make a difference. Besides, it was too late to go to the playground and sniff everybody who looked suspicious. If I could interview every child in the school, I could come up with a theory, after four or five weeks. But the way things were shaping up, it looked like I had only a few days more to detect things. I didn't really believe that Anne would lose her job, but I was certainly in danger of having failed a friend, and that doesn't sit well with me.

Meanwhile, Stephanie Jacobs had not called me back after I'd alerted her to a possible arrest warrant coming her way. That was odd, but I could take comfort in the fact that, on none of my usual web sites had I seen news of Steph being arrested. I assumed the cops would wait until she got back to D.C., if only because Stephanie was a very low risk for flight.

It didn't make sense that the cops were moving on Steph this quickly, unless they had some overwhelming evidence, like a fingerprint, a witness or…

Sitting behind my desk, looking at the Bullwinkle clock tick by the seconds, it hit me. I picked up the phone and speed dialed Abby in her office.

"Abigail Stein."

"Say it again. You know how your voice affects me."

"Robert," she said with an annoyed tone, "haven't I always told you not to call me at the office? What if my husband found out?"

"That's very amusing, dear," I told her. "When I'm dying and my life passes before my eyes, I'll be sure to include this highlight."

"Do you get to hire an editor for that?"

"Abby, how expensive is analyzing DNA evidence?"

Her voice moved from playful to professional in a smooth glide, as opposed to mine, which tends to change moods with all the subtlety of Godzilla dancing "Swan Lake." "Very expensive. It would only be used in a high profile case."

"Like, for example, Stephanie Jacobs and Crazy Legs?"

"Right. Those cops are being watched by the Fox News Channel twenty-four hours a day. If they haven't come up with something to report by lunch, they could be under pressure to resign by dinner. You can believe they have all the resources they need." My wife has the attorney's ability to be absolutely cold-blooded about things, but she manages to do so without the abrasive edge that has earned most attorneys the reputations they so assiduously cultivate. She has a heart, and I get access to it. So I have given her mine.

"Are there specific labs you have to go to for this stuff, or does every jurisdiction have a specialist of their own?" It pays to have someone close to home who knows the ins and outs of criminal investigations, particularly when you're supposed to be conducting one, and you don't know your ass from a garbage disposal.

"Actually, most of it gets farmed out to a few labs. I can look it up for you…" In my earpiece, I heard the rustling of papers and the opening of drawers, and eventually Abigail came back on the line. "The one they'd probably use is the same one the FBI uses, in Arlington, Virginia. It's called HRT Forensic Laboratory." She gave me the phone number.

"Thanks, you sex machine," I said.

"I like to think I do better than a machine would," she said demurely. "Aaron, did you talk to…"

"If you look out your window and see a cop car, it's because Barry Dutton told them to put it there," I told her. "There'll be one near our house most of the time, too."

"Thanks. I don't like being afraid."

"Few people do. Makes you wonder why they keep making those *Friday the 13th* movies." I didn't know how to make her feel better and stay serious at the same time. If anything ever happened to Abby—that is, something I didn't want to happen to her—I would be absolutely adrift in the world. It's selfish, but I need her to be alive and well.

"You saw the letter. What did you think?" she asked.

"Tell you the truth, honey, I could go either way with it. I think it's best to be concerned, but I don't know that we have to panic. He might not have meant anything by it at all."

"I hope you're right."

"Don't worry," I told her. "You have a big strong man to protect you."

"Really? Is Mahoney coming over?"

"I love you, too," I said, and hung up.

Chapter
Twenty-Two

I called HRT Forensic, and sure enough, was immediately told that any ongoing investigations were none of my business, that their activities were not a matter of public record, and that my voice sounded sexy. But I told the guy I wasn't interested.

Barry Dutton called just before the kids normally get home from school. "I've done some asking around about your Preston Burke," he said.

"He's not *my* Preston Burke," I told him. "As far as I know, I don't have a Preston Burke."

"Nevertheless. The State Police, the local police, no matter who you talk to, this was the one time the idiot actually got involved in anything violent. There's no question he shot his girl-friend, but he hasn't hurt anybody, neither before nor since." This may be the spot to observe that few police chiefs in New Jersey, if not the nation, would have added that "n" before the "or." Barry Dutton: criminologist, administrator, linguist.

"Does that mean I shouldn't be worried about the rock through my front window?" I asked.

"No, it means that you can breathe a little easier, knowing this guy isn't a repeat offender with deadly weapons. He's out on bail, conducting his daily life."

"Anybody know where he was at 1:30 this morning?"

"He says he was home asleep. Strangely, since the whole shooting thing, he's had problems finding somebody to sleep with him, so he can't give us an alibi." Barry grunted a little, letting me know he wasn't happy with the way this was playing out, either.

"Where does he live?" I asked.

"Teaneck," said Barry. "Hell of a long way to come and throw a rock through somebody's window."

"No wonder he got here so late. Barry, explain to me why I don't want to go talk to Preston Burke."

"Because it might be the stupidest thing you've ever suggested to me, and you know that's saying something," he said immediately. "If it was Burke who threw the rock, and he is threatening Abby, you don't want to get him mad. If it wasn't Burke…"

"I don't want to give him any ideas," I finished his sentence for him.

"Exactly."

"Suppose I was cagey, and didn't tell him who I was or why I was there." He could probably hear the wheels spinning in my head through the phone.

"Suppose I were from Krypton and could see through Halle Berry's underwear," said Barry.

"I might tell your wife on you," I warned.

"Aaron, there aren't words for how wrong it would be to go see Preston Burke," Barry said.

"I guess."

His voice became more intense. "Tell me you're not going to see Preston Burke, Aaron."

"Barry…"

"*Tell me*," he said.

"I've got to go help Leah with her math, Barry."

"*Aaron!*"

I hung up, but I felt really bad about it immediately after. So bad, I actually went and helped Leah with her math.

Chapter
Twenty-Three

Stephanie Jacobs phoned me well after dinner that night, and I had to avoid the rueful gaze of my wife as I sat and took the call at my desk. Abigail Stein is not to be trifled with. And even though I wasn't trifling with her, she was looking at me as if I were.

"I'm sorry I didn't call sooner," Steph said. "I've been all over the place. First, there was Louis' mother, and then…"

"Listen," I said more urgently than necessary. "I talked to the D.C. cops. They're planning on making an arrest in Legs' murder, soon."

"I know," she said. "They're going to arrest me."

Leah and Ethan were engaging in the traditional "whose-side-of-the-couch-this-is" argument, and I stared at them for a long moment, digesting what Stephanie had just said.

"You know they're going to arrest you?" I said.

"Yes. You know, I hear things, too." She sounded a bit miffed that I assumed I was the only one monitoring her arrest status.

"You sound awfully calm about it," I said. She *was* taking a good deal of the fun out of it for me, and I must have sounded disappointed.

"I suppose I could panic," she said, "but I don't see how that would help. Besides, my attorney is already taking their case apart, and he says he might be able to stop this before it happens."

"That would be a first."

"Aaron, I've set up a time you can talk to Louis' mother, but his brother Lester wants to be there," Stephanie said, her change in tone not nearly as smooth as Abigail's. "Is that okay with you? Louise really hasn't been too strong since Louis…"

"I have no problem with it," I told her. "I wanted to talk to Lester, anyway."

"I don't know if he'll talk to you," she said quickly. "He said he just wanted to be there for the interview with his mother."

I rolled my eyes, since she couldn't see me, anyway. Leah got up from the couch, threw a pillow at Ethan, and ran up the stairs.

"Well," I told Steph, "we'll play it by ear. When and where should I show up?"

She told me, and I wrote it down. I was about to ask how an attorney—any attorney—could stop an arrest before it happens when a bloodcurdling scream came from the upstairs of my house. A small, female bloodcurdling scream—from Leah.

I told Steph I had to go and hung up, and within one frame of film was on my feet, running for the stairs. Abby, running from the kitchen, was just behind me. We exchanged a glance that said: Preston Burke? But that thought was too awful.

I was first up the stairs, and first into Leah's room. The usual tangle of clothes, toys, hangers, books, and CDs was scattered about the floor, and in the center of it was my daughter, crying, holding out the index finger on her left hand.

"It was E-*LIZ*-abeth!" she wailed. "She *bit* me!"

There was such outrage, such a sense of betrayal, in that little voice that I scooped her up into my arms and was halfway to the bathroom before something struck me. I stopped in mid-hallway, and looked at my sobbing daughter.

"Leah," I said, "where is the lizard?" The fact that it wasn't in its tank had just registered on my brain.

"I don't know," cried Leah. "I took her out to play with me, and she bit me. I dropped her."

I handed Leah off to Abby, and as parents, we exchanged another glance which said, "ugh, a lizard running loose in our daughter's bedroom."

While Abigail got Leah into the bathroom and began seeing to her finger, which was not bleeding, I got down on all fours and began searching for the Mini-Me version of It, The Terror From Beyond Space.

I can now definitively report that there is no more rewarding an experience than crawling around on sharp plastic toys and beads in search of a bloodthirsty pet that looks like it just left the auditions for a GEICO commercial.

It took a good fifteen minutes (and that "good" is a subjective term if ever I've used one), during which Leah, her finger washed, dried and bandaged, refused to walk into her own room because she was afraid of her beloved pet, now on the loose. I managed to cut my left palm on the edge of... some toy or another, then crunch a CD jewel box with my knee, bang my head on her bed frame, and get nipped by E-*LIZ*-abeth when I finally found her/him/it hiding in a doll house, lounging on the four-poster bed Barbie used to sleep in before Leah decided Barbie was "stupid."

After a good deal of crying and whimpering, some of it from my daughter, Leah was put to bed. I washed my various wounds and hobbled down the stairs. Ethan, on the sofa in the living room, hadn't moved a muscle through the whole adventure. After all, *The Bernie Mac Show* was on. Ethan thinks he's a riot.

Chapter
Twenty-Four

The next morning, I got out my Bergen County phone book and plucked out Preston Burke's address—(I get most of the books for New Jersey from Verizon every year—they help enormously with *Star-Ledger* work). Then I hit MapQuest.com for driving directions, put on an actual suit and tie, and got into the 1997 Saturn we use when we want to impress people.

Before leaving, I used my "call forwarding" option to bounce any incoming calls to my cell phone. You never know when the school will call about Ethan, or an actual paying gig will turn up—in the freelance biz, it's always better to be near a ringing phone.

Halfway up the Garden State Parkway, the phone rang, and Barry Dutton was on the other end. "You hung up on me yesterday," he said.

"No, I didn't. I had to go help Leah with her math."

"Don't forget who you're talking to, Aaron. Leah's in third grade. Her math homework is way too hard for you." Barry, alas, knew me too well.

"I didn't want to listen to your lecture then, Barry. It's my wife we're talking about."

Barry's voice hardened. "Yeah, and if you're really concerned about her safety, you'll listen to the *professional* here." There was a quick pause, while I tried to come up with an argument against his logic. "Aaron, are you in the car? Did you bounce your calls? Aaron, you're on your way to Teaneck, aren't you?"

"Sorry, Barry, I have to help Leah with her math." I hung up.

The phone rang a couple of times not long after, but I checked the incoming number, and chose not to answer.

Teaneck, New Jersey, is a lovely town in the Northern county of Bergen, where the people with actual money actually live. It is the part of New Jersey where Tony Soprano lives, but not where he works, if you catch my drift. Actually, Tony is more likely residing in Upper Saddle River or Livingston.

Teaneck, which is in the same general vicinity, has both an affluent section and a not-as-affluent-but-hardly-poor section, which is where Preston Burke lived. The clapboard two-family house that matched his address was not at all descript, and didn't look like the kind of place where a wildly violent maniac might reside. Of course, Jeffrey Dahmer probably had very nice mini-blinds in *his* windows, too.

I rang the bell marked "Burke," and waited. A thin, unshaven, balding man opened the door a few moments later.

"Yeah?" A Jersey voice. Slightly suspicious, but not aggressively so.

"Preston Burke?" I tried to sound official, but concerned.

"Who's asking?"

"I'm Aaron Tucker," I said, flashing my Central Jersey YM/YWHA membership card, a finger over the organization's name. "I'm here representing the New Jersey Bar Association."

"Why?" Still not challenging, but not totally accepting, either.

"May I come in?"

He thought about it, but couldn't come up with a reason I shouldn't. "Okay," he said, and moved aside. We walked up the stairs to his apartment, him first.

The place was simple, but it wasn't cheap. There were good rugs on the floors, the furniture was Ikea, maybe, but not Unclaimed Freight. I did not look into the refrigerator to see if there were any body parts, but if there were, they had probably been cleaned up nicely. Things were in their place, which made it look different than my house.

We sat on an overstuffed sofa, and Burke continued to look warily at me. I took out a reporter's notebook and a pen. "I'm here to discuss your recent change of counsel," I said. "We like to investigate some random incidents, so we can determine if there has been any problem with the original attorney assigned or engaged for the case."

Burke wasn't stupid, but he also wasn't used to people talking to him that way. Frankly, I wasn't used to it, either, and I wasn't sure I'd said everything the way I wanted to. In all likelihood, it wouldn't matter.

"You want to talk about my lawyer?" he said. Good. He had accepted and deciphered my babble.

"That's right," I said with my most imperious voice. "You had originally engaged a..." I reached into my inside jacket pocket and took out a Buzbee School announcement about an upcoming round of parent/teacher conferences. I did my best to scan the "official document," and continued. "Ms. Abigail Stein, of the firm Nolan, Delford, and Lincoln, to defend you in the aggravated assault charge. Is that correct?"

"That's right." Burke was clearly not comfortable with the words "aggravated assault."

"But you dismissed Ms. Stein after the verdict and have obtained new counsel for the appeal?"

"Right again."

"May I ask why?"

"Well, she lost, didn't she?" Burke was stating the obvious to a complete idiot.

"A lot of good attorneys lose cases, Mr. Burke. In fact, all attorneys lose cases. Perry Mason was a fictional character. Was there something about Ms. Stein's defense that you felt was incompetent, or showed anything but an honest effort on her part to defend you adequately?"

"She *lost*," he repeated most vehemently. "I didn't do it, and she lost the case. Why should I keep her as my lawyer? So she can lose *again*?"

"So this was not a personality issue, or some problem you had with Ms. Stein's professional demeanor. You would have replaced any attorney who lost that trial." I wanted to hear him agree to that.

"No," Burke said. "There were other reasons I got a new lawyer."

I pretended to perk up, writing incomprehensible notes in my notebook. "What would those be, Mr. Burke?"

The cell phone in my pocket rang. Burke, expecting me to answer it, waited. I looked at the incoming number. Abby's office. If I answered, it could be bad. On the other hand, Burke was waiting. I'd be quick.

"Aaron Tucker."

"Aaron Tucker? Since when do you answer the phone 'Aaron Tucker?'" asked my wife.

"I'm right in the middle of something right now..."

"I just got a call from Barry Dutton," Abby went on. "He says you were talking about going to see Preston Burke."

Burke's eyes flashed at the mention of his name. He must have heard it clearly enough.

"I'll call you back later," I tried.

"Oh my god, you're *there*, aren't you? Oh, Aaron, I could just..."

"Good talking to you," I said, and hung up.

Burke looked at me. "Who are you?" he said.

"I told you, Mr. Burke, I'm Aaron Tucker of the..."

"Oh yeah? Let me see your business card again, Mr. Tucker."

Oops. I hadn't printed any up before I left the house. Funny how you forget those little details when you're trying to misrepresent yourself. I made a show of reaching around in my jacket pockets.

"I seem to have run out," I said. "I'll make sure to send you one when I get back to my office."

Burke stood, and suddenly he didn't seem so skinny and unassuming anymore. "Who *are* you?" he said again, advancing on me. I stood up.

"Mr. Burke, I can see you're getting agitated, and I think perhaps it's time to conclude this interview." I started backing toward the stairs.

"Yeah, you go ahead," said Burke. "I'll watch you leave. And with my binoculars, I'll be able to see your license plate nice and clear. And once I find out who you *really* are, Mr. Tucker, I'm sure our paths will cross again." The very words he'd used in Abby's letter.

I backed down the stairs, cursing myself for parking within sight of Burke's front window. And once outside, I ripped off the tie (how do other men make it through the day in those things?) and jumped into my car, driving away as fast as I could.

Damn. This kind of thing used to work all the time for Humphrey Bogart. I guess he had better writers working for him.

Chapter
Twenty-Five

On the long drive home, I took stock. I turned off the tape I had in the cassette deck (*Invisible Band* by Travis), so I could think more clearly.

First, talking to Preston Burke had been a huge mistake. I couldn't understand why Barry Dutton had been so in favor of the move. It had just gotten Burke mad at me, Dutton mad at me, and worst of all, Abby *really* mad at me. So I was driving away from a man who had probably thrown a rock at my window, and toward a wife and a police chief who might very well throw rocks at my head.

Meanwhile, back in the detective business, the "Case of the Mysterious Stink Bomber(s)" was far from solved. Here, a problem that would have taken Encyclopedia Brown maybe a page and a half to solve, and I was no closer to a solution than I had been a week and a half before. I didn't so much as have a plan of action.

And then there was the investigative reporter business, where I was seriously stumped in my examination of the Crazy Legs Gibson murder. The cops were probably staking out Stephanie's house, other reporters were down in D.C. interviewing actual witnesses and players in the case, and I was in New Jersey, having spoken to a grand total of one person who had been involved at all. Luckily, she was the one who everybody else wanted to talk to, and who wouldn't talk to anyone but me. That, and that alone, was the edge I held in this story. And so far, it had gotten me almost as far as I had gotten in the stink bomb case.

This wasn't turning out to be my October.

My cell phone hadn't rung since Burke's house. This was not a good sign, as it indicated that my wife didn't actually care whether I was in the clutches of a possible serial killer.

I had to concentrate on just one problem at a time, and since $10,000 was riding on only one, I chose Crazy Legs. If there were DNA evidence, it would have to place Stephanie at the scene of the crime to get the cops moving on her so quickly. If it wasn't DNA, but a witness who was actually there, it would be weird. The only people who could be in a place like that would be the killer, the victim, who in all likelihood wasn't talking, and the girl-friend, who had already been interviewed and insisted she'd been in the shower and hadn't heard anything. Maybe she'd recanted her previous testimony. (You freely use words like "recanted" when your nightly bedmate is a lawyer. And when you have impersonated one unsuccessfully in the recent past.)

Could there have been someone else there? Stephanie had definitely been in New Jersey a couple of hours after the killing—I could personally attest to that. If she'd been in D.C. in time for the murder and New Jersey in time for the reunion, she'd have had to fly. But she'd had her car—the D.C. plates were evident on the BMW she was driving at my house that night. For that matter, on my block, the BMW was pretty evident all by itself. And a BMW is not the kind of thing you can place in the overhead bin as a carry-on item.

DNA evidence would rule out Stephanie hiring someone to kill Legs, unless she hired someone who could be directly tied to her, like a member of her family. So it became that much more important that I get some solid information from Abrams as soon as possible.

I'd have to talk to Legs' mother, too. I couldn't imagine she'd have vital information. But you never know where the good stuff is going to come from, so you talk to everybody and rule out most of them.

I was off the Garden State Parkway by then and onto Rt. 27, driving into Midland Heights, when the phone rang. It wasn't a number I recognized, so it was entirely possible it was someone who wasn't furious with me at the moment. I picked up.

"Hello?" I said tentatively.

"Hi, Aaron, it's Stephanie."

"Hi, Steph. Are you in jail?"

She laughed, as if I hadn't meant it. "No," she teased. "I'm at my mother-in-law's house." Ah. So she was putting on a cheery exterior to deal with the old lady. "We were wondering if you might be able to do the interview now. Lester has a business appointment later."

"Now?" I checked the dashboard clock—it was still three hours before the kids would come charging through the door.

"Is this a bad time?"

"No, I can do it now. But you'll have to give me directions. The ones I wrote down last night are still in my office."

She gave me the directions as I made a U-turn on Edison Avenue and risked the wrath of the Midland Heights Police Department, whose chief, already on the warpath, probably had added my scalp to his Ten Most Wanted list. "There's just one thing," she said when she was done.

"What's that?" I always serve up the straight line.

"Lester is here, and he's going to sit in with you two."

"We'd already discussed that. What about talking to Lester?"

There was a hesitation in her voice. "Lester is not willing to talk to the press right now," she said. "I'm sure you understand."

"Sure I understand," I replied. "You tell Lester that I'm not willing to have him sit in on his mother's interview unless he agrees to do one himself. I'm sure he'll understand."

Stephanie stuttered, which was extremely unusual for her. "B-b-b-but Aaron, you said…"

"I never said he could sit in, listen to everything I'm going to ask, then prepare his answers ahead of time and be ready for any possibility. I never said he could gain the advantage before I even enter the room. I never said I'd agree to any of this. All I said was that I'd write a story for *Snapdragon*, and I can do that with or without Lester and his mother. Their participation is entirely up to them. But my participation with them is entirely up to me. I don't exist to act as their public relations manager."

There was a long pause, and I got the impression Stephanie, hand over the mouthpiece, was talking to Lester and/or his mother. When she came back, her voice was different, small and obedient.

"Lester says okay," she said.

"He'll talk to me?"

"That's what I said," and she hung up.

Chapter
Twenty-Six

Louise Gibson lived in a very nice little Victorian with a wraparound porch on a quiet, tree-lined street in Scotch Plains, a Union County town where the people who have money have real money, and the ones who don't probably also have more than me. It was exactly the kind of place you'd expect a mother to live in, with real wood shutters and perfect clapboard siding, nothing plastic (or even aluminum) about it. Flowers were evident in the front garden. It lacked a porch swing, but you almost saw one there, anyway. A real Family Values house, straight out of *Leave It to Beaver.*

Inside was more of a scene from *The Godfather.* Louise sat in a chair with her back to me, looking out a window through the tiny crack of light between drawn room-darkening curtains. I resisted the impulse to kiss her ring, since I couldn't actually see if she had a ring. She did move every once in a while, though, so I was assured it wasn't Norman Bates' mom sitting there with Stephanie throwing her voice from the next room. When you're in the criminal investigation business, you have to watch out for ventriloquism, you know.

Lester, who up close looked even more like Legs, but smaller and smarmier (if such a thing was possible), was hovering to one side, smoking a cigarette like a Gestapo interrogator in a 1940s propaganda movie, holding it between his thumb and forefinger, palm up.

He wore a dark suit and tie, which I thought was a bit much.

Of course, I was wearing a dark suit and no tie, which was about six steps above normal for me. Louise had opted not to sit in widow's weeds, which I appreciated, but was in black. You got the impression she had been in black since Nixon resigned.

Stephanie introduced me, then left me alone with the two Gibsons. Her introduction was simple but flattering, as she called me a "wonderful reporter" who would "understand what you're going through." Personally, I didn't much care what they were going through, but I did understand it. Intellectually.

I won't comment on how wonderful a reporter I am. I think my record speaks for itself, damn it.

When I took the tape recorder out, Lester looked like he might faint, but Stephanie apparently had warned Louise, who nodded, not actually looking in my direction, but aware of every object in the room by radar, or that "eyes-in-the-back-of-the-head" thing your mother used to do to scare you into behaving.

I asked when the last time either of them had spoken to Le… uh, Louis had been.

"I spoke to him the night before he was killed," said Lester, without so much as a blink when his mother winced at the word "killed." "I was thinking of coming down to visit him and Stephanie that weekend, and spoke to him about the possibility of a White House tour."

"Can't you just go up and buy tickets the day you get there?" I asked.

"Not if you want to meet the President," Lester sniffed. I made sure I looked properly impressed, and went on.

"How about you, Mrs. Gibson?"

"I spoke to Louis every day," she said. "He was a good son, and he'd call me every single day to chat." She almost managed not to punch the words "good son" in Lester's presence, but she just couldn't hold back.

"Do either of you know of any enemies who might have wanted to see Louis dead?"

There was considerable silence for a while, but since I wasn't needed anywhere for another two and a half hours, it didn't especially bother me. I counted the change in my pocket—a dollar in quarters, three dimes, four nickels. Pennies were in my back pocket, but I felt it would be rude to start sticking my hand back there.

"There are any number of political charlatans and left-wing extremists who would have wanted to silence Louis Gibson," said Lester, his voice rising to a level that, in a normal man, would indicate he was ordering a cup of mocha java. "His was an important message that many on the other side didn't want to reach the public."

"Easy on the campaign rhetoric, Lester," I said. "Your allegiances are showing."

"I take it you did not share Louis' point of view," said his mother. "Is that correct, Mr. Tucker?"

"My political views are not relevant to this investigation, Mrs. Gibson," I said. I regretted the word "relevant," but otherwise felt I was on solid ground.

She actually turned to face me at that point. Louise Gibson might once have been beautiful, but decades of disapproval (dished out, not taken) had pointed her mouth downward in a permanent frown and clenched her eyebrows into a pucker. "I'm asking if you agreed or disagreed with my son's work, Mr. Tucker."

"And again, I'll have to say that it has nothing to do with the investigation," I tried again, eschewing "relevant." Now I had to mentally deal with the word "eschewing," but I smiled at her in a friendly, non-threatening way.

"You're being evasive, Mr. Tucker," she hissed. "I can tell

what your point of view might be. Your people are famous for their leftist leanings."

You don't often run into such obvious anti-Semitism in Central New Jersey, and it caught me off-guard. "My *people?*" I asked. "You mean short, overweight freelance writers?"

"I mean *Jews*," she spat. "You know that. Like the Rosenbergs. Remember them?"

"Hitler," I countered. "Remember *him?*"

Lester, of all people, ended this lovefest by putting his hand on his mother's shoulders. "Now Mother," he said. "There's no reason for us to be uncooperative."

"He's one of *them*," Louise said, not to be silenced. "He's one of the enemy!"

"Your daughter-in-law is half *enemy*, Louise," I helpfully pointed out. "That makes your grandchildren one-quarter *enemy*."

I snapped up the tape recorder, hitting the "stop" button, turned on my heels, and headed for the door. "Thanks a lot," I said to Louise. "I think I have enough background on Louis' family. Lester, if you ever want to get in touch, Steph has the number." With no better exit line, I walked out, Lester trailing closely behind.

Once in the hall, Stephanie appeared as if she'd been listening at the door. Her face was pale and her eyes wide. "Aaron," she said. "I'm sorry."

"I'm just glad I didn't kiss her ring," I said.

"What?"

Lester appeared behind me as if Steph had twitched her nose and made him appear. "Tucker," he said. "There was no need for you to agitate her like that."

"Agitate her! How, by being circumcised?" I was seeing, you should pardon the expression, red.

"My mother is of the old school," he said, spreading his

hands. "She's of another generation."

"The word is Reich."

In his new role as peacemaker, he ignored that, "She's been through a horrible ordeal. There's nothing worse than burying your own child. Surely you can understand that," Lester said.

I hated to admit it, but he had a point. "That doesn't explain her out-and-out..."

"No," said Stephanie. "It doesn't. But that's always been part of her, and she uses it as a weapon." Lester looked—not appalled, not shocked—annoyed. Steph wasn't following the script he'd written, and he didn't appreciate it.

"Mr. Tucker, to answer your question, which is the one I assume you came to ask," he went on, "my brother had many political enemies, but I can't think of any who would resort to violence when there were other, nastier tricks to pull on him. I can only assume this was"—and he didn't even glance in Stephanie's direction—"a crime of passion."

"So you don't know of anyone to start with," I said hoarsely.

"I'd start with the last bimbo and work my way back, if I were you," he said. "You're bound to hit pay dirt somewhere along the line."

Without another word, he turned and walked back into his mother's room. Stephanie waited until he was completely out of sight and behind the door, then she looked at me and rolled her eyes.

I chuckled. "Has it been this much fun the whole time, or did they decide to spice things up for the rabbinical student?" I asked.

"Well, the bigotry is a new wrinkle, but that's pretty much been the atmosphere around here," she said. "I've lived with it since Louis and I got married."

"Well, look on the bright side. She only hates you half as much as she hates me."

Stephanie laughed, and hugged me. It wasn't a friendly hug, and I didn't understand it. She was trying much too hard to make sure her breasts pressed against my chest.

"Hey, Steph," I said. "Take it easy. I'm still married."

She leaned back. "That's you, Aaron. You'd never do anything wrong, would you?"

Maybe I could distract her. "You're the second person this month who's accused me of being incorruptible," I told her.

"Who was the first?"

"Gail Rayburn."

Stephanie smiled. "Gail Rayburn wore push-up bras."

"Okay, now we're in the area of way too much information." I started to reach into my pocket for my car keys. "I've got to go pick up the kids," I said.

"From what? It's only twelve-thirty."

"Half-day," I lied. "Millard Fillmore's birthday, or something."

Stephanie put a hand over her mouth and giggled. "You're running away from me, Aaron," she said.

"Think of it as walking away in a brisk manner," I tried.

"You'll be back."

"If this is a recurring dream, I sure will," I said, and reached for the doorknob.

By the time I had reached the Midland Heights borough limits, I was relatively sure Stephanie had killed Legs Gibson. I just couldn't figure out how she'd done it.

With all this information rattling around in my brain, I did the only thing a sane man could do: I printed out a copy of my freshly completed screenplay, and mailed it off to my agent. By the time I was back from the Post Office, it really was time for the kids to get home. I dealt with the homework soap opera of the day, listened to the stories, read the note from Wilma, Ethan's aide (she has a separate notebook in which she reports to us on how his day *really* went), and actually wrote a 750-word piece for the *Star-Ledger* on the boating business "down the shore."

When dinner preparation time rolled around, I had almost exorcised the weird events of the day. And then the phone rang.

"Aaron, I'm so sorry," Stephanie was saying, even before I was sure it was Stephanie. "I don't know what came over me—okay, I *do* know what came over me."

"I know it wasn't my animal ruggedness," I said.

"Don't discount yourself, but actually, it was the tranquilizers I've been taking since Louis… died," she said. "I increased the dosage to deal with Lester and Louise, and it made me… I wasn't myself."

All right, maybe she hadn't killed her husband.

"I don't know who that woman was," I told her, "but if I show up in a room with her again, I want to have an elephant gun with me."

"Thanks a lot," she said.

"You know what I mean," I told her. Then, lowering my voice because the kids were in the next room, and listen only when I don't want them to, I said, "I am married, and I intend to stay that way."

At that very moment, the door swung open, and Abigail walked in. The kids swarmed around her, as they always do, and she smiled and kissed them and did everything she always does. But there was something different. The look in her eye.

"I have to go, Steph," I said into the phone. "My wife is going to kill me now."

"Don't joke with me about things like that, Aaron," Stephanie said. "It hits a little too close to home."

"I'm not joking," I said, and hung up.

I walked over to my wife, who was hanging up her coat, and reached over to kiss her. She ducked and walked away. I foresaw scintillating dinner conversation.

We ate, and glared, and didn't talk. The kids noticed—okay, Leah noticed, and Ethan might have caught a loose vibe here or there through his prattle about *The Simpsons*—and ate quickly. They left us in the kitchen alone.

Abigail stood and started to clear the table. "I'll do that," I said, but she went on doing it. I stood up and got in her way on purpose.

"Okay. As boneheaded plays go, this was my best all-time. I was way off base, I never should have done it, I'm a complete idiot, and you should divorce me before the evening is over. Does that about cover it?" She walked around me and put the dishes in the sink. "Abby!"

"I've never been this mad at you before, Aaron, and you're not going to be able to charm me out of it," she said, not looking in my direction.

"I'm not trying to charm you out of it. I'm admitting that it was unconscionable. I was wrong, I'm apologizing, and promising that nothing even remotely like this will ever happen again." I took her hands, and she let me, although she wouldn't look me in the eye.

"If anything had happened to you..." she began, and put her head on my shoulder.

"To *me?* Nothing was going to happen to me. I was there trying to make sure nothing would happen to *you.*"

She held me tight and started to tremble just a little. "You're such a jerk," she said.

"I think we've established that."

"You go through your life thinking you're the one in this marriage who loves the other one more."

It took me a minute to navigate that sentence. "Well, I am. I love you more than you love me. It's only natural."

"Why? Why is it natural?" She stood back enough to look me in the eye. Hers were a little damp.

"Because you're the more attractive person in the relationship."

"So it all has to do with looks?"

"No, I mean attractive in the literal sense of the word. You attract people more than I do. I tend to irritate them. You're the one everybody likes. You're the one all the men follow with their eyes…"

"You want men to follow you with their eyes?"

I ignored that. "You are, in the case of this marriage, the 'catch.' You even make a lot more money than I do. And I had, as you know, a bit of trouble finding women who wanted to know me before we met."

"I've heard the history." She rolled her eyes a bit.

"So it's natural that I should love you more. You are top-of-the-line Porsche, and I'm a used Pontiac. You saved me from the junk heap, and I adore everything about you. Don't you think I see all the dents and dings I've accumulated, physically and emotionally, over the years? But you're still a cream puff." It was, without question, the analogy I have most regretted using in my life.

"Aaron," Abby said, shaking her head and sitting on a kitchen chair. "I fell in love with you. I married you. I have two kids with you. Do you really think I'd do all that with some guy because I felt sorry for him? I'm lucky to have you, and I thank the heavens every day that we met. You don't love me more, and I don't love you more. We love each other. That's why our marriage works."

"So you're not going to kill me?"

"No. But I might maim you a bit. That was the stupidest thing you've ever done, and nothing like that must ever happen again, you understand?" I knelt beside her chair and nodded.

"It won't ever happen again, Abby. I swear."

She bit her lower lip, a sign that she's going to do something she thinks she shouldn't. "So, what'd you think of Preston Burke?" she asked quickly, before she could censor herself.

"At first, I thought you were insane," I told her, "but after a while, I saw how he could come across as dangerous."

"Do you think he threw the rock and made that phone call?"

I sighed. "I don't know. I honestly don't know. Just when I convince myself it couldn't have been him, I recall the look in his eye when he realized I wasn't who I said I was…"

"Aaron!"

"Don't worry. He doesn't know anything about us being married. The fact is, Abby, we'll probably never hear from him again."

And, of course, the phone rang.

I picked it up, and somehow, I already knew the voice would be muffled and masculine. I wasn't sure what the words would be, but they weren't going to be words I wanted to hear.

"I know where you live," he said, and hung up.

I hung up the phone, and looked at Abby. "You know, the kids have Thursday and Friday off for the Teachers Convention," I said. "You think you could take those days?"

"I think so," she said. "Why?"

"I was thinking maybe we'd take a long weekend and drive down to D.C."

Part II:
The
Dog

Chapter One

"A dog?" I was saying to Abby. "What, the lizard thing worked out so well that now you want to get them a larger, more demanding animal?"

Wednesday night, we were packing in our bedroom for the trip to Washington the next morning. It had taken some doing, but I'd managed, through my friends at AAA and my influence with a certain celebrity Washington widow, to find accommodations at a hotel we could actually afford. In fact, we even had a suite, with a separate bedroom for the kids, booked in Georgetown at less than half the usual rate. Sometimes, it pays to know the wife of a prominent dead conservative.

Steph had actually offered to put us up in her house, but I thought that considering her recent behavior, that would be, to say the least, horrifyingly awkward. I politely declined without actually discussing the suggestion with my wife.

"I'm thinking about a dog *because* the lizard thing worked out so badly," Abigail said. "Do you think I need a bathing suit?"

"If you're going to be swimming with anyone besides me, yes," I answered. "You know, I understand the hotel has a pool, but we're only going to be there for what amounts to three days, and I'm..."

"...You're going to be working much of the time, I know," she said. "And while there are plenty of wonderful sights to see in our nation's capital, the kids like nothing better than a hotel pool, so we're going to spend at least some time there." She took a one-piece suit and a bikini out of the assemble-it-yourself piece of furniture she uses for a closet. "Which of these is better?"

"If you're going to be swimming without me, you'd better wear a complete dive suit and an overcoat," I said. "The one-piece. And I'm still waiting to hear how the lizard fiasco makes a dog a good idea."

Leah had flatly refused to feed E-*LIZ*-abeth since the infamous biting incident, but burst into tears anytime it was suggested the little beast might be better off in another home, like the one across the street, where it could play with another of its kind. I had tried to feed the lizard once, managed it without throwing up, and then bravely placed the responsibility in the lap of the person whom I considered most deserving. But Abby didn't want to pluck worms out of a plastic margarine container with a tweezer and watch a refugee from Jurassic Kiddie Park gobble them up, either. So Melissa had been very gamely helping out for a few days.

"You recall that the idea of the lizard as a pet was to encourage Leah's interest in animals," she began.

"I recall that's the excuse you used, yes."

"You know, I still haven't completely forgiven you for the Preston Burke thing. You might try to be a little more agreeable on this." Abby put the bikini in her suitcase.

"Fine. So how does that lead to me cleaning up dog poop?"

My wife, who grew up outside Chicago, took on what she considers to be a New Jersey accent, as if such a thing existed. "Dat's da *beauty* of dis deal," she said. "It *doesn't* lead to you cleaning up dog poop. It leads to our daughter bonding with an animal and taking on the responsibility of its care." I removed the bikini from Abby's suitcase, stuffed it back into her closet, and replaced it with a much more concealing suit—one that would cause most men to weep silently, rather than drool openly, once she put it on. "Hey," she said, but smiled and let me make the replacement.

"So in your heart of hearts, you believe that your daughter will actually feed, groom, and, most importantly, walk a dog, probably a good few times a day, because she will feel responsible? Have you actually been living with this child for any period of time?"

"Ethan will help," she said with a straight face.

"This is not the time for comedy," I told her. "Ethan? It'll take Ethan three weeks to notice we even *have* a dog!"

"Then you're saying it's okay with you if we get a dog?" said my wife.

I sat down on the bed and took her hands, beckoning her to sit next to me so we could talk seriously. Our eyes met, and I tenderly said, "no."

"No?"

"No. Look, Abby, you know as well as I do that this dog is going to end up being mostly my responsibility. The kids will be thrilled to pieces with it for about three days, and then, once February comes and the wind is blowing and there's six inches of snow on the ground, it won't be so much fun to walk Fido anymore. And you're at the office all day, so you won't be able to do it. I'm here, I'm going to feel bad for the poor mutt, and I'm going to end up doing most of the care. So, as the person whose life it will affect most noticeably, I'm saying, no."

Abby stared into my eyes, and saw that I was serious. She took a deep breath.

"*Fido?* You want to name our dog *Fido?*"

"You're beautiful when you're annoying," I told her.

Abigail stood up and went back to packing. "We'll take a look on the Internet when we get back," she said.

"Abby…"

"I said a *look*. We won't do anything until you say it's okay." She reached into the closet again. "Which nightgown should I bring?" she asked.

"How badly do you want me to agree to this dog idea?"

"Pretty badly."

I pointed. "*That* one."

She put it in the suitcase.

Chapter
Two

Driving long distances with children is an experience to be undertaken only by those foolish enough to become parents to begin with. The travel time by automobile from Midland Heights, New Jersey to Washington, D.C. is usually about three-and-a-half to four hours if you go straight through. The actual driving time with a wife and two children is about six hours, and if you listen to what goes on in the back seat, it feels like eight days.

"Stop that."

"Shut up."

"*Ethan!*"

"Get out of my face, you imbecile!" Ethan gets all his best insults from cartoons, which are his major source of cultural information. He thinks people actually say, "curse this traffic!"

We stopped about every half hour so Leah wouldn't get car sick, and made sure to pull into every rest stop because, guaranteed, someone would have to go to the bathroom a half mile after we left. Only a parent can actually force someone to go to the bathroom when they don't want to. We ate bad rest stop food (there is no *good* rest stop food). We listened to an unabridged recording of one of the Harry Potter books, and I did my best to keep the kids engaged along the way.

"Look, Ethan, a sign for the Decoy Museum!"

"So?"

"So, where do you think they keep the *real* museum?"

Long pause. "What do you mean?"

Like that.

Finally, much more battered but no less irritated with each other, we pulled the minivan (which was rumored to hold more luggage than a sedan, an out-and-out lie) up to the parking garage of a hotel that specifically asked me not to mention its name, given the fact that it doesn't want to offer the "Dead Conservative" rate to every family that pulls up with four stuffed animals, a bag full of foods an Asperger's kid will eat, and one suitcase carrying a certain, specifically requested nightgown.

My bag, an overnighter, held three changes of underwear and socks, a few shirts, an extra pair of jeans, my "toiletries," and a copy of my latest script. Maybe being confined in a room with Abby for three nights, I'd be able to force her to read it.

Getting Abby to read one of my scripts is like getting Leah to go to the dentist. She'll do it, but only under extreme duress.

She tells me it's hard to read something when the author is in the room. I've offered to leave the room while she's reading, but she says she can feel my eyes on her the whole time. This is silly of her, since my eyes are on her all the time, but Abby will generally read the latest book she's gotten out of the library, even if she doesn't like it, before my script. Hell, she'll read the side of a cereal box before she'll read my script.

In the old days (before I wised up), I used to wait until she'd read it to send anything out to my agent. Now, I send it to my agent and then suffer the torture of days and days until Abby will crack the cover.

So I had high hopes as we checked into the swanky digs we'd finagled for the weekend that I could do some meaningful interviews, see some sights with my children, and get my wife to pass judgment on my latest work, all in one weekend.

And I believe I may have mentioned the specifically selected nightgown that had made the trip with us.

Before the kids had time to discover Cartoon Network on the in-room cable, Abby spirited them out to see the Lincoln Memorial. I would have liked to have gone, since big Abe in his huge chair is one of my favorite sights, but I had already lined up a good number of interviews for the few days we had. So I was off to see the infamous Cherie Braxton, at the scene of the crime.

I took the Metro, rather than the minivan, because Washington's streets make as much sense to me as New Coke. And after asking only three complete strangers for directions, I found the nondescript, five-story apartment building, and Ms. Braxton buzzed me in.

I couldn't help but think about how many times Legs had climbed these stairs, and whether or not he'd managed to do it without being winded, like I did. Of course, it was just the second floor, but I still took a certain pride in seeing all that work at the Y pay off.

Cherie had the apartment door open already, and she was standing in the doorway, watching for me at the elevator. She was startled when I appeared in the stairwell.

"Mr. Tucker?" she asked in a small voice. I admitted to being me, and she gestured me into the apartment. "I wasn't expecting you on the stairs," she added.

"I'm trying to work off fifteen pounds," I said. Okay, twenty. But no more than that.

"You don't need it," she said automatically. Flattering men who were older than her came to Cherie Braxton as a reflex.

"I hope you don't lie that much when we start the interview," I said, but she didn't smile. I walked inside and was immediately overcome by beige, the clear color of choice among the upwardly mobile in our nation's capital. Beige carpeting gave way to beige walls with beige furniture breaking up the monotony. Amazingly, the ceiling was white. They must have run out of beige paint.

There were cartons everywhere—it was obvious Braxton was moving out. She removed some boxes from an old sofa, and we sat down.

She had, I noticed, decided to dress a little more conservatively for the *Snapdragon* reporter than she had for the cops. Her figure, which was in the top six percent, was still evident, but every button on her silk blouse was buttoned, and her denim skirt fell well below the knee. I clearly didn't represent an upward move in status, so I wasn't being seduced. Just as well.

"You moving because of what happened?" I asked.

"In a way. After the press got hold of me, people began picketing outside the building and everything. Besides, once the pictures ran in the papers and on the news, I started getting better offers."

"Better offers?" For what, her services as murder witness?

"You know, I got asked out by men higher up in the government. And I got a few offers to pose in magazines, but I turned those down." It's nice to have standards. "They were only offering fifteen thousand, and that's not enough to take off my clothes and get my picture taken." No matter how low those standards might be.

"How did you meet Louis Gibson?" I decided was a good place to start.

"Louie came to my office at Housing and Urban Development to try and get my boss to endorse a rider for putting the Lord's Prayer back in schools on a bill that HUD wanted passed in the House," she said, sounding quite knowledgeable. "My boss made him wait a few minutes, and that got Louie pissed. Since we had a common enemy, we got along well right away."

"You started seeing each other."

"We started seeing *all* of each other, if you know what I

mean," she said. "I mean, we were never dating. We just came here to screw."

"You knew he was married."

"Of course." Cherie made a face like she couldn't believe how stupid one reporter could be. "He never shut up about his wife, how she nagged him, what a pain in the ass she was, blah, blah, blah. But he'd never leave her. It'd look bad in the media, this big family values guy throwing over the wife and two kids for a young blonde. And I was glad. The last thing I needed was to be saddled with Louie for the rest of my life."

I feigned surprise. "So you weren't in love with Louis Gibson."

Her laugh was more like an eruption. "Pah!" the sound went. "In love? With Louie? Jesus Christ on a crutch, no! I didn't even like the son of a bitch!"

"And yet…"

"He knew people. And I wanted to know those people. Simple as that. Now, he wouldn't take me to dinner at his friends' houses, but he'd make sure the folks there knew my name. A lot of girls these days don't believe in sleeping your way to the top, Mr. Tucker, but I'll tell you, I don't see anything wrong in it. If men are stupid enough to do stuff for you because you'll fuck 'em, I say, fuck 'em."

Washington is an interesting town. Sometimes, it's as if entire decades of social change never occur there.

"Can I see where it… happened?" I asked.

She led me into the bedroom, which was also full of cartons. The bed was made, since Braxton still lived here, but the only furniture beside the bed were two nightstands with a lamp on each. It was a very beige room, with a beige rug. Near the foot of the bed on the right side, there was a small patch of carpet that was slightly darker, as if it had been rubbed the wrong way. That was the only thing that wasn't quite as beige as the rest of the room. The closet doors were mirrored, and you can bet Cherie Braxton spent a good deal of time looking at her reflection, to make sure she was still a valuable commodity.

"What did you see or hear that afternoon?"

"Nothing," Cherie said. "I was in the shower when it happened. Louie had made some crack about my ass, and I decided to let him wait a good long time for me to come back. Then I was going to dump him, you know, just to see him look surprised. But I was the one in for a surprise, I'll tell you."

"The knife was just sticking out of him when you came in?"

"Yeah, and he had this look on his face, like he couldn't believe it. Not like he was scared, or upset, or even mad, but that he was just so surprised. I guess whoever did it surprised him worse than I was going to."

"I guess so," I said.

Chapter Three

Estéban Suarez, the TV journalist who hosted the program *Left of Center*, was a breath of fresh air, at least compared to Cherie Braxton. Sure, he was just as ambitious and cynical, but he hadn't slept with Legs Gibson, at least as far as I knew.

"I love it when they go on about the 'Liberal Media,'" Suarez was saying. "You get guys like Bill O'Reilly on TV, just to the right of Attila the Hun, and they complain about this liberal bias in the media, *on the air*, as if they weren't in the media themselves."

All of which was fascinating, but it didn't answer my question about his getting into a fight with Legs on the show six days before Legs ended up as a Conservative-on-a-Stick. Instead, he was explaining, without being asked, why his own televised soapbox was named "Left of Center."

"I'm a liberal," he said, having worked up a head of steam. "I think I'm the last one left who's willing to admit it. Everybody else is so busy trying to be 'centrist' or 'objective' that they can't get out of their own way fast enough. Leaves the market wide open for a guy like me, who's got the balls to say it right to your face. 'I'm a liberal.'"

I was starting to wish I wasn't. "That's nice," I told him, "but the question was about the show with Louis Gibson." I gave myself a mental pat on the back for getting a word in edgewise.

"Yeah." He walked around the set of his show, which was as simple as these things get. Two chairs, which were considerably more worn than you might think, a piece of shag rug that went out of style with Nehru jackets and lava lamps, a lot of lights and boom microphones hanging from what appear to be bathtub pipes. Still, like all the other times I've been on a television or film set, I felt perfectly at home. Now if I could just convince someone else I belonged there.

"He came on to talk about his 23rd Psalm in the Schools thing," Suarez said. "You know, the shorthand for 'religious schools getting government money and blowing the separation of church and state out the window.' Gibson comes on, all smoke and mirrors, and gets himself bent out of shape when I call him on it."

"I hear he took a swing at you."

"Yeah. I told him he was working against family values by trying to make the schools only for kids who come from *certain* families, and he, um, took exception to that."

"I'm told you got mad and threw him out, told him never to come to your studio again." Suarez made sure his chair, and not his guest's, had a bottle of Evian water on a small table next to it. "I hear you actually had to be held back by your producer. I hear you told Gibson you'd kill him if you saw him again."

"That's right." There was a rundown sheet on the table next to the Evian water. It was stamped "preliminary," because this was Thursday, and the show would air live Sunday morning. I guess the water was preliminary, too.

"May I see a copy of the tape?"

"I'll make sure my assistant gets you one on the way out," said Suarez, who never stopped smiling.

"Aren't you concerned that a guy whom you threatened on live television turned up dead six days later?"

"Why should I be? I had no motive to kill him."

"You were mad at him for hitting you on your own show," I tried.

Suarez laughed. "Mr. Tucker, are you in show business?"

"I have my aspirations."

"Who doesn't?" He looked heavenward for a moment, deriding amateurs like me as a reflex. "Well, you need to learn one thing about the TV business," Suarez said, taking on an air of condescension only those with disproportionate self-esteem can muster. "You don't ever kill someone who gets you ratings like that. Geraldo got hit with a chair, and nobody remembers what the argument was about, but they remember him with the broken nose. You can't buy publicity like that. It was the same thing with Gibson."

"You mean…"

"Absolutely. It was *great* television."

Chapter
Four

I took a long shower when I got back to the hotel, and then Abby and the kids came in from the hotel pool. My wife, demurely covering up with a pair of sweat pants over her bathing suit, was still enough to melt the fillings in my lower molars.

"Did you cause cardiac arrest in any of the men down there?" I asked her.

"Only one," she said. "Luckily, there were paramedics standing by. Had you warned them I might be swimming today?"

"Yes, I felt it was my public duty."

"Well, it's a good thing I brought the one-piece. They revived him without even using the paddles."

I kissed her, then got the exciting run-down on a day spent looking at a large statue of a man in a chair, then swimming indoors.

"It was spooky, Daddy," Leah said. "I thought he was going to get up and walk toward me."

"I know, Puss," I said. "But he was such a nice man. He wouldn't hurt you."

"It would be cool, though," my son chimed in. "Like a monster movie."

Asperger's Syndrome kids like Ethan—and other children on the autism spectrum—reach a level of maturity during their pre-teen and adolescent years that approximates about two-thirds of their chronological age. Ethan, at twelve, was about as mature as the average eight- or nine-year-old. So he was very much into monster movies right now, as long as they weren't too scary. He loved the original *Dracula*, although he was also addicted to the Mel Brooks version, *Dracula: Dead and Loving It*, which has not yet achieved "classic" status. Mel is a genius, but I'll take *Young Frankenstein* over *Dracula* any day.

Stephanie had insisted we have dinner at her house that night, so we got into our "good" clothes (the only one who looked classy was Abby) and took the Metro to a stop near her brownstone.

I had been prepared for the fact that Steph lived better than I did (I'm prepared for that fact with most people I know), but I wasn't ready for the three-story, original brick, 1800's-era home with Stephanie Jacobs Gibson standing in the doorway.

Keep in mind that I'm not an architecture reporter. I'm used to a house where you're lucky if the walls have no holes in them. This was more like a place where you'd be amazed if the walls didn't have Picassos on them.

Still, it wasn't a museum—it was a home. The house, as far as I could tell, embodied the tug-of-war between Legs' desire to show off what a big deal he was and Stephanie's natural inclination toward living the most normal family life she could provide for her children.

Her sons, she said, would not be joining us that night. Steph and I had discussed that point ahead of time. The conversation would invariably have drifted toward the murder, and that was not something Leah and Ethan needed to hear. So I would meet privately with Jason and "Lou Jr." as Stephanie called him, Saturday.

We sat down to dinner in a large dining room. The food was already on the table—there was no sign of servants, although I was willing to bet Steph hadn't done all this work herself. The conversation began with Halloween costumes (Ethan had been

Dracula—Leah, some Powerpuff Girl or another), and then moved on to the city of Washington, D.C.

"If you like, I can help with the executive tour of the White House and the Capitol," Steph said to Abby, who was smiling a radiant smile I knew meant she thought Steph was showing off.

"No thank you," Abby said. "But I think we want to see everything every other regular citizen does."

"You know, I think that's wise," Stephanie said. Pretty soon, there might be an invisible fistfight in the room, given the looks that were being passed back and forth. Of course, being an idiot husband, I had told Abby about Stephanie's odd behavior at Louise's house, and that might have had something to do with the level of tension. On the other hand, the kids saw nothing, and thought this excursion was just too cool.

Stephanie had asked about their eating habits, and I'd explained that Ethan, especially, was very particular about the way he eats, which is not at all unusual with Asperger's kids. And she had provided exactly what I'd said he'd eat: Hebrew National hot dogs, French fries (pardon me: *Freedom* fries) and water. Luckily, Leah will eat all those things, as well as many others, so we were covered for both kids. The adults were having somewhat more elegant fare—Chicken Kiev on a bed of rice and vegetables.

"What do you think you'd like to see while you're here?" Steph asked Abby.

"Well, since it's Ethan and Leah's first trip, we thought maybe the Washington Monument, the Capitol, and some of the Smithsonian Museums. Air and Space, definitely." Abigail is the only woman I know who can look elegant while eating asparagus.

"All very good choices," Stephanie said, nodding. "Not the White House?"

Abby flashed me a look, and I shrugged the tiniest bit. "I think we'll wait until there's a president we'd rather visit," said my wife.

Stephanie, to her credit, did not react—she just nodded. I had no idea if she agreed with Legs' politics or not, but they had bought her this house and all the things that went with it.

"Yeah," said Leah. "We don't like this president. We wanted the other man to win."

"A lot of people did," said Stephanie. "But I guess we have to deal with what we get."

Leah, waving her ketchup-laden hot dog, decided to elaborate. "We didn't vote for him. How come we have to listen to him?"

"Do you get Cartoon Network?" Ethan piped up.

Stephanie looked from one to the other. She decided Ethan's was the easier question. "I don't really know," she said. "After dinner, you can check, if you want."

Ethan looked at Abby. "May I please be excused?"

"Not yet, Ethan."

"Mom!" Leah sounded wounded. "Ethan just cut me right off! He didn't say 'excuse me' or anything!"

"I know, honey," Abby said. "We'll talk about it later."

"But it's not *fair!*" Leah gestured with her hot dog, which went flying and landed, ketchup side down, of course, on the Oriental rug.

Me: "Leah!"

Leah: "Oops. Sorry."

Abby: "Oh, my. Leah, you've got to be more careful."

"*Now* can I be excused?" I don't think I even need to identify the speaker.

Stephanie, however, was all purpose. Before I saw the hot dog hit the floor, she was up, grabbing a bottle of club soda from the sideboard behind her. With her napkin and the soda water, she managed to obliterate the stain before I could even get out of my chair.

"Wow!" I said. "Do you do windows, too?"

Steph stepped back to admire her work. "If you get to it quickly," she said, "there won't be any mark at all."

"And since you knew my family was coming tonight, you had plenty of club soda lying around."

She stopped, and looked at me strangely. "Actually," she said, "it was for Louis. He used to drink that stuff like it was going out of style. I haven't gotten out of the habit yet, I guess."

"I'm sorry," Leah said in a small voice.

"It's okay, sweetie," Stephanie told her. "Nobody'll ever know."

"No," said Leah. "I'm sorry your husband died."

Stephanie looked at her a moment. "So am I, Leah. So am I."

It turned out Stephanie did have Cartoon Network, so we stayed for a few hours after dinner. The kids went inside to discover the delights of *Cow and Chicken*, while we talked in Steph's living room. Steph and I decided on a time for me to interview her sons on Saturday.

Finally, though, we packed up the brood, still complaining about having to leave while *Scooby-Doo* was on (on Cartoon Network, *Scooby-Doo* is *always* on), and found our way back to the hotel. It was late, so we packed the kids off to bed (although both of us harbored suspicions they'd search for Cartoon Network on their bedroom TV) and then retreated to our own bedroom. It was hard to believe we'd awakened this morning at home in New Jersey.

I lay down on the bed, and reached for my overnight bag on the floor. Abby was getting herself cleaned up in the bathroom, and I could see her through the open door, taking off makeup. I found the script in my bag, and pulled it out.

"I brought some reading material for you," I called to her.

She walked out of the bathroom and looked, saw the script. Abby smiled. "You know," she said, "it's awfully late, and I'm tired."

"You always read before bed."

"Yes, but what I'm saying is, I can either read some of the script, or…"

"Or?"

She walked to her bag and started to rummage through it. "Or, I can put on that nightgown you picked out. Now, which one will it be?"

I am so weak.

Chapter
Five

It had taken a good deal of maneuvering to get me an interview with Madeline Crosby. After all, it was Legs Gibson's rumor-mongering that had kept her off the Supreme Court, so she wasn't likely to acquiesce to a plea from Stephanie. And if Crosby had even heard of *Snapdragon*, it was likely to have been in the context of the odd classical music review they might run to fill space between the headbangers and the rappers.

So, I had had to rely on Mitch Davis, over at *USA Today*, to pave the way. Davis, after much grousing about "giving aid and comfort to the enemy," had made a couple of phone calls and advised me never to call him about this story again. Spoil-sport.

Crosby maintained a home office in, of all places, the Watergate complex, on the assumption that lightning never strikes twice in the same place, I guess. I was buzzed in on Saturday morning while Abby and the kids were out looking at Archie Bunker's chair and the Fonz's jacket at the Museum of Cool Stuff From Television. That Smithsonian is really a fun place.

In her mid-fifties, Madeline Crosby was not (forgive me, Madeline!) a beautiful woman. But she had a face so full of wisdom and wit, and eyes with just the right hint of sparkle, that it never occurred to me she was anything but lovely.

She had been an up-and-comer out of the John Marshall School of Law in Chicago, class of 1970. A year clerking for Justice Thurgood Marshall didn't hurt, and by the late 1980s, Crosby was too strong a candidate for the Federal bench to be denied. It wasn't until the mid-90's, when she was nominated to the Supreme Court, that the allegations of an abortion—a *legal* abortion, it should be noted—were made, not terribly surreptitiously, by Legs Gibson. Her nomination was scuttled within a week, although the abortion issue was never directly cited. Everyone knew Legs' news leak had done the job it had set out to do—it kept Madeline Crosby from being a terrific Supreme Court justice, because her point of view wasn't far enough to the right.

Crosby gave me a curious, but not interested, glance as I walked into her office. She was reading a document on her desk, wearing a pair of half-glasses that I would no doubt need within five years. She gestured to a chair.

"Sit down, Mr. Tucker."

I did so, and took out my tape recorder as I waited. I also had a reporter's notebook and a pen, but they were mostly to give my hands something to do during the interview. I don't trust tape recorders, but I confess that I don't take notes as carefully when I'm using one as I do otherwise.

Crosby put down the document and took off the glasses. She regarded me carefully, trying to determine if I were friend or foe.

"Why am I seeing you, Mr. Tucker?"

"A question I've been asking myself all morning, Your Honor."

She chuckled. "You're here investigating the murder of Mr. Gibson, is that right?" I nodded. "Am I a suspect?"

"Hardly. Although you probably had the best motive I've come across so far. No, Your Honor..."

"Oh, please call me Madeline. 'Your Honor' will keep us here until Tuesday." The sparkle in the eyes hadn't been lying. Madeline Crosby was a real human being.

"Thank you, Madeline. I'm Aaron."

"And you were saying, Aaron, about how I wasn't a suspect,

although you implied that I would be if I'd had any nerve."

She caught me off-guard with that one, and most people have a hard time doing that in conversation. I stuttered for a moment, and felt my mouth open and close.

Madeline Crosby laughed. It wasn't a victorious, "gotcha!" kind of laugh—it was genuine delight in having amused herself. "Oh, not to worry, Aaron," she said when she was finished laughing. "I'm not going to bite you. I just couldn't resist."

"I'm glad to hear it. The fact is, I'm here for background on um, Mr. Gibson, and since he built so much of his reputation at your expense…"

Crosby sat back and sighed. "You figured that I'd have something to say about him. Well, I do. Louis Gibson was an asshole of the first degree. And you may certainly quote me."

Well, I had my lead paragraph for the *Snapdragon* story right there, even if nobody ever found out who killed Legs. When an almost-Supreme Court Justice calls someone an asshole and *asks* to be quoted, you're having a good day as a journalist.

"How did you find out about his allegations to begin with?" I asked.

"The fact is, I read them in the *Post* the day after the *Washington Times* printed them, like everyone else," she said, shaking her head. "But I had been called by other media as soon as the *Times* story broke. That, you must understand, was such a confusing, whirlwind time. You hear rumors that your name might be on the list, then you get them confirmed, then you get the phone call from the President, and then your life is immediately a matter of public record from beginning to end. So I barely had time to think about the issues I thought were *important*, that I might be asked about. This article came from out of the blue."

I nodded. "Did you ever meet Louis Gibson?"

She smiled a bit and put her fingers to her eyes for a good

long rub. "Yes," she said. "Yes, I did. It was years later. By then, Gibson was the head of that bogus foundation of his, and he showed up at a fundraiser where I was speaking. He was there, of course, to try and stir up the opposition, show that there was dissent within the party, even though the only dissent in the room was his, and he wasn't a member of any party I'd ever join." Crosby opened her eyes again and caught me in her gaze. "He walked up to me afterward and offered his hand. Can you imagine? If you have strong enough convictions to sabotage someone's career, the least you can do is stick by them and refuse to act friendly toward her. But, no. Here he comes with his cute little wife by his side, putting out his hand, waiting for the photo op so he can show he's really a nice guy after all. Well, he wasn't a nice guy, and I told him in graphic terms what he could do with his hand."

"In front of his wife?"

"To tell you the truth, she didn't seem to mind," Crosby said. "I remember her chuckling just a bit at the suggestion."

"That's not inconsistent with what I know," I told her. "Madeline, can you think of anyone who would want Louis Gibson dead?"

"I can think of hundreds of people who are thrilled that he's dead. On both sides of the aisle, by the way. Either because he was such an incredible impediment to progress, or because it leaves a big spot open that some reactionary idiot will want to assume. Decent conservatives considered him an embarrassment."

"Can you think of anyone who actually has the guts to kill him?"

"In this town? Not really."

I stood up. "Thank you so much for your time, Madeline. I appreciate your talking to me." I turned the recorder off and approached her. "I hope you'll take *my* hand."

She stood and accepted it, smiling. "Yours? Anytime, Aaron.

You're a delightful change of pace from the usual Washington reporter."

"That's because I'm from New Jersey."

Crosby grinned wider. "A much misunderstood state. Really quite a lovely place to live, in spots."

"I knew I liked you for a reason, Madeline." I turned to leave.

"Aaron," she said, and I stopped on my way to the door. "I'm curious. You didn't ask me…"

"I didn't ask you *what?*"

"If the allegations Gibson made were true."

"That's right," I said, "I didn't ask."

"Why didn't you?"

I considered that for a moment. "Because it didn't make any difference to the story I'm writing, so it's none of my business."

"I knew I liked you for a reason, Aaron," she said. Crosby's smile was ear-to-ear now.

Chapter
Six

I met Abby and the kids at the Air and Space Museum, where we saw the "Spirit of St. Louis," Orville and Wilbur Wright's plane ("The Kitty Hawk"), and my personal favorite, the original "Starship Enterprise." History is different things to different people.

After lunch, my family and I went our separate ways. They headed for the Capitol Building, and I headed for a police station near the zoo.

On arriving, I went through the required ritual. I asked for Lt. McCloskey, was told he was held up in meetings, and was passed on to Sgt. Abrams. Which was where I'd intended to end up, anyway.

Mason Abrams turned out to be a compact man, maybe five foot eight (which still puts him a good couple of inches taller than me), built something like a strong chimp, all chest and arms. I'm built more like a walrus, all flippers and tusks.

He stuck out his hand when I introduced myself, and I took it. I'd felt badly about the way our relationship had begun, but Abrams seemed not to hold a grudge. I said I had more specific questions about Gibson's murder, and Abrams immediately gave me the company line.

"All I can tell you is that the investigation is ongoing. Any details are being held back to aid in the investigation of this crime."

I stopped a moment, raised my eyebrows, and exhaled. "You let me drive for six hours with two children in the back seat to tell me *that*?"

"That's right," he said. "And I'll tell you the same exact thing in the coffee shop at the corner in ten minutes." I nodded, shook Abrams' hand, and left.

It took only five minutes for him to get to the coffee shop, where he didn't tell me the same exact thing. "You wouldn't believe the level of security they're throwing over this thing," he said. "I'll bet the Kennedy assassination didn't get this kind of a shut-down."

"True, but that took place in Dallas."

"That's what they'd like you to believe."

Abrams ordered a coffee, this being a coffee shop. I opted for Diet Coke, since I sincerely thought of it as a Diet Coke shop. As soon as the waitress left the table, he started to talk in a hushed tone. I eschewed the recorder and took notes.

"There was just the one stab wound, in the chest, through the heart. A lovely job, well planned and executed, you should pardon the expression," he said. "The knife was a standard kitchen knife, manufactured by Gerber as part of a set. No fingerprints. A box with the rest of the set, also no fingerprints, was found in a trash can about a block from the apartment. It had, in all likelihood, been purchased in a Hoffritz store about five blocks from the apartment, though the only similar set the shop sold within 24 hours of the murder was a cash transaction, and the clerk doesn't remember the purchaser. They sell seven or eight sets a week, usually."

"No prints at all in the apartment?"

"Oh, no, there were tons of prints. Gibson's, our own Ms. Braxton's, of course. A couple of other boyfriends of Ms. Braxton's—don't bother, they both have perfect alibis, mostly being in bed with other girlfriends at the time."

"This is an awfully friendly town," I observed.

"We're not the Deep South, but we *are* the South," he drawled, saying "South" as if it were "Say-owth."

"What did the autopsy reveal?" I asked.

"What do you think it revealed?" Abrams countered. "He was stabbed in the chest with a six-inch kitchen knife. He died. The end."

"What time did the M.E. say Crazy Legs died?"

"Crazy Legs?"

Oops. "What time did Gibson die?"

Abrams cocked his head to one side and considered me. "The M.E. didn't have to determine time of death. Little Miss Flashdance was only in the shower for twenty minutes. So we know Gibson died between 5:15 and 5:35 p.m. Now, tell me about this Crazy Legs."

So I did.

"You have an interesting history, Tucker," Abrams said. "Nice of you to mention it before."

"What good would my going to school a town over from Legs Gibson do to help the police investigation?" I asked.

"Any information is good information in my business," Abrams said with a smack of self-satisfaction.

"Mine, too. Has Lt. McCloskey looked into the family's finances yet?"

The waitress appeared with the beverages and slapped the check down at the same time. She slapped it down next to me, since she probably recognized Abrams and didn't want to upset him with something so trivial as the bill.

Abrams watched her walk away, and it wasn't in appreciation of her form. He began whispering to me after he was sure she was out of earshot.

"The finances are the reason I had you come down here," he said. "I know you're not one of the pack here, and so far, you've been relatively trustworthy."

"Next time I go to high school with one of your suspects, I'll be sure to tell you, okay?" I said.

"Forget that," he said. "Listen to what I'm telling you. The family finances are, so far, clean as a whistle. But we don't expect that to last."

I could feel my eyebrows meet in the middle. "Why not?"

"Because the books at People For American Values were so cooked we're starting to suspect Wolfgang Puck was involved. So far as the financial guys can tell, the foundation bank account had been skimmed for over thirteen million dollars."

Chapter Seven

Luckily, I wasn't sucking on a straw when Abrams said that, or an ice cube might have gotten pulled up and lodged in my eye socket. *"What?"* I managed to choke out.

He did a very good Cheshire Cat impression. "I thought you'd like that one," Abrams said.

"So, thirteen million dollars is missing from the foundation Legs Gibson started, Legs has a knife sticking out of his chest, and you're going to arrest his wife because... why?"

Abrams lost most of the grin. "Well, that whole arresting the wife thing seems to be going by the wayside at the moment," he said. "We have EZ Pass records showing her entering the New Jersey Turnpike a good four and a half hours before Gibson was stabbed. We don't have any evidence yet that she has the money. She certainly didn't deposit thirteen mil into her checking account."

"And there are no other suspects?"

"There are legions of other suspects," Abrams said. "There are enough people who had access to that funding to keep us interrogating until my retirement. The question is, if someone else was skimming the money, why would they kill Gibson?"

"Because he found out?"

"He didn't seem terribly concerned about it," Abrams said. "There he is, on a Saturday afternoon, losing himself in an administrative assistant in the human resources office of the Department of Housing and Urban Development."

"True," I pondered. "Money. And here I thought you guys had found some DNA evidence you were going to hang Steph out to dry on."

Abrams stopped smiling entirely, and tried to catch the wait-ress' attention so he could get a refill. He was unsuccessful, both at getting more coffee and at throwing me off the scent.

"You *did* find DNA, didn't you?" I asked.

"Keep your voice down," he breathed. "Okay. I'm going to tell you this, but if you ever, *ever* try to attribute or connect it to me, I'll deny not only that I ever met you, but that I've ever even heard of the state of New Jersey. Are we straight?"

"I've always been. I never even experimented in college."

His eyes were not amused, and they were practically boring holes into my forehead. "Okay," I said. "We're straight."

Abrams looked positively intense, which was a 180-degree turn from his usual expression. He was talking in a tone so low I couldn't be sure I was picking up every word.

"We found a hair," he said. "Just one hair, and it didn't match Gibson, Ms. Braxton, or Mrs. Gibson. We ran it through the DNA files of known offenders who've given samples, through the FBI, and we hit a match. A guy from Texas, Branford T. Purell."

"What did Mr. Purell get convicted of?" I asked, in a tone almost as low as Abrams'. Some things are catching.

"Murder. He killed three women in Texas in the late eighties."

I started breathing a little faster. "Did he use a knife?"

"No, a shotgun. Mr. Purell wasn't exactly subtle." Abrams was-n't making eye contact—there was something he wasn't telling me.

"Okay, so let's find this Purell guy. Where is he?"

Abrams set his jaw, and turned his head to make direct eye contact with me. His eyes weren't amused.

"He's dead," Abrams said. "Branford T. Purell was executed seven years ago."

Chapter
Eight

Abrams and I exchanged incredibly unlikely suggestions on how a dead man's hair could make it into a live secretary's apartment seven years after he met his end in Texas, but neither of us was terribly enthusiastic about our theories. Mine, that he had been put to death unbelievably slowly by watching an attractive woman have sex with all sorts of other men, was not entirely serious. Abrams suggested it would lead to a new form of cruel and unusual punishment: death by pornography.

I thanked him for the information, however weird, and went back to the hotel. Abby and the kids were at the pool again, but now I had time to put on a bathing suit and join them, thus delighting my children and disappointing all the other men at the pool, who had been watching my wife and hoping she was a divorcée or a widow. No, I'm not paranoid—they all are truly against me.

We spent the evening quietly, going out to a restaurant and avoiding all mention of Legs or Stephanie. After dinner, the kids retired to their lair to see if Fred Flintstone had come up with anything new to say since 1966 (it was new to them), while Abby and I headed to our bedroom to collapse into two separate exhausted heaps on the bed.

Since my wife is incapable of collapsing into an exhausted heap without doing at least 30 minutes of prep work in the bathroom, I had plenty of time to set the stage. I shut off all the lights in the room except the one over her pillow, then turned down

Abby's half of the bed. The hotel had been kind enough to supply a chocolate for her pillow, and I moved it to a spot just below there.

I stripped down to the boxers with the New York Yankees emblem she had gotten me as a gag gift for my latest birthday, and climbed under the blanket. So when Abby (finally) emerged from the bathroom, she saw a dimly lit, quiet hotel bed, lavishly made up, with a chocolate and a husband.

And, of course, on her pillow, a screenplay.

She laughed, then walked over and sat down, careful to pick up the chocolate first. She looked at me and determined that I was not, in fact, asleep. Then she looked at the script, and chuckled again.

"*The Minivan Rolls for Thee?*" she asked, looking at the title.

"Hemingway," I said.

"I understood the reference," she admonished. "I'm just wondering if it's about…"

"It kind of is," I said. "And it's kind of not. You decide."

Abby lay down, her short pajamas showcasing her magnificent legs. She picked up the script and opened it.

"You realize I'm not going to read it all tonight," she said.

"Of course," I told her. "I'll be glad if you get past page one."

She bent her magnificent legs to make a reading stand for the script, and got to work. I did my best not to watch, but then she chuckled, and I tried to catch a glimpse of which page she was on, to see what was funny, and whether it had been intentional.

"Stop watching me," she said. "You know it makes me nervous."

"I wasn't watching you," I told her. "I was ogling your legs."

"That's different."

She went back to reading, and I lay there, eyes ostensibly closed, appreciating her. Okay, so I was watching to see if she'd find anything else amusing.

"You're making this difficult," she warned.

"Me? I'm as quiet as a mouse."

"A mouse with a pair of binoculars."

"They're still quiet," I pointed out.

Abby tried valiantly, and I even turned away at one point, relying on the inevitable closet mirror to watch her. She caught me looking at her in the mirror, and closed the script.

"Don't stop," I said.

She leaned over and put the script on her nightstand, then turned off the light and reached over to me. Abby pulled me close to her and kissed me with an impressive amount of passion for a woman who'd spent all day shepherding two children around our nation's capital.

"C'mere," she said.

"Two nights in a row? You'll do anything to avoid reading that script with me in the room, won't you?"

"Pretty much," she said.

The next morning (ahem!), I got up early to meet Stephanie and her sons at Steph's house, and left a note for Abby saying I'd meet her and the kids at the hotel before checkout time.

By the time I navigated the minivan into a parking space near Stephanie's house, I was a wreck. If you have a car, Washington makes even less sense than most cities. They even have streets that are one-way at certain times of the day, and two-way the rest of the time. Now, that's entertainment.

So I was a wee bit late when Steph opened the door. She had been kind enough to put out a basket of muffins and bagels on the table, along with a pot of coffee and, in my honor, a smaller pot of real hot chocolate. The woman had class, I'll give her that.

Stephanie introduced me to her sons. The taller one, Lou Jr., looked me straight in the eye. He has dark, straight hair and no doubt is his grandmother's favorite. You couldn't find Semitic blood in this kid if you went in with a sewer snake.

He shook my hand like he was damn glad to know me, and even smiled—the same smile Legs had in all the newspaper clip photos. I tried not to dislike the kid too quickly on the basis of his accidental similarity to a noted asshole.

"How can we help you, Mr. Tucker?" My god, the private schools really had done a bang-up job on this one. He'd be President of the United States by the end of the week.

"Well, if your mother will be so kind as to leave us to our business…" Stephanie nodded unhappily, took a worried glance at Jason, which I noticed, and closed the door behind her. I looked back at Junior.

"You two have been away at school, is that right?" Always best to start off with something easy, unless you have only one question to ask.

"Well, I've been at college, but it's just Georgetown," Junior began. ("Just Georgetown." That's like saying, "I have a car, but it's just a Porsche.") "So I'm around here pretty frequently. I have an apartment near school, but that's not far from here, either."

I turned to Jason, who had been standing near the window, but unlike his grandmother, facing into the room. He was lighter in complexion and hair, and his eyes looked wary. Clearly, the better interview, because he wasn't as sure of himself, and might say something he wasn't supposed to.

"How about you, Jason?"

"Pringley. It's in Annapolis." It wasn't a mumble, but it might just as well have been. Jason wanted out of this room, and now.

"Is it too far for you to visit often?" Now I sounded like my own mother.

"No, I come down once a month or so."

"When did you see your father last?"

There was a bit of eye contact between the two before Junior decided to answer for both of them. "I saw him the night before it… happened… and Jason was here the week before that," he said.

"Anything unusual? Did he seem tense, or distracted?"

There was no hesitation this time. "No."

"Anything going on between him and your mother?"

"No." Jason still hadn't moved a muscle, nor was he attempting to answer for himself.

"What kind of relationship did you have with your father?"

Junior looked surprised. "He was my father," he said, with a degree of "how-stupid-are-you" in it.

"Marvin Gaye's father shot and killed him. What was *your* relationship like?"

"I respected him," Junior said, his eyes burning death rays into my skull. "He had accomplished an enormous amount, and he was still a relatively young man."

"How about you, Jason?"

I have no doubt that Jason was about to acquiesce to my brilliant line of questioning, but he never had the chance. The dining room door opened, and Lester Gibson walked in. Both boys seemed uneasy, almost alarmed, at his entrance, and now they both fell silent.

"So, how have the boys been doing, Mr. Tucker?" Lester asked, all bonhomie and good feelings. You'd have thought that we hadn't exchanged epithets the last time we met. Politics, it would seem, is a genetic condition.

"They've been doing just fine, Lester," I said. "Thanks for dropping in to check." I flashed a look toward the door, but he wasn't buying. He actually sat down, just to Jason's left. Junior's eyes never left Lester, but Jason was doing all he could not to look at the man.

"Good to hear. We wouldn't want to hold anything back from the press, now, would we?" Lester took a croissant from the basket that I would have sworn had only bagels and muffins (it was a sure bet he wouldn't take a bagel) and bit off a corner. He appeared pleased, and nodded his head, as if the maitre d' was in the room, agonizing over whether Lester's croissant was adequate.

"That's a very refreshing attitude, Lester," I said. "Now, if you don't mind..."

He waved a hand, minor royalty giving the commoners permission to continue their drab, dreary lives. "Not at all. Pretend I'm not even here."

"I'd prefer not pretending," I told him.

Jason's eyes rotated in their sockets a bit, and Junior looked positively shocked. "How dare..." he began.

"I don't see how my presence would cause a disruption," said Lester, cutting him off. He wasn't looking at me—his eyes were admonishing Junior for his near-outburst.

"Your presence has already caused a disruption," I explained in a calm tone. "You've ruined the admittedly lousy rapport I'd established with the guys here, and now you're making it impossible for me to continue with this interview. Was that your goal? Because both times you've been in the room, my interviews were cut quite short."

Lester didn't so much stand as rise—it was a smooth motion that appeared to have less to do with legs, which have all sorts of bones and joints that can make for jerky motion, and more to do with the perfect, ethereal right of the privileged to their indignation.

"You will leave this house *immediately*," he hissed.

"Since when is it your house?" I purred at him. "Get Stephanie to tell me to go."

Lester looked toward the door, considering, but this time, Junior cut *him* off.

"That won't be necessary," he said. "This is still *my* house, and I'm asking you to leave, Mr. Tucker."

So I left. I drove the minivan back to the hotel, met my lovely wife and children, packed up everything we could legitimately call our own, and checked out. By the time we hit the Beltway, I had my cell phone in hand, and was pushing the button to call Mahoney.

"Hello?

"Mr. Mahoney."

"Mr. Tucker. How was Washington?"

"I'm still there, but I'm on my way back. I have an assignment for you."

"Broken fan belt?"

"No. I'm getting a handle on the Legs Gibson thing. But I'm going to need to consult with a panel of experts."

"Such as…"

"A carpet expert, a medical expert, a political expert, an accountant, and someone who understands the workings of a major airport."

"Aha."

"Precisely. Set up an evening with The Guys."

Chapter
Nine

In case you were wondering, driving from Washington, D.C. to New Jersey with two pre-teenage children is no more enjoyable than traveling from New Jersey to Washington, D.C. with two pre-teenage children. Harry Potter had finished his tale by the time we left Maryland, which left the 15-minute tour of Delaware, and about a two-and-a-half hour stretch of our home state, to survive without the aid of an apprentice wizard. The scenery didn't help, either. I believe it was Charles Kuralt who once said, "thanks to the Interstate Highway System, it's now possible to travel from coast to coast without seeing anything."

Somehow, though, we managed to make it home in four pieces, and for once, I was actually glad for the extra room in the minivan, which had made it possible for Leah to spread out on the back-back seat while Ethan played Gameboy in the back seat, thus avoiding any serious bloodshed among the progeny. We pulled into our lovely crumbling driveway at about seven in the evening, just in time to unpack and make dinner for four before collapsing into a sniveling heap on any available sofa. Luckily, Abby did the cooking.

You have to understand the freelance mentality. We are an exceptionally paranoid lot. We are convinced that, once we finish one assignment, we will never get another paying job for as long as we live. So immediately after the bags were lugged in the door, and while my wife bravely attacked the food supply in our refrigerator, and my children busied themselves with television, video games, and trying to kill each other, I checked my phone answering machine and my email.

I had not checked my messages from the road, since Abby gives me a funny look when I do that during a vacation, and there were twelve messages from the four days we'd been gone. The first was from my agent, Margot Stakowski of the Stakowski Agency of Cleveland, Ohio.

"Aaron!" As usual, she sounded shocked. "Didn't I tell you there was no market for mysteries? Oh well. I'll read it and call you back."

Margot sounded as enthusiastic as if I'd written a screenplay about athlete's foot, but that's Margot. Hey, if I were some big-name screenwriter like Charlie Kaufman, I wouldn't be represented by someone in Cleveland.

There were two messages from my mother, who apparently had forgotten I'd told her we were leaving on Thursday. She was considerably more frantic in the second message than the first. There was a message from Lydia Soriano at *Snapdragon*, not at all frantic but asking for a progress report. Leah's gymnastics teacher called to ask where she was (I'd forgotten to call and cancel). Ethan's friend Chris mumbled something about coming over to play Play Station. Melissa asked if Leah could come over and play. An editor at the *Star-Ledger* asked if I might be interested in a story about the latest in the commercial and industrial real estate market. A telemarketer asked if we wanted to refinance our mortgage. And Barry Dutton asked me to call him as soon as I got back.

I was just about to do that when the last message kicked in. "This is Preston Burke," the whiny little voice said. "I'm looking for Abigail Stein, but that was a man's voice on the machine. Am I calling the right number? I'll call back."

Thank goodness Abby didn't hear that message, as she was in the kitchen turning whatever dross we had left over into something that would be magnificent to look at and delightful to taste, much like herself. I stared at the machine a moment, then dialed Barry Dutton's home number.

"Dutton."

"Barry, it's Aaron Tucker. I just heard a message…"

"Aaron. I wanted you to know, I heard on Friday that the charges against Preston Burke had been dropped."

My voice sounded like I'd been swallowing razor blades again. "I *beg your pardon?*" I rasped.

"You heard me," Dutton said. He actually sounded a bit amused, the swine. "You're gonna love this one."

"I'd be willing to lay money I won't."

"Let me see if I can't make you feel better," he said. "It turns out that Burke actually didn't do it."

"Wait a second," I said, and put him on hold. I beckoned to Abby in the kitchen. "Pick up on the wall phone," I told her. "Preston Burke's charges have been dropped."

"*What?*" She walked to the phone double-time and picked it up. I pushed the button on my desk phone.

"Go ahead, Barry. Abby's listening in."

"Okay, here's the deal. I got a call from the Bergen County prosecutor on Friday. Turns out Burke really didn't shoot his girlfriend at all, just like he's been saying."

"That's impossible," Abby told him. "Six different witnesses all saw him do it."

"That's the funny part," Barry said. He waited, but neither of us was in a laughing mood. "It turns out there's this guy, Waldrick Malone."

"Waldrick?"

"Shut up, Aaron. I'm talking. Yeah, Waldrick Malone. Same size as Burke, same general build, and—get this—same face. People who have seen them side-by-side swear they could be twins, but they're not even distantly related."

"Oh, come on," Abby said. "You're telling me these two guys look so much alike that people standing in broad daylight couldn't tell them apart? People who knew Preston Burke thought this Malone guy was him?"

"I'm telling you, Abby. I saw both mug shots, and *I* would have sworn it was the same guy."

Abby sat in one of the kitchen chairs. "How could I have missed this?" she said. How could she have missed it? How could she have *found* it?

"Hold it, Barry," I said. "So this guy looks like Burke. Let's say for the sake of argument he sounds like Burke, too. How did he happen to get mad enough at Burke's girlfriend to shoot her?"

"That's how the case came apart," Barry said. "Turns out the girlfriend was sleeping with Malone first. She's known him for a couple of years. They have one of those relationships where he gets mad at her every once in a while and gets abusive, she leaves, then comes back because she mistakenly thinks there's no alternative. Then one night, she's in this bar and she meets Preston Burke."

"And she thinks he's Malone," I suggested.

"At first, but after a few minutes, it becomes obvious he's not. So now Barbara figures, hey. Best of both worlds. She has a guy who's a carbon copy of her boyfriend, but without the violent tendencies. Problem is, after they've been together a little while, Malone finds out about Preston Burke, too."

Abby shook her head. "He never came for Burke, though. He just went for the woman."

"Ain't that always the way," Barry said. "He's going to punish her for wanting a better version of himself. And he's going to set up Burke for the crime. So he goes around to the bar and a few other places for a day being Preston Burke. Letting everybody see

him as Preston Burke. And the next morning, he collects Barbara
outside Burke's apartment. *She* can tell the difference after a second, but by then, it's too late. He drags her into an alley after
making enough noise to attract witnesses, and shoots her."

"Why didn't she name Malone, and not Burke, in the complaint?" I asked.

Abby knew why. "Fear," she said. "She knew Burke would
never hurt her, but if she put Malone in jeopardy, he'd kill her for
real this time, right?"

"You're good at what you do, Abby," said Barry.

"Not good enough. I should have gotten this. No wonder
Burke was so mad at me."

"You can't be right all the time," I told her. "Nobody could
have seen this coming."

Barry's voice sounded uncomfortable, like he was intruding
on a private moment. He cleared his throat. "Anyway, Malone
hears that Burke has been convicted, so he gets cocky, shows his
face a couple of times too often when Burke is in jail, and the
next thing you know, somebody's calling the cops. The gun
shows up in his apartment. They've got fingerprints, everything.
He even confessed. I just wanted to let you know Burke is off the
hook," he said. "I don't know if you still have to worry about any
more rocks flying through your window, so I'll keep the patrols
coming by for a couple of days, okay?"

"Thanks, Barry," I said, and we hung up. Abby sat down in a
kitchen chair and stared for a long while. I looked at her, walked
over, and stroked her cheek. She took my hand and held it.

"I hate screwing up someone's life like that," she said. "I was
so sure."

"Don't beat yourself up. You had all those witnesses. Apparently Burke looks just like this guy Malone. That happens once
every millennium or so. And after all, Burke's life wasn't ruined.

He spent a few nights in jail That's it. You did what you thought was right, and you did try to defend him."

"It's just… I thought… I could have…" She banged her fist lightly on the table.

I knelt down to look into her eyes, but for the first time since Ronald Reagan was elected president, I couldn't think of anything to say. Luckily, Ethan ambled in, assessed the situation, and knew exactly what to say.

"Is dinner almost ready?"

It took a moment, but Abby sputtered, and started to laugh. She reached an arm out for our son, and he let her hug him, although he certainly didn't understand why.

"What are we having?" he asked, figuring he could compound the good cheer.

We stood there, me kneeling by my wife's chair, her holding our son with one arm for a few moments. Then she got up and started making his dinner.

I went to check my email.

Chapter Ten

That night, Abby and the kids spent an hour on my computer in the den/playroom, surfing pet adoption sites for available dogs that weren't so big they'd need their own wing added onto our house. Given her state of mind about Preston Burke, it was hardly the time for me to tell my wife I thought a dog was a truly awful idea for our family. And she knew it. She didn't know it was also a lousy time to mention that Burke had called our house while we were away, and I wasn't about to tell her. By bedtime, they had at least twelve possible dog candidates, and I had acid reflux.

Monday morning, I went to see Anne Mignano. I felt she deserved a progress report, despite the fact that I hadn't made the least bit of progress.

Ramona, the school secretary, looked a little surprised when I appeared in the office, and asked if there was trouble with Ethan. I told her no, I was here to see Mrs. Mignano on an unrelated matter, and Ramona's eyes narrowed. There's nothing Ramona hates worse than gossip when she's not in on it.

She didn't have time to grill me further, however, because Anne appeared in her doorway and waved me in. She didn't look happy, and what I was going to tell her wasn't going to lighten her mood any.

I sat down in the visitor's chair and looked unhappy. Anne sat in her desk chair, and didn't look any cheerier. We sat and assessed each other for a few moments.

"You don't look like you're here with good news," she started.

"I'm afraid not. Anne, I'm sorry."

She stood up and checked again to make sure the door was closed, which she knew it was. Anne started to pace, which is something like saying that Jennifer Lopez is the shy, retiring type. The words don't go together.

"It's not your fault, Aaron. There's no way a simple prank should cause this much pressure, anyway. I'm sure I'm just being overdramatic."

Hearing the word "pressure" from Anne Mignano was a startling experience, like a punch to the gut when you weren't prepared for it. Anne usually handles pressure the way most of us handle breathing. I wasn't sure how to respond.

"I just don't have any leads to go on," I said. "Nobody saw what happened, or if they did, they aren't going to rat out a friend. You investigated it yourself each time, and now weeks have gone by and the trail is cold. I'm just... I wish I had something else to tell you. *Anything* else."

The fact that I hadn't actually interviewed anyone, because I couldn't think of anyone to interview, didn't seem like the kind of information I especially wanted to share at this moment. Anne kept walking back and forth behind her desk, playing with a rubber band in her hand. For someone as perfectly controlled as she usually is, this was the equivalent of tearing her clothes off and running naked through the hallways. I was actually frightened.

"It's not your failure, Aaron. It's mine. I appreciate your trying."

So I was defeated, then. I'd let a friend down, and it was going to cost her, if not her job, then something equally precious to her—her dignity. It wasn't exactly my finest moment.

"How much time do you have left?" I asked.

"A day or two, but no more than that," Anne replied. "The board meets on Thursday, and they'll expect a report by then. I don't really think they'll terminate me, but they *will* give me a slap on the wrist in private, and everyone will know about it before I leave the room. Besides, you know, my contract is up next year, and in this town, the people will remember something like this."

She flopped down in her chair. I was starting to wonder if maybe there were someone who looked exactly like Anne Mignano, and was impersonating her now, because this woman's behavior was completely opposite that of the principal I knew.

Come on, it had worked for Waldrick Malone. For a while.

"Well, don't do anything until that meeting," I told her. "I have two days. I'll come up with something."

"Aaron..."

But I was already on my feet and at her door. I nodded to Ramona on the way out, and now she was *really* steamed about not knowing what I was up to.

Halfway out the door, though, it occurred to me that there was someone who might have some insight into the stink bomb incident, and I might as well seek him out while I was here.

Reese McElvoy, the Buzbee School janitor (pardon me, cus-todian), took any physical assault on what he referred to as "his" school building personally. Reese had been employed as a certi-fied public accountant for a chain of tax-preparation storefronts before the whole adding-and-subtracting thing got to be too much for him, and he ditched it to work among children. He'd never had any of his own, and didn't have to pay for anyone's college tuition, so Reese and his wife could afford to live on what he made in a civil service job as a janitor (pardon me, custodian).

Oh. Did I mention his wife is CEO of a small brokerage house?

I caught up with Reese near the gymnasium, which he watches like a hawk to make sure no one scuffs the floor, which is always freshly waxed. He was watching a class going on inside, during which some fifth graders were playing Dodge Ball, and looking concerned. Nothing scuffs a floor like Dodge Ball.

"Hey, Reese," I said, and he turned his head for a millisecond to see who was speaking. "How you doing?"

"How you doing, Aaron?" he said. "Would you look at that kid? Black shoes. Running on my gym floor wearing black shoes. And do they stop him? No. You know what that's going to do to my floor?"

"Maybe the kid can't afford a separate pair of shoes for gym, Reese," I said.

He snorted. "In this town? Kid could probably afford a separate pair of shoes for each class in the day." I didn't have the heart to tell him my son's shoes had needed replacing for a month and a half.

"Hey, Reese, what do you know about this stink bomb thing? Did they ever figure out who did it?" I had to protect my source, and clearly, if "they" had found out, she'd know about it.

He turned, looking me up and down for a second. "That was the damnedest thing," Reese said. "I couldn't figure it out."

"Were you here each time?"

"Of course I was here," he said, as if the idea of the school being open without him was patently absurd. "I was near the locker room when it happened, even. Heard some running as I turned the corner. The girls inside were already screaming. Felt like I let them down, you know."

"You can't be everywhere."

"No, but I should have been there. Kids put their trust in you, Mrs. Mignano puts her trust in you, you should be able to pro-tect…" It was clearly a personal affront to Reese that some 10-year-old had decided to patronize the Kwik N' EZ and have some fun.

"Anything you can tell me that might point me in a direction?"

"Why, Aaron?" he asked. "You writing about it?"

"Maybe," I said. (Sure. I'm writing about it. You're reading about it, aren't you?)

"The first one was the gym," Reese said. "That wasn't that bad, because it was just one bomb, and it's such a big room, with doors that open to the outside, it didn't make that much of a stink."

"But the parents did," I suggested.

He widened his eyes. "Oh, you better believe it!" Reese said. "Anne got calls all that morning—the phone was ringing before the fumes cleared. It's amazing how fast they work."

"The second one was the boys' room?" I asked, trying to keep him on topic.

"Yeah, that was probably the worst one," he shook his head. "Small space, tiny window. There were three boys in there at the time."

"Did you see it?"

"No," he lamented, shaking his head. The man looked as if someone had suggested he'd betrayed his country and cheated on his wife. "I was downstairs cleaning up where some little third grader had gotten sick."

"You can't be everywhere at once," I repeated. "Tell me about the locker room."

"Well, I'll tell you," he said. "I didn't see anybody in the area before, and naturally afterward, all I heard was screaming and footsteps. But I can tell you one thing."

"What's that?"

"Whoever did it had on the right sneakers. Wasn't a scuff mark on that floor. No, sir."

Somehow, that observation didn't seem like it was going to be a tremendous amount of help to me.

Chapter
Eleven

Because my faith in my agent was roughly equivalent to my faith in my cable company to lower its rates, I spent much of the morning going through the *Hollywood Creative Directory*. The *HCD*, as we just-barely-outsiders call it, is an exhaustively detailed list of production companies in Hollywood (or thereabouts), their personnel, their credits, and little details like their addresses, phone numbers, faxes, and email addresses. And if that sounds like it ought to cost you a pretty penny, rest assured that it does. Three times a year.

What you do is, you go through the *HCD* in alphabetical order, looking for companies which you believe might be interested in the letter-perfect screenplay you've just completed. You compile a list of those which have done something similar in the past, or are run by an actor/actress/producer/director whom you think might be just right for the material in some way. Once you've narrowed your list down to the merely implausible, rather than the ridiculous, you can begin the "pitching" process, long distance style.

I should point out that absolutely none of this is done until you have filled out the appropriate forms, printed out a copy of the opus, written a check for $35, and made sure you send all that to the Registrar of Copyrights at the Library of Congress in Washington, D.C. Since I had just come back from said nation's capital, I had dropped the package off on Independence Avenue personally. The truly dedicated screenwriter should also do all that stuff and send a copy to the Writers Guild of America, which registers screenplays in roughly the same way the Copyright Office does. This facilitates all sorts of nasty lawsuits should one be lucky enough to be plagiarized later on.

It took about two hours to compile the pitch list for "Minivan," since there are a lot of production companies in Hollywood, and I am an ambitious bastard. Once I had it properly compiled, I wrote another in a distressingly long series of brilliant cover letters, which emphasized the story, and not what a swell writer I am, and urged the producers on the list to hurry the heck up and request a copy of the script this very second, before the guy in the next cubicle became a mogul by leaping on the material first. The first rule of Hollywood is: Paranoia is your friend.

After spending a good deal of time learning how to use Microsoft Word for the Mac to personalize form letters, I was ready to start printing out cover letters. But strangely, all this time, my mind had not been on the script—I'd been thinking about the stink bomb, the rock through the window, and the hair from a dead man that was found in Cherie Braxton's bedroom.

My leased Epson printer spit out letter after letter, and I began the process of faxing the ones that could be faxed. Faxing is quick (although not as quick as email) and relatively cheap (five cents a minute, rather than 37 cents a letter), and makes me feel better, because I don't have to wait five days for a letter to get to California from New Jersey before I can expect the bidding war to begin on my phone. Hey, we must cling tightly to our dreams.

It struck me that I hadn't made any progress on anything. While I mindlessly faxed letter after letter, I wasn't any closer to finding out who the stink bomber was. Preston Burke may or may not have chucked a stone through my unexpectedly expensive front window, but if he hadn't, who had, and why? And how in the name of Sydney Greenstreet did the hair of a man who had died in the Texas electric chair seven years earlier find its way into a Washington, D.C. secretary's (oops, administrative assistant's) bedroom while a violent crime was being committed?

At least on the Madlyn Beckwirth story, I had been able to excuse myself because I wasn't, and still am not, a private investigator. I could overlook the fact that I didn't know what I was doing because I wasn't *expected* to know what I was doing. I had spent so much time telling people I wasn't a detective that I very nearly missed many of the most obvious clues in the story.

This time, though, I wasn't being asked to do anything a good reporter shouldn't be able to do. Yes, I was reporting in areas that were out of my normal expertise, but the technique of reporting remains the same no matter what the subject matter. I should have been able to get farther along than *this*.

Was Mahoney right, that I was letting 25-year-old lust for Stephanie cloud my judgment? Honestly probing my feelings, I had to say that wasn't the case. For one thing, I had much greater lust for Abby these days, and besides, the rest of Legs' family was so creepy that the murderer could have been any of them and not disturb my fantasy lust at all. So I discounted the Mahoney Theory.

Maybe there was just too much to think about—the knife, the stink bomb, the window—could be I was just spreading myself too thin and not doing justice to any of the things I should have been investigating.

I had to better organize my day. Then I'd see if I couldn't tackle one thing in the morning, like the stink bomb, then devote the time before the kids got home to the front window investigation.

The last producer fax was crawling its way through the machine when the phone rang, and Mahoney, sounding like he was calling from Calcutta, was on the other line.

"You have a cell phone?" I asked incredulously.

"Of course I have a cell phone!" he roared through the sea of static. "I spend my day in a rickety van on the road all over New Jersey, picking up other cars that have broken down on the side of the highway in god knows what isolated area. If I didn't have a cell phone, I'd be a complete idiot!" This from a man who complains because he can't find current 8-track cassettes to play in his van.

"So what have you accomplished?" I asked.

"It's nice talking to you, too," he said. "How was Washington?"

"A lot like Detroit, but for all the politics," I told him. "The usual amount of unpleasantness and backstabbing."

"Or, in this case, frontstabbing."

"Good point."

"I've gotten The Guys together, and we're meeting at a restaurant near you Wednesday night. That's tomorrow. That okay with Abby?" Mahoney didn't much care about keeping things convenient for me, but he would lay down his life to save Abigail thirty-five cents on a melon at Stop & Shop. I've known him for 27 years, and she's known him since she met me. Loyalty is a funny thing.

"I'll check with her, but I think it's okay. Where are we meeting?"

"That place J.P. Mugglebuggle's, or whatever."

"R. W. Muntbugger's?" It figures. I go out to eat twice in the same month, and it turns out to be the same restaurant.

"Yeah, is that okay, or do you want to go to the Ethiopian place?" Mahoney is an advocate of international dining.

"I don't understand the concept of Ethiopian cuisine," I said. "Isn't that where they're always having famines?"

"You, sir, are a vulgarian," he said with an upper-crust accent that a true Harvard graduate couldn't tell from the real thing.

"I have been called worse things," I said. "Just out of curiosity, how would you find out who threw a rock through your window?"

At just about that moment, I could practically see Mahoney stretching his massive, powerful body behind the wheel of that van and knitting his brow.

"I'd look for the stupidest person I could find."

"Why?"

"Think about it," he said with a snarl. "Would you throw a rock through *my* window?"

That didn't help much, either.

Chapter Twelve

I spent my lunch hour on the Internet, looking up the shining life record of Branford T. Purell. A lovely man, Mr. Purell had roamed the highways of West Texas, particularly the area of Midland/Odessa, where he had once worked on an oil rig, or as they call it in the Lone Star State, an "all reeig." Once the area's oil business, um, dried up, Purell took the whole unemployment thing personally, and vented his frustration on virtually any woman who happened to be walking along the road alone. He shot five of them, three fatally, for no discernible reason. The two he didn't kill eventually recovered. Not having the same concerns as Preston Burke's girlfriend, they fingered him pretty quickly, and his trial had roughly the same outcome as Burke's. The difference was, Purell's conviction stuck. Something to do with the fact that he was actually guilty.

Purell had been the kind of guy who would blame everyone else for his problems. To the day he died, he claimed the women were "asking for it by walking out there alone." As we all know, the international symbol for a woman who hopes to die by shotgun blast is one who walks alongside the highway. It makes perfect sense when you have the right point of view.

Virtually nobody except the most vehement death penalty opponents tried to stay Purell's execution. His own sister, contacted by his attorney, refused to put in a clemency request to the governor. Of course, this was Texas, and they'd just as soon execute somebody there as go out for a hamburger, so it's possible

Purell's sister was just looking to spice up an otherwise dull Tuesday evening. Hey, some siblings are closer than others.

Lucille and her son Avery were the only "kin" Purell left behind, and from the look of it, they were not a close family. Lucille attended the execution, but brought a date, and after it was over, signed autographs outside the prison for a good long while seeking out television reporters and granting interviews. She made her 15 minutes of fame last more than twice that long.

It wasn't a difficult thing to get Lucille Purell Watkins's phone number from directory assistance. These days, you just dial 411 and James Earl Jones will tell you anybody's phone number, so long as you're a Verizon customer. Except his own. Maybe Verizon wants us to believe that 411 *is* James Earl Jones' phone number.

Lucille wasn't home, but miracle of miracles, she did have an answering machine, one that played "The Yellow Rose of Texas" while she instructed me to "go ahead and leave a message." So I went ahead and left one.

I had nothing left to do except run down the parents of the usual suspects I'd taken out of the "Find-A-Friend" directory, and that was just a millimeter above nothing. But I had only a day and a half left, and I'd stupidly promised Anne I'd have something for her before the Board of Education meeting Thursday night. Sometimes, being gallant is overrated.

Trying my best to gather enthusiasm, I checked the clock. Two hours before the kids got home—plenty of time to see at least two parents. Why call ahead?

I got the list from my reporter's notebook, put on my denim jacket, and headed out the door.

Standing on the sidewalk in front of my house, gazing into the lovely garbage-bag-and-cardboard patch I'd made from the remains of my front window, was Preston Burke.

Chapter
Thirteen

We stared at each other for a long moment. "What are you doing here?" Preston Burke asked me.

"Isn't that supposed to be my line, Preston?" I asked.

He looked positively stunned, standing in the sunshine outside my house. He squinted up at me, trying to make sense of it all. "Isn't this Abigail Stein's house?"

So that was it. He'd looked up Abby's address somewhere, maybe in the state's lawyer's directory, and come down here to do whatever mischief he'd planned for this visit. He hadn't expected anyone, least of all me, to be here while he left her his flaming bag of dog poop, or toilet papered her tree.

The one thing I had to do now was convince the man he'd made a mistake. I wanted to be sure he never came looking for Abby again.

"This is my house," I said, honestly enough.

"Then, why did the reverse phone book list this as Abigail Stein's house?" Burke wasn't challenging me. He was asking a sincere question.

"I couldn't begin to tell you," I said, which was also true. At least, I couldn't begin to tell him if I wanted to protect my wife.

He sat down on the front steps, and I thought he was going to cry. "How am I going to find Abigail Stein?" Burke said, seemingly in despair.

"Why are you looking for Ms. Stein?" I asked, as innocently as I could muster. "I heard the charges against you had been dropped. I assume your business with her is done."

Burke did a double take Soupy Sales would have envied. "Oh, it is," he said. "I'm not here in a professional capacity."

"You're here on an amateur basis?"

"No, you don't understand." The understatement of the week. "I'm looking for Abigail Stein on personal business." He sucked in his breath, screwing up his courage. "I'm in love with her."

I'm ashamed of myself, but I do recall letting out a laugh. "You're… in love with Abigail Stein?"

"Is that so amusing?"

I walked down and sat next to him. "I'm sorry, Preston. You have to understand. Abigail Stein is my wife."

To truly empathize with the look in Burke's eyes, you have to know what it is to be in love with Abby. To have aspired to someone so close to perfection, and then have the rug pulled out from under you… it's a feeling I hope never to actually have myself.

"Your wife?"

"Yes," I told him. "We've been married for fourteen years. We have a twelve-year-old son and an eight-year-old daughter." I actually reached into my jacket for my wallet, and showed him pictures of my children. This, to a man I was pretty sure five minutes ago was a dangerous maniac.

"Oh, my…" Preston Burke was coming apart at the seams, and I felt awful for him. "All that time when she was working on my case, the only thing that got me through was thinking, 'once this is over, I'll go and I'll ask her out.' And now…"

It occurred to me that he should have seen Abby's wedding ring during all those visits, but some people are less observant than, let's say, eighty percent of the population. "I understand how you feel," I told him. "I'm sorry. I got to her fifteen years before you did."

"I thought you said fourteen." Ah. Now it was becoming even clearer. Preston Burke was, in all probability, an adult Asperger's Syndrome patient, and he didn't even know it. It happens all the time, and after you've lived with it for a while, you can spot them a block and a half away.

"We dated for a year before we got married, Preston."

"How come she's not Abigail Tucker?" Burke was trying to trip me up, prove that Abby wasn't really my wife.

"Not all women change their names when they get married."

He absorbed that. It was all coming down on Burke at once, but he was used to readjusting his expectations. He stood up. "What happened to your window?" he asked.

I didn't have the heart to tell him. Until very recently, I thought *he* had happened to my window. "Somebody threw a rock through it," I told him.

"Why?"

"I have no idea," I answered honestly.

He walked over and examined the tic-tac-toe pattern of the window. It looked like we had been playing Hollywood Squares in our front window, and somebody had thrown a rock through Paul Lynde and Charley Weaver.

"You have somebody look at this yet?" Burke asked.

"Yeah," I said, bewildered.

"How much they charging you for it?" It was my turn to stare at him for a while.

"They quoted us two thousand." I didn't want to tell him, but I couldn't think of a reason not to.

Burke looked like his head would explode. His eyes widened and his mouth dropped open like a wide "O." "Two thousand dollars to fix this window?" he gasped.

"No, two thousand dollars to replace the window. The guy said it couldn't be repaired." I was talking to a six-year-old.

"The guy lied. This window is easily repairable. I could do it for four hundred." No, *Burke* was talking to a six-year-old.

"You could?" (Really, Daddy? It just needs new batteries?)

"Sure. Didn't your wife tell you? I'm a contractor. That's how I make my living. This, here, is maybe a one-day job. Four hundred, including materials."

"Three hundred," I said. "You're in love with the owner of the window."

"Five hundred," he countered. "She's married, to you."

"Split the difference," I said magnanimously. "Four hundred."

"Deal." We shook hands.

Preston examined the window and made some measurements with my tape measure. He kept talking to himself and nodding, since apparently he agreed with what he was saying. I walked over when he appeared to be finished.

"When do you think you could do it?" I asked.

"I'm not working now," he said. "Too many people still think I'm a serial killer. I can start this afternoon and finish tomorrow."

"You're a fine human being, Preston," I said. This was not how I expected this conversation to end up.

"Just one thing." Uh-oh. Here came the catch.

"Yeah?"

"You're not from the Bar Association. Who are you, really?"

I let out my breath and told him the whole story. Burke seemed shocked that we suspected him.

"You thought it was *me?*" I was personally offending him. I think he was considering raising the price of the repair again.

"Well, there was that letter and… look, Preston, that's over now. And I just have one question to ask you."

"Name it."

"You're not really Waldrick Malone, are you?"

Preston Burke smiled. And shook his head.

Chapter
Fourteen

The encounter with Burke left me no time to interview potential hooligan parents before my kids got home, so I decided to do that first thing tomorrow. The kids came barreling in just about the time Burke showed up with some wood, panes of glass he'd cut to size, putty, and other equipment. He borrowed a ladder from my garage and set to work.

Leah burst in the door and dropped her book bag on the floor. "Who's the man on the ladder?" she demanded.

"He's fixing the window. Go feed your lizard." She rolled her eyes and flung herself on the couch, her latest in a series of defiant gestures.

Ethan was a few steps behind her. He stomped noisily into the house and dropped his book bag on the floor. "Can I go on the Internet and look for dogs?" he asked.

"Do your homework."

He shrugged, got his books out of the bag, hung the bag up on the banister, and got to work on his homework, sitting on the floor next to the couch and working on the coffee table (in this case, the homework table). He had to avoid sitting on his sister, who was writhing on the couch now, since just flinging herself onto it had not produced the desired response.

"Leah, feed the lizard and do your homework."

"Ahhhhhhhh!" The sound that emanated from her throat can't be accurately translated into letters and punctuation. It was the kind of thing that took the sound effects artists who worked on

The Exorcist three months to produce, with layer upon layer of wild animal noises, squeaky doors, and the transmission of a 1942 Nash. But she got up and stomped into the kitchen to fetch the tasty treat for Little Zilla.

While she was upstairs, the phone rang. "Hi, Aaaaaaron," said a minuscule voice. "Is Leeeeeeah there?"

"Hi, Meliiiiiiisa," I said. "She's feeding the liiiiiiizard."

But Leah was already harrumphing down the stairs, still glaring at me, and I pointed to the phone in my hand, then to the one on the kitchen wall. She didn't smile, but nodded.

She and Melissa were deep into conversation when I heard a loud scuffle outside the window. I looked out, and two Midland Heights police officers were holding Preston Burke's arms. They'd clearly pulled Burke down off the ladder, and were talking to him. He appeared perplexed.

I opened the door and called to the one I knew. "Hey Crawford," I said. "It's okay."

"Isn't this the guy the chief told us to watch for outside your house?" Crawford said. "He was doing something to your front window."

"Yeah," I said, walking down the stairs to them. "He's fixing it. I hired him."

The two cops looked at each other, then Crawford shrugged. They let Burke's arms go. "That's what he said," Crawford reported. "But you can understand..."

"Don't worry about it," I told him. "You did your job exactly right. I'll tell the chief."

"Can I come in for a minute?" Crawford asked. I knew he was just checking to see if Burke had, in some way, taken my children hostage and was coercing me into letting him repair my window, so I waved Crawford into the house while his partner continued to question Burke.

Crawford looked around and saw one 12-year-old boy, approaching his father's height, with his knees on the floor, his hands on the coffee table and his feet on the sofa, and one eight-year-old girl, approaching the height of the average lawn gnome, sprawled out flat on the floor in the kitchen, phone cord tracing to the wall five feet above her head.

In other words, the usual at my house.

"Situation normal," I told Crawford. "He's telling you the truth. But I appreciate your concern."

He collected his partner and drove off. I made a mental note to call Barry Dutton and commend their work. Burke walked over to me as soon as they drove off.

"This is one secure community," he said. "I should think about moving here."

We went on like that for the rest of the afternoon. Melissa invaded for a while, and the two girls played on the swing I hung off the roof of our patio (we don't actually have what you'd call a backyard), doing tricks designed to give me a massive coronary, until it was time for me to start cooking dinner for the kids.

I got out some pieces of frozen fried chicken for Ethan, since he refuses to eat virtually anything that is cooked under our roof, and put them in the oven on a cookie sheet lined with aluminum foil. Then I cut some potatoes very thin, sprayed them with cooking oil, and put them on another cookie sheet, similarly prepared, to "fry" in the oven. For Leah, I dredged a piece of boneless chicken breast in matzo meal, then seasoned it with the Colonel's recipe of eleven herbs and spices, eight of which are salt, and put that on the same sheet as Ethan's dinner. The sound I heard off in the distance was James Beard spinning in his grave.

Just about the time I started calculating my children's cholesterol levels, the door opened and Abby, looking as flustered as I've ever seen her, came in and pointed at the door.

"Isn't that... do you know who... why is... Aaron!"

It was so cute, I could barely stand explaining the situation to her, but by the time I got to how Burke was saving us $1,600, Abby was grinning. We sat in the kitchen until Burke knocked on the door to say he was leaving, and would be back in the morning. Abby and I waved, and he sighed (I like to think) and walked out.

"It's a shame," I said. "That there aren't two of you to go around."

"Maybe the guy who looks like him has a sister who looks like me," Abigail said.

I snuggled close to her and kissed her on the cheek. "Looks are not all there is to you," I said. "She'd have to be the most wonderful woman in the world, too."

"Aaron, you make such lovely use of hyperbole."

Silly woman. She thought I was exaggerating.

Chapter
Fifteen

The next morning, I was all set to start interviewing parents of miscreants, but by the time I got back from the Y, helped Burke get set up, took a shower, and got dressed, it was too late even to consider such a thing (okay, so it was 9:30, but I just couldn't think of a way to do this gracefully). Freelancers are without question the finest, most diligent procrastinators on the planet.

Still, there were at least two other mysteries to be solved, and one of them was actually a paying job, so I called Lydia Soriano at *Snapdragon* to keep the boss happy. That was easier said than done.

"I called over the weekend, Aaron, and today is Wednesday," she said grumpily. "Couldn't you have called sooner?"

"I was away in Washington, actually doing interviews for the story," I told her. "My wife doesn't let me check in for messages while we're away."

She laughed. "Well, she's a wise woman. What have you found out so far?"

I filled her in on my minute progress, and told her about the hair and the gathering I had organized for the evening. "At the very least, I figure I can get the guys to talk about what Legs was like in the old days," I said.

"It's decent background," she said. "But if I want to get it into an issue that's going to be at all relevant to the event, you're going to have to write something soon, Aaron."

"How soon?"

"Like, Monday."

I believe something akin to a sharp intake of breath took place on my end of the phone. "Okay," I breathed.

"It's been over a month since the assignment," Lydia reminded me. "I know I haven't been breathing down your neck, but if I hold this much later than the January issue, it's going to be such old news that my readers will wonder why we ran it at all."

"It's okay," I said. "But does there have to be a solution to the mystery in the article?"

I have no idea what Lydia Soriano looks like, so the image of a woman pursing her lips in thought is probably just conjecture. Besides, the woman looked a little like Abigail.

"I don't want to press you for it, Aaron, since any arrests will hit the papers long before we run a story, but if we run a story that doesn't at least speculate on who killed Gibson, and arrests are made in the interim, we're going to look awfully foolish."

"Okay, Lydia. I'm close. Really. I'll have something for you Monday."

"Thanks, Aaron. And, if this works out, there may be more we can do in the future." We hung up.

Four days to unravel Legs Gibson's murder, and all I had was a hair from a dead man and a whole lot of missing money.

Piece of cake.

Not that I had any idea what to do, but a piece of cake sounded like a good idea. I walked into the kitchen in search of one before I remembered that Preston Burke was watching through my front window, and used him as an imaginary diet cop to stop myself from becoming obese. It was even too early in the morning for a Diet Coke. Luckily for me, the phone rang.

Lucille Purell Watkins had a Texas twang that could snap a rubber band. And if it was 9:45 a.m. where I was sitting, it was 8:45 where she was, so the slurred words and thick pronunciations that come with drinking were even more jarring than they normally would be.

"Is this Mr. Aaron Tucker?"

"Last time I checked."

"This is Lucille Watkins. I'm Branford Purell's sister." At least, I'm pretty sure that's what she said. I activated my tape recorder as quickly as I could, but even after multiple subsequent listenings, Lucille was not easy to decipher.

"Mrs. Watkins, thank you for calling back."

"You can call me Lucille. But I don't understan' why you're calling me about my brother, Mr. Tucker. He's been gone for seven year'."

"I know, Lucille. I'm writing a story about someone else for *Snapdragon* Magazine, and your brother's name came up, so I need some background on him. And you can call me Aaron."

I got up and started to pace, which is a habit I have whenever the call I'm on is not routine, or I have to be on my best behavior. Like when my mother calls.

"I don't know what I can tell ya, Aaron. My brother was a bad guy who killed some women and paid the price for it." Lucille was nothing if not to the point.

"Well, tell me. Did he ever mention a man by the name of Louis Gibson?"

"No. He did know a Marvin Gibson, I think. Worked in the Mobil station on Route…"

"I don't think that was him, Lucille. Did Branford ever go to Washington, D.C.? Ever give any money to political causes, get involved in groups against abortion, anything like that?" Okay, so I was grasping at straws. I was hanging by a hair, literally.

"No, sir. I don't think Branford even noticed there was politics. Only time he ever joined anything was when he joined the gun club, and I think that was just to meet girls." I did my very best not to speculate on the kind of girls one meets at the gun club, and pressed on.

"How did Branford make a living after the oil rig shut down?" I asked. "That must have been tough."

Lucille took a long pause, which I initially thought was reflection. After repeated playings of the tape, I finally discerned a long pull on a bottle of some beverage. From the burp that followed, I'd guess beer.

"Well, it was rough," she agreed. "He never really held a steady job after that. Just bummed around, picked up money doing odd construction work, but there wasn't much of that, either. He actually sold his blood a couple of times for medical research at a lab near here. Then, he just took to driving around, and as it turned out, to shooting people."

"Can you imagine why DNA evidence would surface that suggests your brother was in a Washington, D.C. apartment a little over a month ago?"

This time, the pause was out of sheer confusion. "Did I hear you right? There's DNA of Branford in Washington last month?"

"I can't be sure, but that is the indication." I was still pacing, and I'm willing to bet Lucille was on her feet, too.

"I can't tell you, Aaron," she said. "I saw the man fry more than seven years ago, with my own eyes. If he was in Washington last month, it's only because he rose from the dead, and I don't think that's all that likely."

"No, ma'am," I said.

Chapter
Sixteen

Branford Purell's perplexing insistence on staying dead was not improving my day in any way, shape, or form. Luckily, Preston Burke was doing his very best to cheer me up, and had finished his task by 11:30. I stood back on the sidewalk in front of my house to admire his hardwork.

"You do nice work, Pres," I said. "If it was painted, I'd never know there'd been any damage."

"I could paint it, Aaron," he countered. "Another two hundred, and I'll scrape and paint the whole thing."

I weighed the two hundred bucks against the mental image of me on a ladder in front of my house on the weekend as the weather turned colder, scraping the thin wood between window panes. It wasn't even close.

"Go for it, Preston," I said. He happily went off to Haberman's Hardware for some sandpaper and paint.

The only thing to do now was have lunch. I was still trying desperately to lose that last nagging twenty pounds, so I went to Hallie's Coffee House for a grilled chicken salad, which I brought home in the environmentally disastrous Styrofoam package that all New Jersey diners consider *de rigeur*.

You may have noticed that nowhere in that paragraph did I mention going out to investigate the stink bomb incidents. You are a remarkably astute reader.

The fact was, I couldn't bring myself to de facto accuse little kids without a shred of evidence to back up my claims. I needed something, *anything* to hang a theory on, and I had absolutely nothing.

So I pondered, which is what I'm best at before two in the afternoon. I read Fax McCloskey's latest missive, detailing with exhaustive thoroughness the Washington, D.C. Police Department's examination of FBI files that had virtually nothing to do with Legs Gibson's murder. But it was nice Fax continued to write. It made me feel part of the D.C. police family.

If I were nine or ten years old, and bought a stink bomb at the Kwik N' EZ, why would I choose the girls' locker room, the gym, and the boys' room at school to try out my purchase? Well, two of those locales, at least, had a common overseer. A grudge against the gym teacher, of course (I suppose you have a better idea?). I headed for Buzbee to seek out Hester Van Biezbrook.

Hester, the prototype for all gym teachers, was roughly 400 years old, and could still put me through a cinderblock wall if the spirit moved her. She stood about six-foot-three, had triceps Arnold Schwarzenegger would find intimidating, and spoke in a voice high enough to qualify as a dog whistle. She was supervising a game of volleyball when I arrived, breathless from my two-and-a-half block walk.

"The stink bombs," I managed.

"What about them?" she asked. Hester wasn't much given to small talk, and since Leah had never so much as stepped out of line once in her class, she didn't know me very well. The parents of the squeaky kids get the grease.

"Did somebody have a gripe against you? Some reason one of the kids would have wanted to get back at you that day?"

She regarded me with a look approaching pity. "You think that a fifth grader needs a *reason* to throw a stink bomb into a bathroom? Any ten-year-old boy worth a damn would throw it into the locker room just to watch the girls run."

"Yeah, but that's the point," I countered. "He didn't stick around to watch them run. He threw it and ran. Maybe he was trying to make a point about the school. And because this is your part of the school, maybe about you. What do you think, Hester?"

She thought about it. "There are tons of troublemakers in those classes," she said thoughtfully. "I can't single one out just because he pisses me off. And there wasn't anybody who specifically had a gripe on those days. Nope, this was the nasal equivalent of joyriding, Mr. Tucker." And before I could go on, she was off to dock one team of girls a point for spiking the volleyball, something I was impressed they could even do.

You'd have thought the whole stink bomb thing would have died down by now, anyway, but I'd seen an article in the *Central Jersey Press Tribune* detailing a meeting of the Buzbee PTO in which it was actually suggested that the girls' locker room be padlocked *while the girls were inside* to prevent further incidents. It wasn't until someone in the crowded meeting yelled the word "fire" that the padlock suggestion was tabled indefinitely.

I went home and caught the spectacle of Preston Burke carefully painting my bow window, which was quite a sight. With a very thin brush and a straight edge, he was avoiding any splash of paint on the window glass itself. I felt I was intruding on a private moment.

Inside, the answering machine was flashing, and there was a message from Stephanie. "I'm sorry about the scene with the boys and Lester," she said. "If you want to re-interview them, I'll set something up on the phone."

I didn't think Stephanie's sons knew much of anything about the murder, although there were clearly undercurrents to this family that Carl Jung would find scary. And there was, now, a pretty tight deadline, and no reason to waste time. So I called her back and said I didn't see a need for a new interview, that the waters had been muddied enough by the first one, and let it be known that if I never actually came into contact with Lester again, I wouldn't weep into my pillow at night.

"He can be a trial," she admitted. "I can't wait until all this is over, and I can go back to having a life again."

"I've never been involved in the death of a public figure before," I told her. "How long do you think it'll take before you can put this behind you?"

"It would be a big step if they found out who did it, so I didn't have to worry about being arrested every waking minute," said Steph. It must be an awful bother to have to plan your day around being arraigned and making bail, and never knowing when such activities might be coming up.

"Who do you suspect?" I'd never actually asked.

"Tell you the truth," Stephanie said, "I think the woman he was sleeping with did it herself. And knowing Louis in situations like that, I'm not entirely sure I blame her."

I didn't bother to tell her that the police had almost definitively eliminated Cherie Braxton as a suspect, for one thing because she lacked the upper body strength to get a kitchen knife through Legs' rib cage and into his heart. Besides, she didn't like Legs enough to kill him, from what I could tell.

"Well, I'm supposed to write about it by Monday," I said, "and I haven't a clue what I'm going to say."

"Well, if you need any help, you know who to call," she said, and we hung up.

By the time the kids got home, I'd exhausted all my best ways to procrastinate, Burke had quit for the day, and my children were mystified at my insistence on helping them with their homework, despite their not needing any help. Leah went so far as to retreat to her room, turn on the CD player, and close the door, all to keep out the guy who still does long division the old way. It's hell being middle-aged.

Abby got home a little early, and I went upstairs to get dressed for the conference with my brain trust. She walked into the bedroom and started changing from her work clothes.

"Did Burke finish the window?" she asked. I told her about the fine job he'd done, and how we had devoted an extra couple hundred to the beautification of our front window. She nodded. "He's still pretty creepy, though, isn't he?"

"I don't know. I'm starting to like him."

"He's not in love with *you*," she pointed out.

"Well, it's no wonder he's crazy about you," I said, embracing her. "You drive me wild, walking around in various states of undress."

"Luckily, I don't do that very often at the office," she said. "Besides, I could probably drive you wild if I dressed like the Michelin Man."

I considered that. "Wait. I'm picturing that. Wow. Yes, you could."

She broke the clinch and put on a sweatshirt and sweatpants. "I'm just still a little concerned about Burke," she said. Abby waited, but got no response. "Aaron, are you listening?"

"No, I'm picturing you dressed in tires."

"It's driving you wild, isn't it?"

"Just as you knew it would, you tease," I said.

"You're a very scary person, Aaron," she said. "Now, get dressed and go talk to the boys from Bloomfield."

Spoil-sport.

Chapter
Seventeen

"**O**kay, so Stephanie Jacobs is smashing her boobs into you, and you're telling her to cut it out?" Mark Friedman was shaking his head, incredulous. "What's *wrong* with you, Tucker?"

"I'm terminally married," I said.

We were sitting around a large table, the five of us. Muntbugger's had been warned ahead of time, but took no reservations. So I'd had to wait for about fifteen minutes while the troops gathered (I'd gotten there first, feeling some responsibility for the occasion). Now, all of us having ordered and already downing a beer, I was getting the others up to speed on the state of the Legs Gibson investigation. Apparently, my conduct during a crucial episode was somewhat disappointing to my friends, or at least Friedman.

"I'm married, too, but I'm not *that* married," Friedman said.

"You were at Aaron's wedding," Mahoney said. "Don't you remember Abby?"

"I was pretty drunk," Friedman noted.

I took a picture of Abigail out of my wallet and showed it to him. Friedman's voice dropped to a rasp. "Okay," he said, "I see your point. Can I keep this?"

"No." I snatched it out of his hand and put it back into my wallet. I'd have to clean it off later.

"It's not that I don't want to see pictures of your wife," Greg Wharton said, "but I don't think that's why you asked us to come here, is it, Tucker?"

"No, thanks, Wharton. I have one question to ask each of you, and I'd appreciate it if you'd each think very carefully about it before you answer. There may be follow-up."

I took the tape recorder out and put it in the center of the table. And the four of them burst into such a storm of laughter that people at tables in all directions around us looked over, shook their heads, and despaired at the state of middle-aged men in America.

"What the hell is that thing for?" Mahoney gasped through guffaws. "We going to sing later?"

I was prepared for the outburst. "I'm working," I said. "If I'm going to quote you idiots, I need to get it right, and I don't plan on taking notes all through dinner."

"Is *Snapdragon* paying for dinner?" McGregor wanted to know. "I didn't order the filet mignon sandwich, but if they're buying, I could always change."

"Maybe they are," I said. "If what you guys tell me is any help at all, I'll put it on my expense sheet." There was much hand-rubbing, smiling, and eye-widening at that remark. Friedman ordered himself an Anchor Steam. McGregor didn't change to the steak sandwich, but he did add steak fries to his order. They make them waffle style at Muntbugger's.

It was McGregor who finally sat back and put his hands behind his head in a gesture of relaxation and preparedness. "What are your questions?" he asked. Thank god for McGregor. Otherwise, we'd have sat there all night trying to make each other laugh, and succeeding most of the time. High school friends are easy.

"I'm going to start with Wharton," I said. "He gets two questions, one for being a politician, and another for being a doctor."

"Osteopath," he corrected.

"What is an osteopath, anyway, Greg?" McGregor asked.

"Sounds like somebody who attacks you with the bones of his last victim."

"That's very amusing," Wharton said sourly. "We're the most misunderstood branch of the medical profession. Why, if internists had to know half of what…"

"Save the electioneering for the politician question," Friedman said.

I saw my opening and dove in. "Let's say somebody in Washington wanted Legs Gibson dead," I started. "What kind of idiot would they have to be to do something about it?"

"A big idiot," Wharton said immediately. "You don't kill the people you disagree with. You make their lives miserable and then make sure you smear them so much they can't get re-elected and have to go work for a living. Killing them is just way too quick. There's not enough suffering. Besides, there's the whole 'getting caught' thing that can put a crimp in your campaign."

The waiter brought our dinner, so I turned off the recorder until everyone was well hunkered down. When I turned it back on, numerous groan-worthy puns later, I was asking Friedman about carpets.

"Let's say we're in a room with a light beige carpet," I started.

He cut me off. "What kind of carpet?" He asked.

"Light beige," I repeated.

"Deep pile, shag, shallow pile, wall-to-wall, area rug, old, new, Scotchguard, no Scotchguard, what?" Friedman's tone indicated that he was talking to a complete moron, and was exasperated for having had to explain himself further. "Polyester blend, wool, what kind of material?"

"I'd say deep pile, wall-to-wall," I started. "It's a rental apartment, so my guess would be that every unit has the same rug."

"Carpet," he corrected. "A rug is something that doesn't go

wall-to-wall."

"Or something that Wharton could use on that bald spot," McGregor noted, to some hoots.

"Better than that comb-over Legs was doing, from what I could see on the news," Mahoney chimed in.

"Let's not stray too far from the topic at hand," I urged.

"Topic at head," McGregor interjected. I ignored him, and pressed on.

"The carpet, Friedman, the carpet."

"What about it?"

"Okay, so it's beige, right? And whatever pile I said it was, and a rental apartment carpet, so it's probably not the most expensive one left in the warehouse."

"Okay," Friedman said. "So?"

"So let's say, for the sake of argument, that there's one area on the ru... carpet that's a little bit darker than the rest of it. What does that tell me?"

Friedman looked at me with disdain. "You don't have to be a carpet expert to figure that out," he said. "Something's been spilled on the rug."

"Carpet," Wharton corrected.

"I'm willing to bet that area was a little stiffer than the rest, no matter how many times it had been vacuumed, right?" Friedman asked.

"That's right," I said, prompting him to pontificate on the art of rugging a little more. Reporting isn't about talking. It's about getting others to talk. It's something the TV people have never fig-ured out.

"And it stood up a little bit more, didn't it?" he said, essentially repeating himself, but I let him go on, to see if he'd reach the conclusion I wanted. I nodded. "So then, something was spilled on it, but there was no stain, right? I mean, no discoloration."

"No, that's right. It was a little darker, but not a different color than the rest."

Friedman smiled a smug smile. The wise old expert on Aladdin's mode of transport would now dispense his hard-earned expertise, if we were men with sufficient sense to stop chewing long enough to hear it.

"So what happened was, something was spilled on the carpet," Friedman began.

"And we don't have to be Einstein to figure out what that was," Wharton said. I gave him the patented stare I give my kids to shut them up, but on Wharton, in this case, it had the opposite effect than the one my children employ: Wharton actually shut up.

"And whatever it was, it was mopped up just about immediately," Friedman went on, ignoring both Wharton and the byplay that had gone on between Wharton and me. "Because you're right, Tucker, if it's in a rental, it was probably a cheap carpet, so if it had been left to stain for even a couple of minutes, it probably would have left a noticeable discoloration."

"What do you use to mop up liquid on a rug?" I asked, not being well schooled in the art of cleaning. And if you don't believe me, come to my house sometime.

"Best thing right away is club soda," he said. "So it doesn't leave a stain, but the fabric is left with a change in texture, and that's why you can notice it, if you look, and feel it, if you touch it or walk on it."

"Whart," I said, "if someone is stabbed in the heart, I assume that would cause a pretty massive blood loss. Would I be wrong?"

"Well, there'd be a lot of immediate spurting," he said. "You have to figure that a wound to the heart, if the heart were contracted, or beating, at the time, would last for a few beats of the heart, expansions and contractions, at the very least. So blood would be spraying all over for at least a few seconds."

"The police report indicated that there was a good deal of blood on the bed," I said. "Would that be consistent with the kind of wound you're talking about?"

Wharton thought for a moment, chewing carefully on his cheddar burger. Finally, he regarded me and pointed a finger. "Can I have one of your fries?" he said.

I handed him one, probably without even thinking. "What about the blood, Whart?"

"You told us to consider our answers carefully, didn't you?" he asked through a mouthful of potato. "I'm considering."

"Not to mention raising your intake of carbohydrates by about six zillion percent," Friedman added.

"From what you've told me, the wound was a single wound, delivered through the rib cage and into the heart," Wharton said finally. "That's a strong person pushing that knife, or a really, really angry one pumped up by adrenaline."

"So there'd be a bunch of blood?" I asked, trying to get him back to the question.

"Not as much as in the first few seconds of a head wound," Wharton said. "But for maybe ten or fifteen seconds, the blood would be flying, and not in any predictable pattern. It wouldn't be pretty in the room, I'll tell you that."

"If he's stabbed while he's lying on the bed, would it fly far enough that there'd be a stain almost at the foot of the bed, and to the side, like where you'd put your shoes, if you were neat?"

Wharton thought about that for a while, too, until I realized he wanted another French fry. Given that, he said, "No, I'd say probably not. The heart would pump out blood, but not in arcs. It would fly up, miss the bed, and then hit just the one spot at the foot of the bed. There would have to be a lot of other dark spots on the rug to indicate that was what happened."

"So if there is just the one spot, and a relatively large one, at the base of the bed, what does that tell us?" I asked.

"One of two things," Wharton said, washing down his pilfered potato with some of McGregor's beer. "Either he was killed near the foot of the bed and fell down…" he tailed off.

"Or what?"

"Or that wasn't blood that got washed up at the foot of the bed. Could be other bodily fluids."

Emitted was a loud group grimace that you can actually hear on the cassette tape, and Mahoney made a comment about not discussing such things in front of open food. I turned to McGregor.

"Okay, Alan, let's talk money." McGregor brightened considerably, about to show us his level of expertise. Everyone was glad not to be discussing bodily fluids.

"What money?"

"About thirteen million dollars that's missing from the Legs Gibson 'You'd-Better-Have-My-Values' Foundation. If I want to see where that money came from, and even more fun, where it went, what do I have to do?"

McGregor grabbed his beer back from Wharton, who looked annoyed, and took a long drag on the bottle. Then he put it back down on the table, out of Wharton's reach.

"Ask," he said.

"Ask? Ask whom?" I was showing off my grammatical expertise here. I was an English major in college, you know.

"Ask the Foundation. Believe it or not, Gibson's American Values thing is a not-for-profit organization. That means the books are a matter of public record, and anybody can ask for an accounting whenever they feel like it. You gotta love America." McGregor grinned at that.

"So if I just call up and say hi, I'm a member of the public,

and I'd like to see your books for the past three years, they have
to give them to me?" Wheels were spinning in my head that I had-
n't used since freshman economics, a class I almost never attended.

"That's right. Of course, if there was illegal activity, I'd be surprised to see it labeled that way. Somebody had to find a way to
skim off the money without being obvious about it." McGregor's
eyes got dreamy, like he was trying to come up with the right way
to do such a thing. If this went on too long, he'd be trying to get
Max Bialystock to invest in a musical about Hitler by the time
dessert came.

"If you saw the books, would you be able to figure it out?"

He came back to earth. "I don't know," McGregor said. "It
depends on how clever the person doing the skimming was."

"Let's say the person was Legs Gibson."

"Twelve seconds," McGregor said without boasting. "Less, if
Legs was distracted."

Mahoney had been sitting, semi-quietly, at the other end of
the table all night, but all the activity had gotten to him. "Why am
I here, again?" he asked. "Was it just to make sure that Friedman
doesn't break the bank ordering exotic beers he couldn't recognize without the labels?"

"I resent that," Friedman said, draining an amber with a Hun-
garian label. "I don't deny it, but I resent it."

"You are here," I told Mahoney, "for a number of reasons.
First of all, you organized the evening, so it's only fair you should
have to suffer through it like the rest of us. Also, you are my closest and largest friend, and therefore are necessary in case a fistfight breaks out over the last French fry. And last, but certainly not
least, you are here because I have a question about the operations
of Newark International Airport, which as I recall is your base of
operations, professionally speaking."

He took on a smile which could only be described as beatific. "So it is," Mahoney said.

"How often does a shuttle run from Newark to Washington, D.C., and vice versa?" I asked.

"About every fifteen or twenty minutes, if you factor in all the airlines running them," he said. "It's a short flight, only a little over an hour, and lots of business guys go back and forth all the time, so that's where the airlines make their money."

"How about on Saturdays?" I asked.

"It's not all that different," Mahoney answered. "Some business guys are coming home from the Friday meetings that run late. Some tourists go down for a weekend. Some other business guys go down there to get ready for the Big Meeting that's coming up Monday morning. The weekend schedule isn't very different from the weekly one."

"How long does it take to rent a car at the airport?" I said. There were groans all around the table, and Mahoney's eyes narrowed.

"Not that long," he said with too much emphasis, defending his chosen profession with authentic zeal. "If you have one of those club cards, where you can do everything over the Internet or on the phone, you can literally take a shuttle to the gate, pick up the car they told you to take from the lot, and leave. With the shuttle or the monorail at the airport, maybe twenty minutes, tops. More if you're waiting for baggage."

"You spend a lot of time on the roads in our beloved state," I said. "How long from Newark Airport to Scotch Plains on a Saturday late afternoon/early evening?"

"Maybe half an hour," Mahoney estimated.

"So if I were in D.C. at five, I could conceivably be in Scotch Plains by seven-thirty without breaking a sweat?"

"It'd be close," Mahoney said, "but if you planned ahead, it's possible. There's one problem with your theory, Inspector," he added.

"What's that?"

"Well, if you're assuming that Stephanie killed Crazy Legs, then got right on an airplane at Reagan, flew to Newark, hopped in a rental car and drove to the reunion, you're forgetting that she had her own car when she pulled into the lot in Scotch Plains."

"You noticed that?" I asked incredulously.

"Sure," Mahoney said. "It's second nature now. I see a car, I check the plates, and I look for a sticker or a number that would indicate it's from a rental company. Got to keep up with the competition. And Stephanie's car was definitely private."

I thought for a while about that. "That leaves a few possibilities," I said. "But one thing's for sure."

"What's that?" asked Mahoney, always dependable to deliver a straight line when you need one.

"Well, you gentlemen—and I use the term loosely—have answered your questions very well, so *Snapdragon* is definitely picking up the tab for dinner," I said, reaching for my American Express card.

There was a good deal of cheering while I calculated the tip, and how to convince the people at surrounding tables that I'd never met these men before in my life.

I got home after Leah was in bed, but Ethan was still up, wreaking havoc with my computer by playing Internet games on the Nickelodeon site. Abby, with a Sphinx-like look on her face, told me he had been on the Internet pretty much all evening.

We sat in the kitchen, she having a cup of decaf and me having a couple of tablespoons of Maalox. And the idiot grin that kept trying to conceal itself on my wife's face finally got the better of me.

"Okay," I said, "tell me about the dog."

"It's so *cute!*" she gushed. "We found it on the site for this shelter in Hackettstown…"

"Hackettstown!" I groaned. "That's an hour and a half drive easy."

"You only have to do it once," Abby said. "He's so adorable, Aaron. Part beagle, part basset hound."

"A bagel. Very appropriate."

"You have to see. As soon as Ethan's done playing, I'll show you the picture."

"Don't show me anything," I said. "I don't want to be infected with cute dog disease like the rest of you."

"You are a very difficult man," my wife said. "Believe me, once you see the picture, you'll fall in love."

"I might fall in love tonight, but in February, when the wind is blowing and it's twelve degrees outside and Mr. Adorable wants to be walked, I'm not going to be so in love."

Ethan called in from the den. "I'll do it, Dad," he said. "You don't have to walk the dog."

Abby and I looked at each other, but our looks were saying two different things: hers was all about "see?" while mine was very clearly stating, "famous last words."

Chapter
Eighteen

After the Y the next morning, I decided to let bygones be bygones and go get a water bottle at the Kwik N' EZ. In my stinky sweats, I didn't want to inflict myself upon anyone at a real store, and besides, I thought with a certain malevolent glee, they were used to things that didn't smell especially good around there.

Not paying attention to the staff, I just walked over, picked up the bottle of Poland Spring, and headed for the counter. The owner, Mr. Rebinow, was eyeing me warily the whole time, but he wasn't working the register. I noticed that he had taken the box of stink bombs off the counter as soon as he saw me walk in.

I paid for the sports bottle, took the top off, and raised the bottle in his direction, which I considered a conciliatory gesture, and left. But he made no sign, no movement, no nod in my direction. Some people—you mess up their store for two stinking days (literally), and they never forgive you.

When I got back to the house, Preston Burke was there, admiring his work. He had finished painting the window frame, and it looked better than at any time we'd lived in the house. The man lacked social skills, but he could certainly fix a window, which was more than I could say for myself.

"Oh, Pres, I forgot to take the money out of the bank. Do you mind if I give you a check?" I could do an online transfer of the money from our savings account later.

"It doesn't matter, Aaron. You ever think about painting that front door? It really doesn't match the window anymore." Burke looked sideways at me, trying to convince me this was a spur-of-the-moment idea.

"Come on, Preston. You're becoming the Contractor Who Came To Dinner. Besides, painting the door is something I can do myself, and I've blown my annual home repair budget on you already."

He thought about that. "No charge," he said. "I'd hate to leave the house looking like that. I could take pictures, and use it for promotion to get more work." I hesitated, and he knew he had me. "Just take a couple hours, maybe half a day."

Before I knew it, he was scraping the front door in preparation for painting. As we've established, I'm damn easy.

The phone was ringing as I walked in the front door. Abby sounded as excited as she's been since the first pregnancy test came back positive thirteen years ago. You'd think she'd have learned.

"I called the shelter, and they're holding Warren for us," she exhaled.

"Warren?" Who the hell was Warren? I pictured Warren Beatty in a homeless shelter, and that seemed wrong.

"The bagel." Beat, two, three, four...

"Oh, the *dog!*" Give me enough clues, and I'll still generally fail to solve your mystery for you.

"Can you get up there?" To Hackettstown? Now? When I had such an enticing assignment, like parents to harass?

"I can, but..."

"Oh, Aaron, go ahead. We'll talk about it later. Once you see that face..."

I put on my Serious Husband voice. "Abigail, you listen to me. I need you to understand that I am not in favor of us getting a dog."

"Aaron…"

"No. If this is going to happen—and I'm getting the awful sense that it is—you have to understand that this is *not* my dog. I take no responsibility for it, I don't want it, I won't walk it, and the first time it takes a leak on the rug in my office when I'm the only one who's home, I'm going to kick its little canine butt out into the street. Do you understand that?"

"Sure. Now…"

"Abby, *do you understand that?*"

There was an appalled pause. "Yes. I understand it."

"You know it to be true? You acknowledge it?"

A little growl in the voice this time. "Yes."

"Okay, give me the address of this shelter."

She did, and before I could have a rational thought, I visited MapQuest on the Internet and gotten semi-reasonable directions to the current home of Warren the Bagel. MapQuest estimated it would take me one hour and twenty-three minutes to reach my destination, and it's rarely wrong.

I bounced the calls from the land line to the cell phone in case school called, and got out the minivan. If I was going to bring home something whose toilet habits were unknown to me, I'd rather have the van.

There are no good tapes in the van, and I'd forgotten to transfer one from the Saturn, so I kept the cassette player turned off, rather than have to suffer through the Backstreet Boys, Smashmouth, and whatever other bands my daughter had picked up from the radio station her friends told her she liked. I remember when the kids were big Beatles fans, because I told them they were. Times change.

I had enough time during the drive to bounce around a few ideas. If there was in fact a bloodstain at the foot of Cherie Braxton's bed, that probably meant Legs wasn't killed while he was lying down. If that were true, why would the killer bother to arrange him on the bed? Why not just let him fall where he stood?

That was the problem with this story—every answer led to another question. I couldn't think of a reason to move Legs after he was stabbed. Maybe he lay down by himself, just to get comfortable when he died. Uh-huh. Maybe he did a quick fox trot while he was bleeding, too.

And if the stain on the rug was Legs' blood, why didn't the police get DNA on it? Abrams had told me the only blood found was on the bed, and that it had soaked through the mattress to the box spring, which Cherie Braxton had told me forced her to get a new bed, which she expected the government to pay for. Fax McCloskey, on the other hand, had already put out a release stating that Ms. Braxton was not entitled to relief from the government. It was the only useful information he'd ever sent to me, or anyone else.

Did the fact that the carpet might have been cleaned with club soda *really* implicate Stephanie? After all, she wasn't the only one who used that stuff to clean stains—Friedman had known about it. It was just the swiftness with which she had wiped up Leah's ketchup that had impressed me—that and being able to think on her feet so rapidly. That didn't make her a murderer. Necessarily.

The big question, though, was where was the thirteen million, and who had taken it? Stephanie was living well, but not well enough for that. Legs was probably not using the money, what with being dead and all, and that left...

Branford T. Purell, killer, bon vivant, corpse. There was absolutely no explanation for a hair of his to be in Braxton's apartment, and yet, there it was. Could it have ridden in on the killer's pants or something? Was the killer carrying it around for seven years, waiting for the right moment to drop it and confound the living hell out of law enforcement officials and freelance reporters? Maybe the killer was the Texas state executioner, a man who never had his clothes cleaned. But now, I was just grasping at hairs.

Just then, the cell phone rang, and the number was not recognized by the caller ID service Verizon gives you whether you ask for it or not. So I picked up. And there was The Voice.

"Stop what you're doing. It's none of your business."

"You know," I said, "this is getting tiresome. Who are you, and what is it you want?" I thought I was starting to recognize The Voice, and I wanted to keep him talking.

"Stop," said The Voice, and the phone went dead.

Driving up to pick up the dog I didn't want, I thought: All in all, I wasn't really getting much out of this day.

Chapter
Nineteen

The Hackettstown No-Kill Shelter (HNKS) turned out to be someone's house, with a huge L-shaped wing built onto its side and extending back into the property for about a hundred yards. That, I assumed as I drove up, was where the animals were being kept. I looked at the digital clock in the van: it had taken me an hour and twenty-one minutes to drive this distance. Two minutes less than MapQuest had allowed. I must have been speeding.

The front door was locked, but there was a bell, which I pushed. A little window in the door opened. A pair of eyes filled it from the other side, and they had to look down to find me.

"Yeah?" the voice, of indeterminate gender, growled at me. It's nice to deal with humanitarians.

"Swordfish," I said, but there was no response as the eyes looked me up and down, which, alas, didn't take long. "I'm here to see Warren," I added. The door opened, and in I went.

Inside, there was the usual office with dog food, dog toys, dog accessories, and a huge donation box, which bore a sign that said, "Help us keep these animals alive!" But hey, no pressure.

The voice turned out to belong to a woman of about five-feet-and-eleven inches, which, with help from her Jersey hair, made her just a fraction shorter than Michael Jordan. She examined me again and said, "You the one who called about Warren before?"

"My wife," I said in the deepest voice I could muster. I'm a manly man, dammit. I would have spat, but there was no receptacle in sight.

"He's in the back, number thirty-six," she said, handing me a key and pointing to a door. I used the key on the door, and miraculously, it worked. I walked into the animal shelter.

It was dark, and I hit a light switch on my left side. As soon as the lights came on, about two million dogs began barking their brains out all around me. The room was a long, long hallway, with what amounted to cells on either side going all the way back. From the look, the sound, and the smell of the place, it was full up.

Luckily, the stalls were numbered, and it didn't take long to find thirty-six, on the right side and about halfway back. There, sitting and looking hopeful, was the only dog not barking to beat the band.

He was, as advertised, an attractive animal. Big, basset eyes, long basset ears, but otherwise beagle-like, Warren was the poster puppy for dogs. "Take me home," his gaze, from a head tilted to one side, said. "I'm a good dog. See, I'm not barking like those other demented animals. I'll be a fine companion for your children."

The woman in the office had given me a short green leash, and I opened Warren's stall and attached it to his collar. He promptly stood up and walked out just at my left heel. He probably would have shined my shoes for me, too, but I was wearing sneakers.

"How gentle is this dog in real life?" I asked the woman.

"What do you mean?"

"I mean, I have a twelve-year-old son and an eight-year-old daughter, and they have to be able to walk him," I said. I wanted a clear picture for me and for the dog.

"Well, my son has been walking him every morning for the past two months," she said.

"How old is he?"

"He's five."

"Okay, the dog's gentle. But do I have to call him Warren?"

She scratched her head. "Nah, that's just the name we gave him here. He was a stray from the Bronx, and they were going to euthanize him, so we brought him here. You can change his name to anything you like."

"How much to adopt him?" I sighed. If you're going to have a dog, you might as well have one a five-year-old can walk, I always say.

It cost about $120 to adopt Warren, what with the fee from the shelter ("it keeps us going," said the woman), the leash, the collar, the food bowl, the water bowl, the bag of dog food, the dog treats, the dog toy, the dog pillow, and the dog tag. So I'd go a week without eating—Lord knows, it would probably do me good.

The dog and I got into the van and started home. He didn't want to get into the van, as he was quite happy walking around the parking lot and sniffing every blade of grass individually. But I managed to force Warren into the back seat (I'd had practice with two toddlers at various stages of my parental career) and close the door behind him. He didn't relieve himself as he climbed up onto the seat, which I took to be a positive sign.

On the way home, since Warren was not an especially talkative dog, I made a mental list of phone calls to make as soon as we arrived. They included one to Lucille Purell Watkins, one to Mason Abrams, one to Alan McGregor, and one to Barry Dutton about my latest vaguely threatening phone call.

It took slightly less time to navigate the distance this time, because I knew the way from highway to highway now. New Jersey is the kind of state where you can do really well if you never have to drive on a local street.

Two blocks from our house, Warren lost his lunch on the

back seat. Luckily, I had put a blanket out to cover the seat under him, so cleanup was somewhat easier, but I was already noticing how much caring for this dog (for which I took no responsibility) was eating into my day.

Warren trotted out of the van as if he hadn't just made a deposit on its back seat, and set out exploring his new neighborhood. It was a good thing I had the leash to hold him, or he'd have explored all of New Jersey and I'd have been out $120.

Preston Burke was finishing work on the door when he saw us approach. "Watch his tail by the wet paint," Burke said. "I didn't know you had a dog."

"I didn't," I told him. "Now, I do. It's been that kind of morning."

Burke knelt down and started to stroke Warren. "Nice dog," he said. "He doesn't mind strangers, does he?" Then he looked into the dog's eyes. "No you don't, do you? Do you?" he said. People ask dogs questions like that all the time, as if they're expecting an answer. "No, I don't mind strangers," the dog would say. "I just like it when they give me some bacon."

Warren relieved some pressure on his bladder out in the front yard, which was my plan. So I closed the screen door, preventing him from running out, and put down his food and water bowls, filled both, then showed him where they were. He seemed unconcerned, and went to explore the house. Finally, he settled on the rug in my office, four feet from where I was working, and went to sleep.

I was about to call Abby when the phone rang. It was Margot the Agent, informing me that four production companies out of the seventy-five or so that I'd faxed had requested a copy of the script. It was better than nothing, but not much. In the middle of the conversation, the call waiting beep sounded, and I blew off Margot for, as it turned out, McGregor, who sounded excited.

"I've been looking over the books for People for American Values," he said. "I found the thirteen million."

It took me a few seconds to absorb that. "That fast?" I gasped.

"I told you it wouldn't take long, especially if it was Legs who hid the money."

"Was it Legs?"

"No," McGregor said. "It was done much too cleverly for it to be him. Maybe someone who worked for him, because it certainly looks like it was done at his bidding."

"Why?"

"The money came out of separate, private accounts Legs and his vice presidents had established to use for fund-raising, entertaining pols and donors, paying for travel, that sort of thing," McGregor explained. "This has been going on for years, which is why nobody noticed. They never took more than five or six thousand at a time, but eventually, it added up."

"I'll say. To me, the five or six thousand sounds good." Doing mental arithmetic (which was never my best subject, it should be noted), I estimated that it would take... uh...

"How many of these five thousand dollar skims would it take to amass thirteen million, Alan?" I asked him.

"Two thousand, six hundred," he said.

"So if they did it every week for fifty years, they'd have enough?"

"Well, that's the thing," McGregor said. "It was five thousand, but five thousand from each of ten accounts at a time. So it would only take five years if they did it every week, which they didn't. They took more like ten years, and did different accounts at different times. No pattern, no huge withdrawals, no noticeable crime, for a long time. If Legs hadn't gotten killed, it's possible this could have gone on longer, and made whoever did it even more money."

"Wow. So maybe whoever killed Legs is pissed off now, because the attention from the murder cut off the gravy train."

"Maybe. Or maybe whoever killed Legs decided to do it because they had enough money to do whatever they wanted now, and they didn't need him anymore." McGregor has a devious side you rarely get to see in certified public accountants outside an IRS audit.

"You care to take a guess at who was skimming, Alan?" I asked. "Any style to the crime that could point to one person or another?"

"That's the beauty of it," he said. "It could be any one of those ten vice presidents, or it could be Legs."

"I think we can disqualify Legs as a suspect," I said.

"Yeah," McGregor chuckled, "that's just what they want you to think." I thanked him and hung up.

I was starting to formulate a theory, and the best way to confirm it was to call Lucille Watkins. She answered on the third ring, and appeared to be sober. She even remembered who I was.

"I don't know there's anything more I can tell you, Mr. Tucker," Lucille said. "My brother's been dead seven years, and he couldn't possibly have been in Washington last month. That's all there is to it."

"Maybe," I said, "but I'm wondering about something. You said there was a time when things got so bad that Branford sold his blood to make some money."

"That's right," she said. "Drank it all up, fifteen minutes after he got the money."

"Did he ever sell anything else?" I wasn't sure exactly how to broach the subject.

"Anything *else*?" Lucille asked. "Like what, a kidney or something?" She laughed rudely, having been surprised by the question, and by her response to it.

"I was thinking more of his hair."

She stopped laughing, and came back after a few seconds, sounding mystified. "You know, Mr. Tucker, I'd forgotten about it, but there was this one time he had a bunch of hair cut off—you know, Bran wore a long pony tail for a while—and sold it to one of those 'real human hair' wig places. He got a good price for the hair, too. How did you figure that out?"

"The hair was where the DNA came from," I told her. "Whoever was in the room was wearing the wig that the company made from your brother's hair."

"Eight years later?" she asked in wonder.

"Some people wear those things for thirty years," I said. "Do you think Tony Bennett's fooling anybody?"

She was aghast. "*Tony Bennett?*" she asked.

Lucille gave me the name of the company in Odessa, TX that bought Branford Purell's hair. It had gone out of business, but the records it left were still available to local authorities, so I'd call Abrams later and fill him in, but I was willing to bet I knew what they would say.

One person who wore a toupee was involved in this affair. One person who had sabotaged every attempt I'd made to find out more in his presence. One person who might have had Legs' confidence, and could easily have been helping him skim money away from his own foundation.

Branford Purell's hair had ridden in on Lester Gibson's head.

Chapter
Twenty

Preston Burke finished painting the front door just before the kids got home that afternoon. He had done a much better job than I would have, sanding and smoothing the entire surface before he applied primer and then two coats of paint. I was impressed, and ashamed.

All that took a back seat to the touching scene when Ethan walked in the door, hung up his backpack, and walked directly through the living room and past the hyperventilating dog without noticing anything out of the ordinary. Warren looked mightily disappointed, but I explained to him about Asperger's Syndrome, and he nodded his understanding. Ethan went right into the bathroom and turned on the exhaust fan. It was anybody's guess how long he would be in there.

Things were different when Leah walked in. The dog practically rushed the door this time, and Leah fell to her knees, yelled "He's *here!*" and gave the dog the biggest hug since Charlie Brown met Snoopy. "Daddy, he's here!" she repeated, sincere in her belief that the dog had merely gotten our address from the shelter people, hopped into his car, and driven all the way to our house on his own, without my knowledge.

"I know, Puss," I said. "But you know he's going to be a big responsibility, right? You're going to have to walk him every day after school."

"Every day, Daddy," she said.

"Like today, right?"

"Today? I have six pages of homework!" Leah fretted prettily, but to no effect on her hardhearted father.

"Today. Here's the leash and here's a bag." I handed her a plastic bag from the supermarket.

"What's the bag for?"

"What do you *think?*"

She thought about it. "Ewwww…" she said.

"You got it."

"You mean I have to…"

"You sure do," I said. "There are laws in this town, and this is the kind of town where they're serious about those laws."

She grumbled, but took the leash, and led the dog outside. We settled on a specific route—one that would require crossing no large streets, and a brief visit to the park. That, I figured should give Warren the time and varied scenery he would need.

While she was out, Ethan came out of the bathroom and started on his homework. I was about to impart the news of the dog, but the phone rang, and I went to answer it.

"Mr. Tucker?" The voice was shaky, and vaguely familiar. I braced myself for the latest threat. "This is Jason Gibson."

Whoa. If you'd told me Marcel Proust was going to call out of the blue, I might have found it just a tad less likely than a call from Legs Gibson's younger son. But this was a lucky break, since Marcel probably didn't speak English all that well, even when he was alive.

"Hi, Jason. I'm surprised to hear from you, but I'm glad you called." I was trying as hard as I could to sound somewhat jovial. "What's up?" If I got any more jovial, they'd probably have me committed.

"I just wanted you to know," Jason began. His voice was urgent, and somewhat hushed. I couldn't tell if he was on a land line or a wireless phone. "About what my brother and I were telling you the other day. It wasn't the truth."

"Jason, where are you? Are there people listening to this conversation?" I got up to pace.

"No, I'm back at school. They don't know I'm calling you. But I just wanted you to know."

"What wasn't the truth, Jason? You guys didn't tell me much that could be lies. You didn't tell me much at all."

He paused, thinking about how to say this without getting himself in trouble, or saying anything that could be traced directly back to him later. "Well, I *was* there the week before the stabbing, but..."

I was going to wear out a path in the rug. "But *what?*"

"Don't believe anything they tell you, Mr. Tucker. Every word of it is a lie, okay? I don't want to leave the country, so I'm telling you now. You can't trust anything they tell you."

"Who, Jason? Your mother? Your Uncle Lester?"

Jason chuckled a chuckle with no humor in it. "My uncle's never going to tell you anything, Mr. Tucker, so you don't have to worry about him lying to you. But everyone else is a total liar, okay?" He hung up.

The front door opened and Leah walked in with Warren on the leash. He was panting happily, and she still had the plastic bag, which was empty.

Warren looked at me as Leah took his leash off. He seemed to grin, but that was just the panting from his exciting walk. Then he walked onto the rug in my office and relieved himself right next to my chair.

Ethan walked in from the kitchen and took a look. "Dad!" he said. "Did you know we have a dog?"

Chapter
Twenty-One

In the abstract, it's easy to kill a dog. You just think of it as something that has invaded your house and intends to make your rug smell bad. In the concrete, material world, you have to look into those big brown eyes and watch those floppy ears, and the fact is, you just can't do it. And bringing back a dog to the shelter is a lot like bringing back a used car. Once you're out the door, "The merchandise is your responsibility. But we'd be happy to sell you some floor mats and a pine tree deodorant you can hang from your rear view mirror."

Ethan and Leah were introduced, that day, to the wonderful world of rug cleaner and paper towels, and the fun-filled uses to which they can be put. They complained, but the dog was still new to their lives, and they did what was asked of them. I knew this trend would not last long, but I was powerless to stop it.

I called Mason Abrams that afternoon to tell him about Branford Purell's hair, but he wasn't in, and I was condemned to voice mail. I would have told Fax McCloskey, but I was relatively sure he didn't exist, and was just an illusion run by a man behind a curtain employed by the Washington D.C. Police Department. If I ever did get in to see him, I'd ask him for a brain, or a heart. Or some height.

After that, I tried getting through to Stephanie. Naturally, I wasn't going to blow Jason's cover for him, but I did want to see if she had any suspicions about Lester, and that would require my talking to her when she was alone. She wasn't in, and that settled that, for the time being.

When Abby got home, she too fell under Warren's spell. Of course, she didn't have that far to fall, since she had pushed me toward the shelter to begin with. If it had been that easy to get her to fall in love with me, we'd have married a year earlier. Women are funny that way.

We had dinner, which Warren watched with great interest, and the kids did their best to interest him in his dog toy, which was a rubber ball in the shape of a shoe. Never give a dog a toy shoe to chew up, because that encourages them to go after the real thing.

After dinner, the three of them went to play with the dog, and I cleaned up the dishes. I was distancing myself emotionally from Warren, since I didn't want to feel bad when the urge to kick him out the door overcame me, and besides, I hate to admit that I've been wrong. After all the public bitching and moaning I'd done about not having a dog, actually enjoying the dog would have made me look silly. Okay, sillier.

I did preside over a family meeting, at which the issue of a name for the dog came up, and the overwhelming winner in the election was: Warren. Go figure.

It was just after seven, and at that moment it hit me: in less than two hours, Anne Mignano would be facing the wolves at the Board of Education meeting, and I had done nothing to help. I hadn't even failed, because in order to fail, you have to put out some sort of effort. All I'd done was question a gadfly on exercise equipment, a janitor, and a gym teacher, none of whom could actually be considered a source of information, since none of them had any.

I sat down at the kitchen table and slammed my fist down like Bogart in *Casablanca*, except I wasn't mad at Ingrid Bergman. Why hadn't I just gotten up the courage to go talk to those parents? Was there still time to call them on the phone and tell them to go ask their kids if they were delinquents? This was probably going to lead to Anne losing her job after her contract was up, and after all my talk about what a good friend I am and how I appreciate all she's done for Ethan, I had done nothing.

I was a bad friend. I was a bad person. I didn't deserve to own such a fine dog.

The dog chased his ball into the kitchen, picked it up and ran out again, to much laughter. Leah, who had been chasing him, stopped giggling when she saw the look on my face. She suddenly reverted to the adorable six-year-old she used to be, and sat on my lap. I held her close, trying to forget that I was the scum of the universe.

"What's the matter, Daddy?" she asked, stroking my cheek.

"I'm just a little upset, Puss," I told her. "I promised someone I would find something out for them, and then I couldn't, and I'm upset that I let them down."

"Oh," said my daughter. "That's too bad."

Yeah. That's too bad. And wait until your next principal is some discipline-obsessed Nazi who'll probably give your children detention for being cute. Luckily, I wasn't blowing this out of proportion.

"I know," I told Leah. "I'm sorry I'm not being happy about Warren. I'm just upset with myself, not anybody else."

She gave me a Leah hug, which is rumored to be able to cause a smile on clinically depressed people for whom Prozac is a breath mint. I smiled weakly and hugged her back. Leah got up off my lap and headed out of the kitchen. No sense sitting here with a big old drag like this guy when there was a fun dog to play with.

At the edge of the dining room, she stopped and looked at me. "What were you supposed to find out, Daddy?" she asked.

I sighed. There was no point in trying to evade the question. "I was supposed to find out who threw the stink bombs in your school," I told my daughter.

She got a strange look on her face, one that indicated that I must be on an intellectual level just a hair below Warren's. "Susan Mystroft threw the stink bombs," she said in a voice dripping with superiority. "Everybody knows that, Dad." And she turned and walked out of the room, as I heard Abby yell, "no, no, Warren, not *there!*"

Chapter
Twenty-Two

I blinked a couple of times, then stood up. "Ethan!" I yelled. "Get in here!"

"What'd I do?"

"Nothing! Get in here *now!*" He showed up in a few seconds, over Abby's pleas for paper towels and rug cleaner. Ethan looked worried, like I was going to kill him whether he'd done something wrong or not.

"Ethan! Who threw the stink bomb in the girls' locker room?"

He narrowed his eyes. "Susan Mystroft. Why, did somebody say that *I...*"

"No!" I handed him the rug cleaner and paper towels. "Give these to your mother."

He did that while I raced to the wall phone. I pushed the speed dial button marked "Melissa," and waited until Miriam answered the phone.

"Hi, Aaron," she said breezily. "What's new?"

"No time," I told her. "Put Melissa on the phone."

"Melissa?"

"Your daughter," I reminded her.

"I *know* who Melissa is," Miriam said brusquely. "Why do you need to talk to her?"

"Miriam, I've got no time. Please. Melissa, *now!*"

In seconds, Melissa's usually confident voice came on the line, sounding like a tiny bear cub looking for its mother. "Um, hi, Aaron," she said. "Is Leah there?"

"Melissa, who threw the stink bomb into the girls' locker room?"

"Not me," she said. "I wasn't even there that day."

"I don't think it was you," I told her. "I need to know who it was."

"Susan Mystroft. Everybody knows that. She thought they'd close the school down and she wouldn't have to take her science test, but she did it over the weekend, and the only thing they closed was the locker room."

"What about the other ones?"

Melissa's voice took on confidence, as she realized I wasn't mad at her, and was proud she knew something a grownup didn't. "The one in the gym was because she doesn't like Ms. Van Biezbrook," she said. "She made Susan do sit-ups, and Susan doesn't like sit-ups."

"And the boys' room? Why do the boys' room?"

"I dunno," Melissa said. "Maybe they come three to a pack."

I thanked Melissa and hung up. Running for the door, I grabbed my coat.

"Where the heck are you going?" Abby asked. "Are we out of something?"

"I've got to go to the Board of Ed meeting," I told her. "I'll be back in an hour and a half. I've got a stop to make first." And I was out the door before she could point out that the dog would need an evening walk.

At a house two blocks away, following a hurried explanation, a small girl broke down in tears, and to their credit, two parents did not try to shift the blame. They blamed each other. But they agreed I could take their daughter, as part of her punishment, with me.

Midland Heights is a small enough town that virtually everything is within walking distance, assuming you're not a native

New Jerseyan, and therefore bred to take a car even if you're visiting your neighbors next door. Still, parking at the municipal building, where the Board of Education meeting had started fifteen minutes ago, would be a nightmare, so I double-timed the three blocks and arrived to utter chaos. The little girl didn't want to come inside, but she didn't want to stay outside by herself more, so she did as I requested. Her father, who had come along, had something to do with her decision.

The chaos in the building didn't bother me, because even when I was a municipal reporter covering three towns at the same time, I never attended any public meeting that *wasn't* utter chaos. You just get used to it, and move on.

As we walked in, the issue being discussed was an appropriation for the Middle School library to buy two new computers to be devoted to Internet use. One father whom I did not know was arguing that the money was being used "to give our children access to pornography," and was being instructed in the ways of site blocking, and in-class supervision.

Anne Mignano was sitting by herself in a seat far from the entrance, in one of the back rows on the aisle. She looked absolutely composed, a woman completely content to accept what Fate had decreed for her.

As I was snaking my way through the room toward her, the discussion on access to porn was tabled for further research, and Board President Michael Lanowitz announced that the next item would be the "breakdown in security at Buzbee School." I made it to Anne and sat down next to her at that moment.

I gestured to her, and she leaned over to hear me whisper. "Susan Mystroft," I told her. Anne's eyes widened, and I nodded "yes." "My sources are impeccable," I said quietly. I pointed to Susan and her father, Brad, who were waiting at the door.

Anne smiled just a bit and nodded to Lanowitz, who was asking for her report. She stood.

"I have very good information," she smiled, not looking at me, "that would indicate we have solved the security breach in question," she said to the president. He looked surprised.

"Can you mention names?" he said.

"Certainly not in an open meeting," Anne replied. "But if you wish for me to speak in executive session, I might be able to be more specific."

Lanowitz looked around at the board members, including Faith Feldstein, who was showing off her exercise-enhanced body in a tight T-shirt and jeans. They nodded, and he called for a vote to adjourn to executive session, which was unanimously passed.

I gave Anne the information and explanation I had before she had to get up and walk into the anteroom where the executive session was held. She nodded. "I knew it," she said, "but I couldn't prove it." Then she thanked me and walked, head held very high, into the session. The doors were closed, but any good reporter can tell you to stay near them in case any sound leaks through. Susan and her dad walked in quietly when no one except me was looking.

After about a minute, sound leaked through so plainly that the level of murmur in the main meeting room, where I was standing, dropped to silence. Faith Feldstein's voice yelled "*what?*" loudly enough to be heard through cinderblock, wood paneling, and steel doors, followed by Faith herself, who exited the meeting, muttering to herself under her breath.

About seven minutes after that, the Board members came out, followed by Anne, who to her credit was not looking like a triumphant administrator who had stuck it to her bosses. She actually wore an expression of concern. The board president immediately suggested that the issue of Buzbee School discipline be tabled indefinitely, and the board agreed unanimously, with one member absent. No doubt, there would be hell to pay in the morning.

Anne and I walked out together, as the board took up the pressing issue of gum in the school water fountains. She allowed herself a small smile, and looked at me as we stood outside, enjoying the chilly air after the claustrophobia that accompanies any public meeting.

"You certainly are the cavalry, riding over the hill in the nick of time," she said. "Thank you, Aaron."

"I got lucky," I told her. "My children just happened to know what was going on."

"We like to foster communication between parents and students," Anne said with the hint of a sly grin. "In any event, I owe you a favor."

"No, you don't," I said. "You've been the best principal I've ever dealt with. Ethan isn't an easy kid to have in your school."

"No," she agreed, "but I've seen a lot worse. At heart, he's a very sweet boy. And he's never boring."

"Tell me about it. Will you have trouble with Faith and her cronies?"

"A little," Anne admitted, "but not more than I can handle."

"Imagine," I said, "all this over a couple of stink bombs. Imagine if there were real problems to worry about."

"There are," said Anne. "But they don't generally come to the surface until it's too late, I'm afraid."

She thanked me again, and we went our separate ways. At least I'd managed to save the day for Anne. Now, all I needed was to solve Legs Gibson's murder and find out who was threatening me, and I'd chalk this one up as a good week.

I got home a few minutes later, and found Abigail on her knees with a can of carpet cleaner and a roll of paper towels. Warren was sitting on his dog bed in the living room, surveying all that was his.

"Hi, honey, I'm home," I ventured.

"What was that all about?"

"I saved Anne Mignano's job for another year or so," I informed her. "Based on information I got from our children and Melissa."

She stood up and assessed the damage. "Warren has been a busy boy," she said.

"That's one way of looking at it. You know, the carpet still smells."

"I was hoping you wouldn't notice," Abby said. I have a notoriously bad sense of smell.

"Crazy Legs Gibson would notice. Are you sure we want a dog?"

"I'm sure. Are you sure you want a carpet in here?" She was already eyeing the threadbare wall-to-wall with the eye she generally reserves for things whose days are numbered. Luckily, she has not yet fixed that gaze on me.

"I'm sure I don't want to move my desk, the computer, my file cabinets, the bookshelves, and everything else in the room to move the rug," I said.

"Well, it looks like I need to call Mark Friedman and ask him what takes the smell out of an old, old carpet," said Abby.

"I'll call him. He's seen a picture of you, and may actually pant on the phone."

"That hasn't happened to me in weeks," my wife teased.

"Well, I can't call your office *every* day," I said.

Friedman was home, luckily, so I didn't have to spend much time talking to his wife Marsha, who doesn't like me. I don't know why she doesn't like me, but she snarls whenever I call, even when she's saying things like "so, how's life treatin' ya?" It's hard to snarl through a phrase like that, but Marsha manages.

This time, she didn't even answer the phone, so I could avoid all that and get right to the point. "I have another carpet question for you," I said.

"More blood?"

"Not this time. It's not related to a crime, unless you consider rescuing a dog from the shelter to be cruel and unusual punishment."

"Uh-oh. Dog urine." Friedman was completely in his professional mode.

"Among other things."

"The other things you can clean up and forget about," he said. "The urine is a problem. What kind of carpet?"

I was prepared this time. "Wall-to-wall, shallow pile, looks to have been installed sometime during the Vietnam War. And now it doesn't smell so good."

"You're screwed."

I waited. "That's it? I call the carpet maven and I get, 'you're screwed?' What about some magic compound I can cook up in the basement that will take out the smell and make the rug look like I just bought it last week?"

"It doesn't exist. You're screwed. Face it. Dog urine on a rug like that isn't going to come out. It's powerful stuff. Pull up the carpet and get the floors sanded, if the stain doesn't go down too far." Friedman doesn't pull punches. I could have used a few pulled punches right around then.

"You're not helping, Mark."

"Superman couldn't help you. Face it, the carpet's a goner. Come on in, Tucker, and I'll give you a deal."

"It's cruel to try and drum up business among friends," I pointed out.

"Don't blame me. I didn't make you go get a dog." I glared at Abby, who was pretending not to be looking at me. She walked into the living room and started reading my script, which I had left on the coffee table. She must be feeling really guilty if she's willing to do that, I thought. Wonder what else I can get out of it...

"Well, thanks anyway, Friedman," I said. "I'll call you if I decide to get another rug."

"Whatever. Hey, did the Legs thing ever work out? Did you find out about the stain on the carpet?"

"Not yet, but it's close. That bastard didn't die the way he was supposed to, writing his killer's name on the rug in his own blood. Would have made it so much easier to solve."

Friedman laughed. "He never did have any redeeming social value, Legs," he said. "No qualities to recommend him."

"Well, he was taller than me."

"Not really." Friedman's voice had a tease in it.

"What do you mean, 'not really?' Legs was at least three inches taller than I am."

"No, he wasn't," said Friedman. "I played basketball with him once, and we changed in the same locker room."

"So?"

"Didn't you know?" Friedman asked incredulously. "Legs Gibson always wore lifts. That's why his legs always looked longer than they should be. It's the reason we called him 'Crazy Legs.'"

Chapter
Twenty-Three

Ethan actually got up at six-thirty the next morning to walk Warren, who had miraculously made it through the night without fouling any more of our furnishings, although he did show a preference for our living room sofa over his dog bed. We solved this problem by completely giving in to the dog, and throwing a blanket over the couch in case he shed. So much for my being the alpha dog in his pack.

Now, given three days to come up with five thousand words for ten thousand dollars, I decided to forego the Y Friday morning and concentrate on work. Writing is always the least of the job—it's gathering the information that takes all the time. And I had gathered information, all right. It just fit together like a jigsaw puzzle put together by a klutzy moose.

What I had was a theory that fit the facts I'd discovered, but no evidence whatsoever that the theory was correct. In fact, the proven information on this story would indicate to any sane person that the theory was ridiculously improbable. Luckily, there were no sane people in my office, only a freelance writer. Our usual motto is: "When the facts don't fit, make sure you get your money in advance." Of course, I hadn't done that, so the facts had to fit.

Preston Burke came by that morning for his check, which I wrote out to "Cash," and handed to him. Then, somehow Burke managed to convince me that the cast iron railing on my front steps needed to be sanded and painted, and before I knew it, he was back at work, happy as a clam, assuming that clams enjoy physical labor in the presence of the husband of the woman you think you're in love with. You never can tell with clams.

It occurred to me that the best way to put off worrying about who killed Legs Gibson was to worry about who threw a rock into my since-repaired front window. This would be the same person who called my house periodically to make extremely general threats that were sounding increasingly weak these days. If a threatening phone caller can't even muster up a good scare in a short Jewish freelance writer, he really should give up the pursuit and take up botany, or something.

I called Barry Dutton to see if the rock-throwing incident was still his Number One crime priority, and amazingly, it had dropped down the list. Barry said a couple of bicycles had been stolen from people's garages, and there were numerous reports of motorists exceeding the twenty-five mile-per-hour speed limit that infests Midland Heights, so the whole rock thing had faded as quickly as Jean-Claude Van Damme's fame. Muscles from Brussels, indeed.

After Barry, I called my other law enforcement buddy, but Mason Abrams had chosen a very inconvenient Friday to begin a long weekend. Since we in New Jersey often go to Washington for three-day excursions, I assumed Abrams would be on his way to beautiful downtown Newark, whose reputation is not entirely deserved, but whose reality ain't exactly Venice, either.

All this, and *still* no additional producers had called to express interest in buying the script. It was enough to discourage a normal man.

There was only one person left to call for business purposes, and I had admittedly been putting it off until it could no longer be avoided. But that calendar on the wall was showing Monday coming up rather quickly, and there was no avoiding Stephanie

Jacobs Gibson any longer.

I hate having to call people when I don't have good news for them. I especially hate it when they are people who loom large in my past, even if the reason they loom so large is driven less by deep feeling and more by hormones.

Actually, that was no longer true. When I was eighteen years old, Stephanie could easily have held me enthralled simply by showing up in the right T-shirt. But now, she represented less a legitimate erotic fantasy and more a symbol of an era that I, to be honest, have remarkably little affection for. I'd much rather be the person I am today than the one I was then. And while Steph could still wear a T-shirt with the best of them, I was married to the best of them, and didn't have the same empty longing I'd had in high school. But as symbols go, Stephanie was a pretty strong one, and I hated disappointing her. Giving Steph bad news—which in this case could be characterized as no news at all—wasn't my favorite thing to do that morning. So, I avoided it.

Instead, I called Mahoney on his cell phone. He was, it turned out, halfway between Atlantic City and Newark, traveling between emergency calls for his rental car bosses. He had the phone on speaker, which was evident from the level of noise on my end of the line. But his hands were free. I imagine one of them was probably even being used for steering.

"There's going to be trouble tomorrow," I told him. "You want to come?"

"What kind of trouble? Minor household repairs, or foundation work?" Mahoney is, to me, what Bob Vila is to everybody else. Except he's not on television.

"Neither. Remember the night you spent in my closet?" Of course he remembered. I'd almost gotten shot, and he'd managed to beat up a kid almost thirty years younger than himself. It was quite an evening.

"I believe I do recall a night like that," Mahoney said.

"It'll be more like that," I said.

"Legs Gibson?"

"One and the same," I told him.

"What the hell. I haven't faced death in close to six months. What kind of snacks should I bring?" We discussed the menu, he said he'd drive, and we decided to firm up the rest of the details for our brush with mortality later on.

Finally, I couldn't put off the call to Stephanie any longer. She was at home, and sounded tired and more subdued than usual.

"What have you found out, Aaron?" No small talk, and the tone was less inviting than it had been since this whole thing began. I was starting to feel like an employee.

"Not a huge amount, Steph. But I do know that Lester was in the room when Louis was killed. I can't tie him to the crime yet, but…"

"Lester? Are you sure?" She sounded truly shocked, which surprised me. Ten minutes with Lester in the most casual circumstances could convince you he was capable of violence. Just the way he smiled when he was trying to look friendly was enough to wake me up in the middle of the night for weeks afterward.

"I'm sure, all right. There's DNA evidence that can't be explained any other way. Now, where the connection is, I don't know, but Lester was definitely there. Also, there's some evidence that Louis may have been illegally funneling money from his foundation into his private accounts. Did you notice any extravagant spending, any financial things that you couldn't explain, in the past few months?"

Stephanie thought for some time, and answered, "no." I waited, but there was no elaboration. Just, "no."

"There's more," I told her finally. "I have evidence that Louis might have been killed standing up, and then laid out on the bed to make it look like he'd been there all along. Can you think of a reason someone would do that?"

Again, "no," this time sounding smaller and more meek.

"We need to meet, Steph. Are you coming up to Jersey for the weekend?"

I got the impression she had her hand over the mouthpiece, but Stephanie came back very quickly. "I hadn't been planning on it," she said, "but it sounds like it's important we see each other."

"I have to finish the story by Monday for *Snapdragon* to print it on time," I said. "That's why there's some urgency in the timing."

"Okay," Steph said, starting to sound more normal. "I'll come up. Do you know the Hyatt Hotel in New Brunswick?"

"Sure. I can practically see it from my bedroom window."

"I'll be there tomorrow. I'll call when I have a room number. We can meet there."

Stephanie Jacobs in a hotel room—there was a time when that would have answered every prayer I'd ever care to offer up, if I was the prayer-offering-up type. Now, it was not quite as exciting as I would have hoped. It was, in fact, just a little bit scary. After all, the woman had come within inches of being arrested for killing her husband, and for all I knew, she *had* killed him.

But I didn't think so.

Chapter
Twenty-Four

The dog continued his assault on the rug in my office, completely ignoring every other carpeted area in the house. I began to think he had a particular grudge against me, since I was the only one who hadn't taken him for a walk yet. Warren loved a walk more than most other males like staying at home and watching the game on a plasma TV with the remote in their hands and a beer close by on the table. It's the advantage of being a dog, I guess, that one's pleasures are so simple.

Leah, at least, had fallen so completely in love with Warren that she was pleased to take him out when she arrived home from school on Friday. She said "hi" to Preston on the way in, having totally accepted him as a fixture in the house, and he tipped his painter's cap at her and smiled as she walked by with Warren, making sure the dog's tail didn't brush against the black paint on the railing. Burke was nothing if not thorough.

Friday night my mother came to have dinner with her grandchildren, and in the process, to see Abby and me. She laughed at virtually everything the kids did, whether it was funny or not, chuckled when they were being especially obnoxious, and told the adults tales of incompetent internists and unscrupulous produce managers at the Foodtown. That is, the produce managers were at the Foodtown. I'm not clear on where the dopey doctors were, since I was only listening with one ear.

My mind was on Stephanie and Legs and Lester. Clearly, Lester had been in the room when the stabbing took place. He had been scheduled to visit the Gibsons that weekend, and his DNA, or that of the man whose hair he was borrowing, was found in the room. Someone had cleaned up some stains on the floor, which may or may not have been blood.

"...two for ninety-nine, when clearly it should have been labeled two for fifty-nine," my mother was saying. Abby was doing a much better job of looking fascinated than I was, but Abby, generally speaking, is a nicer person than I am. And she wasn't going to confront a murderer in a hotel room the next day. Or a non-murderer.

Meanwhile, back at the window, there was something about that last threatening phone call that had bothered me since I'd hung up the phone. I can't say I had recognized the voice, but there was a certain familiar cadence to the sentence being uttered that I couldn't deny. I'm very good at remembering sound—I have a "photographic ear." I can remember lines of dialogue from movies I saw when I was a child, but my eye is not nearly as talented, and quite often, I forget what I've seen. Never, though, what I hear. So there was something about that sound, the syntax, the tone of voice, which I'd heard before. I just couldn't quite place it, like the bass line of a song that runs through your brain until you can dredge up the melody and identify the music. It was nagging at me.

"...and he never even checked to see if I'd been in before for a hiatal hernia," my mother continued, disgusted with the state of medicine these days. The fact that these days were undeniably better than those days wasn't really relevant. The fact that the days two hundred years from now would inevitably be better than now, and that she wouldn't be here to see them was annoying. I could sympathize with that.

The children were devastated when their grandmother left, which is to say that Leah tried to turn one hug into seventy-five, and Ethan actually called down from his room, where Play Station was, to say good-bye. The dog, whom my mother had met earlier, followed her to the door, tail wagging eagerly, assuming that she was going to take him for a walk. Instead, Abby did the honors after my mother left.

I had trouble sleeping that night. It wasn't dread, since I didn't really think I'd be in much danger no matter what happened (but then, I'm usually wrong about such things), but more a feeling of disappointment that kept me awake until one-thirty. Abby slept peacefully, even though I had told her about my plans for the next day and she, supportive spouse that she is, had informed me that she would never speak to me again if I got myself killed, which seemed reasonable.

Warren was up when I got out of bed at seven-thirty, after having tossed and turned fitfully, while sleeping just a bit overnight. Everyone else was still asleep, and the fact was, he did have nice big brown eyes and floppy ears, and his tail wagged quite adorably when he thought you were going to take him out. So what the hell—I took him out.

Much as I hate to admit it, I found the experience to be pretty enjoyable. You could think more clearly when you were concerning yourself with nothing more than the toilet habits of an animal considerably lower to the ground that you are. And since very few humans are lower to the ground than I am, I found a certain comfort in Warren's short little legs attached to the big basset hound paws. He was disproportionate, which seemed just about right for my household.

Damn mutt was growing on me.

It was during the walk through Edison Park, two blocks to the east of my house, that the facts of the Legs Gibson story all came together in my head. There was only one way it all made sense, and even though the sense it made was pretty nonsensical, as that other great freelance writer Sir Arthur Conan Doyle used to put it—and I'm paraphrasing—when the impossible is eliminated, whatever remains, no matter how improbable, must be true. Sir Arthur used up all the good lines for the rest of us.

By the time I reached the house, carrying my plastic bag with Warren's contribution to the walk inside it, I had convinced myself that I was right. So I dumped the bag in one of our outside garbage cans (no sense bringing that stuff into the house), marched inside, and called Barry Dutton's office. Strangely, at eight on a Saturday morning, the chief of police wasn't in. Barry and Mason Abrams were proving that you can't ever find a cop when you need one.

I left Barry a message detailing what I had planned for the day, then called Abrams' number and left him the same message, knowing he wouldn't be back until Monday. Maybe he'd check his messages. In any event, the cops should know what a freelance writer knows, whether the writer really knows it or not.

Abby came downstairs a few minutes after I got off the phone, dressed for her morning run around the park. She, of course, looked ravishing, but in an athletic way. I gave her a kiss and held her too long.

"I have to take Mr. Dog for a walk," she said.

"Mr. Dog and I just got back," I informed her, and her eyebrows rose a couple of feet from their normal position.

"Oh, really?" she said, her voice indicating amusement. "So you're starting to like Warren, huh?"

"I never minded Warren," I said, using all the spin techniques I learned during my disastrous six months in public relations. "But I don't want to be the first line of responsibility for him. It was the concept of a dog I opposed, not the particular dog himself." I gave my wife another squeeze for good measure (and because I wanted to), and she went off to exercise, laughing to herself at how easy I am to manipulate.

On Saturday, you can count on Ethan to sleep until roughly Sunday, so I wasn't expecting him downstairs anytime soon. Leah, however, rarely sleeps late, and sure enough, Abby was barely out the door before she came downstairs, brushed past me like I was part of the furniture, and launched herself at the dog, who looked positively terrified at the sight of this eight-year-old female projectile advancing on him.

"Look at that *face!*" she cooed, and went about informing the dog, at great length, of how adorable he was.

"Nice to see you, too," I said to my daughter, who at one time in her life, however briefly, had believed me to be the most wonderful person on the planet.

"Good morning, Daddy," she replied by rote, and set about petting the dog until surely his fur would be worn off.

I hadn't expected Stephanie to call until late in the afternoon, but the phone rang about eleven in the morning, when Ethan was just coming down the stairs, dressed in the boxer shorts and Star Wars T-shirt he had slept in. The kid was born to live in a frat house. I pointed to my clothes and then upstairs, indicating that he should get dressed. He walked past me into the kitchen.

"I'm in the car, and I just passed Baltimore," Steph said. "I called ahead to the Hyatt, and I'll be in Room 716. Check in time is three, and I should be there by three-thirty. Can you meet me there as soon as I get in?"

"Sure," I told her. "Call me as soon as you're in the hotel. I'm only a few minutes away."

She agreed and hung up, choosing not to make small talk. The tension in her manner was palpable, and I wondered if she were afraid that I knew something, or afraid that I didn't. I had my suspicions, but I couldn't be sure.

Abby, fresh from a shower, could cause most grown men to

weep openly, but I have grown hard-hearted in the fourteen years we've been married, and only got a trifle teary-eyed. I told her about Stephanie's call, and gave her the timing for the rest of the day. She wasn't happy about it, but agreed that I had the right idea. Then I called Mahoney and told him. He'd been in his garage, where he has every tool in the world and a set of free weights, pumping iron and planning to construct a built-in stereo cabinet for his home theatre. I asked him if being perfect took up a lot of his time, but he said I'd have to ask his wife.

He showed up at my door in the Trouble-mobile, his work van with the bald tires, old dents, and only half of all the tools in the world, at 1:45, as planned. I gave Abby a kiss, a long one, and she gave one to Mahoney. A short one, I was pleased to note. The kids were attempting to wash the dog with a garden hose and a bucket, and finding that beagle/bassets do not much care for water, and are downright averse to soap.

Mahoney walked over and touched Warren under the chin. The dog looked up, and immediately sat. His tail wagged, but he never moved. Mahoney told him to stay, and walked back to where I was standing with Abby. The dog didn't move.

"Nice dog," Mahoney said.

We got into the van and drove the enormous distance into New Brunswick in about four minutes. The Hyatt is just past the Raritan River, over the bridge from Midland Heights, and we were in the lobby (luckily, there is self-parking at the Hyatt, or we'd have had to endure the horrified look of a valet at the sight of the Trouble-mobile) by two o'clock on the nose.

"Have you figured out how to get into the room before Stephanie gets here?" Mahoney asked casually.

"Follow my lead," I said. "If check-in time is three, they're cleaning the room just about now."

We took the elevator up to the seventh floor and walked

down the aisle to Room 716. Sure enough, both 716 and 718, next door, had their doors open, and the cart with the cleaning supplies was parked between the two.

Vacuuming could be heard from 716. Mahoney and I looked into 718, saw what we needed to see, and walked inside.

The rooms were adjoining rooms, and the doors were open on both sides so the maid could get in and out of either room whenever she needed to. At the moment, she was busy working on the rug in 716, and didn't hear or see us in the adjoining room.

"Has she done the bathroom yet?" I hissed at Mahoney. He stuck his head in and nodded, yes, the bathroom had been cleaned.

We scuttled into the bathroom. Fortunately, the shower had a door, not a curtain, and we both managed to get inside and wait without causing so much commotion that the maid, in the next room with the vacuum going, would notice.

"This is not my idea of a great Saturday afternoon," Mahoney said. "If I'm going to spend time in a shower with someone, I'd prefer it not be you."

"Quiet," I told him. "We have to make sure we get out before she locks those adjoining doors."

Sure enough, after about fifteen uncomfortable minutes (being fully clothed in a small shower with another man is, at best, awkward), the maid in the next room seemed finished with her work. I signaled Mahoney, and we crept out of the shower and into Room 718.

The door was still open, but I saw the cart move past it and toward the next pair of rooms. She was getting ready to finish up.

Mahoney and I scampered through the adjoining door and into the shower in 716, just to be safe. Within a minute, the adjoining doors were closed and locked, and so was the door to the room we were stuck in. I looked at my watch.

"We've got about an hour and fifteen minutes," I told Mahoney, and we walked out of the shower, no cleaner than we had been before we got in, and into the room.

I reached into the canvas bag I'd brought and took out the snacks we'd agreed upon. Wow! Fat Free Chips for me, a box of Ring Dings for Mahoney. I had a bottle of Diet Coke, and he satisfied himself with orange soda. We were an elegant pair.

It was, of course, a classier hotel room than I'm used to, since our family budget doesn't always allow for a wet bar, a Jacuzzi, and a king-size bed.

"We should have used the honor bar instead of bringing our own," I said. "Then we could have charged Stephanie for the snacks, at about three bucks for a bag of peanuts." I sat down and arranged the food on the table. "Plenty of time."

"Great," said Mahoney. "I'll brush up on my canasta."

Instead, he actually lay down on the bed (after removing his shoes—ever the gentleman, my best friend) and went to sleep, leaving me an armchair in which to ponder the meaning of life in its many permutations for a little less than an hour. I would have gone to sleep myself, but Mahoney's snoring could probably be heard in Princeton, NJ, a good sixteen miles to the south.

That's why we were caught so completely off guard when the hotel room door opened and the dark trench coat, the dark glasses, and the awful toupee told me that Gibson had entered the room. He was concealing a gun in his right hand.

"Come on in, Legs," I said. "Sit down. Relax. Take off your hair."

Louis Gibson tore off the dark sunglasses and stared at me. "I've always wondered why you called me that," he said.

Chapter
Twenty-Five

Mahoney was barely awake, and shoeless, and therefore not a terribly useful deterrent to violence. He sat up and started glaring at Legs, who stood in front of us with the hotel room door closed and the gun fully visible now.

"Actually, it was the reason I knew you were alive," I said. "But I'm never going to tell you why we call you that."

"How will I go on?" Legs said with what he uses for sarcasm.

"You were right, then?" Mahoney asked.

"Yeah. Legs, here, has been alive the whole time. You killed your own brother to cover up your embezzlement and give the cops no reason to look for you, didn't you, Legs?"

Gibson didn't answer, but he did take a roll of duct tape out of his trench coat pocket, and motioned Mahoney into the desk chair. Mahoney didn't move right away, so Legs put the gun closer to my face and cocked it. That convinced my bodyguard that it might be a good idea to sit in the chair.

"See, Legs here"—and I could tell every time I used that name it annoyed him, so I resolved to use it as often as possible— "skimmed thirteen million off all the sincere conservative maniacs who sent him money, and he needed to be able to cover it up so he could go on living with all the money, even after the cops or the IRS found out about it, right Legs?" He was trying to figure out how to tape Mahoney to the chair while still holding the gun, and was having a hard time doing it. "You want me to hold the gun for you while you do that, Leggsy?"

He pointed the gun at me. "Stop calling me that!" he said.

"Just trying to help." Legs went back to pulling on the edge of the tape with his teeth, while moving the gun back and forth from me to Mahoney. I don't know why, but the image of Legs holding a gun on me just wasn't all that frightening. Maybe because it was Legs. He'd always been annoying. He'd always been a self-congratulating pest who never conceded that anybody but he could be right, but he was never what you'd call scary. "I can understand your need to cover up the theft, Legs, but your own brother! Isn't that just a little cold?"

"You didn't know him," Louis Gibson said. "He was the most self-satisfied, egotistical, ill-tempered, pompous…"

"In your gene pool? Who would have thought it?" Mahoney chimed in.

"He wasn't the kind of brother you think twice about," Legs continued, his face a little redder.

"So you stab your brother in your girlfriend's apartment after sex, and you dump his body on the bed, put on his clothes, pull the extremely unconvincing toupee off his head and put it on your own, and assume his identity so you can be dead and still have more than thirteen million dollars. Now, *that's* family values," I said.

"I guess you *can* take it with you," Mahoney added. He looked at me. "But wouldn't the cops do fingerprints, that sort of thing, and find out it wasn't Legs?"

"No," I said. "The medical examiner wouldn't have a reason to take prints if Cherie Braxton—who didn't know him very long, and couldn't tell the difference—and later, Stephanie, both identified the body as Louis Gibson. Lester looked enough like you to pull it off, right Legs? And once you took his shoes, the ones without the three-inch lifts in them, you were walking around at your real height, instead of the one everybody was used to. So you looked more like him."

"DNA?" Mahoney asked. Legs was looking at whomever was speaking, as if he were a spectator, enjoying the show. After all, we were talking about how clever he was—what's not to like?

"All they got was a hair from the piece of cabbage Legs has on his head," I said. Legs involuntarily touched himself on the head to make sure it was still there. "That actually worked to his advantage, since the cops got a DNA match on a guy who was executed in the state of Texas seven years ago, and that totally confused them. It always pays to get a real human hair wig, doesn't it, Legs?"

"I said, stop calling me that!" he bellowed.

"Did you know that you were wearing a murderer's hair, Legs?" I asked. "That's kind of, I don't know, symmetrical, isn't it?"

"So, where did the money go?" Mahoney asked. "The cops didn't find it in any of his accounts."

"They won't find it in my accounts," said Legs, pleased to pat himself on the back for his own ingenuity. "My mother is laundering it for me."

"Forty-four years old and still doing his laundry at Mom's," Mahoney said, clucking his tongue and shaking his head. "Pathetic."

"Clearly, Stephanie knows about all this, or she wouldn't have led us to this room for you to shoot us, right Leggsy?" If I could get him angry enough to make a large movement before he taped us to the chair, Mahoney or I (better Mahoney) could rush him.

Legs laughed. "Yeah, Stephanie knows," he said.

"How'd you get her to go along with it?" I asked.

The voice from the doorway was one laced with nostalgia and sex. "Go along with it?" Stephanie asked. "Do you really think he was smart enough to think this all up *himself?*"

She stood in the doorway in a matching trenchcoat, although

hers was more of the tan-colored Humphrey Bogart type. Of course, it flattered her. I thought in that moment that the old hotel keys were better. These "slide-the-card-through-the-machine" things just didn't make enough noise, and someone could sneak in on you like this.

"I knew Mr. Mahoney would be here," she said. "You have a habit of hiding him in the closet, don't you, Aaron? Sorry Louis got here so early."

Stephanie's face was hard and emotionless, and I had never seen her look like that before. She walked in and took the gun from Legs without so much as a blink. He gave it to her, and actually seemed to flinch a little as she reached for it.

"Tie them up," she said. "I'll hold the gun."

"So it was your idea, huh Steph?" I asked.

"Naturally," she said. "Louis couldn't come up with a decent plan to get himself from one room to another. You have to blame yourself for this, Aaron. If you hadn't found out more than you were supposed to, and then told me what you knew, we wouldn't have to shut you up on our way to the airport. But we have to buy a few hours before the flight leaves."

"I'm disappointed," I admitted. "I thought better of you than this."

"Why?" she asked. "Because I was the girl from high school with the big tits that everybody wanted to go to bed with? We never really knew each other all that well, Aaron, so that's the only image you could be clinging to."

I'd been thinking quite a bit about it, so I was ready. "That wasn't it at all, Steph," I said. "You're right that the image I had from twenty-five years ago was the one I was using, but it wasn't just about sex. I never seriously considered sex with you, because I thought I was out of your league. That was before Abby taught me about leagues. I was a skinny little kid who didn't fit into any group, and you used to talk to me sometimes. You, the coolest girl in the class. So that was what I wanted. If I could impress the cool girl, then maybe I could be cool, too."

"Sorry to disappoint you," she said as Legs finished taping Mahoney to his chair. "But you're never going to be cool."

"Big news," said Mahoney.

I cut him off. "Why me, Steph? Why'd you insist that I write about the murder, instead of just taking off with the dork and the money?" I pointed at Legs.

"There were some financial details that hadn't been completed yet, and we needed to stay in the country for a few weeks to make sure no one suspected Louis was still alive," Stephanie said. "Louis, get the legs." Gibson almost reacted at the word "legs," then started in on Mahoney's with the tape.

"But you didn't answer why you needed me," I reminded her.

"You were insurance, Aaron. I could get information on what the police knew through you, and I could control which way the press was going by controlling you. You got just enough information to keep you going."

Damn it! I wasn't just going to get shot. Now I had to tell my wife she was right, too. Boy was I was having a day!

"But you didn't control me," I said. Got to get some of your own back.

"I did for a while. Long enough," said Steph. Her eyes were devoid of emotion. "Besides, you were a great witness. You'd seen me at the reunion, and you could testify I was in New Jersey only a few hours after poor Louis had been killed."

"Should I put tape on his mouth?" Legs asked Stephanie, pointing to Mahoney.

"Hopefully, it won't be necessary," she said. "Start taping Aaron." Legs obediently walked over and started wrapping duct tape around my arms and the armchair.

"I get the better chair," I teased Mahoney.

"Could you please tape *his* mouth?" Mahoney asked.

Once Legs had me securely fastened to the chair, Stephanie put the gun into her coat pocket. "You're not going to shoot us?" I asked her.

"Not unless we have to," she said. "We're not cold-blooded murderers."

"I think Lester might disagree," I said. "How did you get him to show up at Cheri's that day?"

"The way I get any man to do anything," she answered. "I told him I was going to have sex with him, told him I was getting revenge on Louis for all his affairs. Then we got in with a key Louis had made. Lester showed up with his tail wagging and his tongue hanging out of his mouth."

"I have a dog like that," I said. "Did Lester pee on the rug, too?"

"That's very funny, Aaron," she said, and a shiver ran down my back.

"Must have been a shock to you, Legs, when they show up and you're already naked on the bed. Talk about your *interruptus.*"

"I knew they were coming," said Legs. "I was just expecting them later."

"It wasn't anything I hadn't already seen," Stephanie said. "And believe me, it isn't really worth looking at."

"Ouch," said Mahoney. Legs actually winced a little. I was glad Abby never talked about me like that. At least not in front of me.

"So you drove up to New Jersey, immediately parked near, but not at, the airport, flew back down to D.C., killed Lester, and then flew back up to Jersey, so it could be established you were up here when the cops figured Legs had been killed?" Mahoney had the itinerary all worked out.

"Very good," said Stephanie. "I thought that part would be enough to throw everyone off, but you've become a real problem, Aaron. You didn't even respond when I tried to seduce you, and that always works."

"I'm seduce-proof. Except for my wife, who can seduce me pretty much by breathing." Competition brings out the best in women.

"That was the moment when we first started thinking that you might not be totally controllable," said Stephanie. Of course, it doesn't bring out the best in *all* women. That didn't bode well. Best to distract her.

"So you couldn't get Lester to lie down," I continued, "and you stabbed him right there, next to the bed. You had to work fast to mop up the blood, didn't you, Steph?"

"Good thing I had my club soda nearby," Legs chimed in, proud of himself for having gotten something right. Stephanie rolled her eyes a little.

"How'd you make sure he didn't have any clothes on already?" I asked Stephanie. "There were no fibers on the knife."

"We had our... foreplay in the living room," she said. "Lester already had his shirt off before we went in to consummate the relationship. The poor man, he really was awfully confused."

"You took a big chance that old Cherie would take a shower at just the right time," Mahoney pointed out.

"Not really," said Legs. "The original plan was to make it look like she killed me. But she took long showers all the time after we made love."

"I can't imagine why," said Mahoney.

"Now that we've answered all your questions, boys, I'm afraid we'll have to leave you." Stephanie motioned Legs toward the door, and he obeyed. "We have a plane to catch." To Legs: "we'll take my car."

"A plane to a place without an extradition treaty with the United States, I'm sure," I said. "You're traveling under false names with very, very expensive counterfeit passports, right? And I'll bet Mom has already funneled the money out of whatever accounts she was hiding them in and into a numbered Swiss account."

"Cayman," said Legs, and Stephanie flashed him an angry look.

"Your mother is really a case," I told Legs. "You kill her own son, and she actually helps you get away with it."

"She's getting a decent cut of the money for her trouble," Legs boasted. "She'll be a wealthy woman for the rest of her life."

"You're lucky she doesn't have a conscience," I said. "Of course, she's modeling her life on that of Eva Braun, so…"

"Not everyone can be as morally perfect as you, Aaron," said Stephanie. "Louis, it's time."

He turned and walked out of the room. Stephanie walked over to the chair where I was restrained. She knelt to make sure she was making eye contact.

"Don't think about screaming your way out," she said. "I need enough time to get us to the airport. So I requested a room with no one on either side, and the upper floors here have better soundproofing. They don't want to annoy the guests who pay six hundred dollars a night."

"I don't get it, Steph," I said. "Was this all about the money? You're going off to live the rest of your life with a guy who cheats on you on a daily basis, away from your children, and you can never come back. Is the money worth it?"

She reached into her pocket and pulled out a wad of cash. "Let's see what money is worth," Stephanie said. "Here's the ten thousand dollars you were going to get from *Snapdragon*. I'm willing to bet that you won't tell them the whole story, and they won't print it, so I'm reimbursing you ahead of time. You won't want to admit your embarrassing role in this, and you won't want to soil the reputation of good old Steph Jacobs, who's been on your pedestal since you were sixteen. Here." She put the money in my inside jacket pocket.

"You think my taking the money proves that I'm as bad as you? That I'd kill an innocent man and live my life with a lizard like Legs Gibson for money?"

She knelt back down next to me, and whispered in my ear. "It's not just the money," she said. "I actually love him." I looked at her, and couldn't stop myself.

"*Why?*" I asked, and she shrugged. Then Stephanie stood up and started toward the door. She stopped, turned, and walked to Mahoney, who looked up at her in wonder. Then, Stephanie leaned down and kissed him hard on the lips for a long moment. When the kiss was finished, she turned on her heels and walked briskly out the hotel room door without looking back.

Mahoney and I stared at each other for a while, then he broke into a wide grin.

"See?" he said. "I *told* you she liked me better."

Chapter
Twenty-Six

We didn't bother to scream for the longest time, although Mahoney did make one spirited attempt to wiggle his chair over toward the desk and dial the phone with his tongue. When that didn't work, we sat and waited. I screamed once, but that was only because I hadn't gone to the bathroom before they taped us to the chairs. When he found out why I was screaming, Mahoney gave it a try, but neither of our hearts was in it.

Lucky for us, Barry Dutton checks his voice mail on Saturdays, and two Midland Heights cops (with two New Brunswick cops along for the ride) found us in the room about an hour and a half after Stephanie and Legs had left. I told them what had happened, but even Mason Abrams (who also checked his messages, and had called Barry in the interim) couldn't get the Feds to Newark Airport before whatever flight they had taken was long gone.

The cops cut us loose. I told them about the money in my jacket, that it was a bribe meant to keep us quiet, and they took it for evidence. I made sure it all went into a plastic bag, and was counted before it was marked. I didn't want anyone to think I'd taken a dime.

It did make me wonder about Gail Rayburn, though. Here, someone had asked me to compromise my values, and offered me a good deal of money to do it. I had given serious thought to keeping my mouth shut about it, and Mahoney would have backed me up.

Ten grand is a lot of money in my neighborhood. But the thought of having ten thousand of Legs Gibson's dollars paying for my son's summer camp just didn't feel right.

We got home about five, and Abby made both Mahoney and me tell the whole story out of the kids' earshot. This was easy, since Ethan was in his room playing video games and Leah was at Melissa's house, handing over E-*LIZ*-abeth, whom she decided scared Warren too much. Warren had, in fact, refused to walk into Leah's room, causing her much mental anguish. So the lizard went to live across the street, with another of its own kind. Those worms didn't stand a chance.

"You two really are a pair of detectives," she said with great sarcasm. "If Ms. Cleavage and her husband hadn't decided to let you live, I'd be explaining to the kids how their Daddy would not be coming home anymore." She actually got a little moist in the eye at that suggestion, and she clenched her teeth with anger at our foolhardy actions. Then, being a Jewish woman, she began cooking. She started water boiling for pasta.

"We had a backup plan," I said. "I was going to be so witty and charming that she'd fall in love with me and ditch Legs."

"But she liked me better," boasted Mahoney.

"Nice plan," said my wife.

"What can I tell you, Abby?" I said. "I relied on my feelings. I never really thought that we were in danger. They were much more intent on showing us how superior they were than in killing us. And they've gotten everything they wanted."

She thought about that. "Yeah, you and your keen sense of human nature," Abby snarled. "You kept insisting Stephanie didn't kill her husband."

"Well, she didn't."

"So she killed her brother-in-law. That's a minor distinction," said my wife. The water was close to boiling, and she started creating an Alfredo sauce that would cause me to expand by a belt notch or two.

"Actually, we never really did establish which one of them killed Lester," I pointed out. "They were both there. They both knew the plan. It could have been either one of them."

Abby turned and gave me a "give me a break" look. "You know perfectly well that Louis wasn't strong enough mentally to do that to his brother. You know that it was Stephanie's plan from the beginning. You know, deep down in your heart, that she killed Lester Gibson without so much as a second thought."

"I don't know that at all," I said. Off her look, I added, "I might *suspect* it…"

While Mahoney called his wife, Abby started the pasta in the water and finished the sauce. I sidled up to her while she was stirring something, and put my arm around her waist.

"You really do love me as much as I love you, don't you?" I said.

She turned and studied my face. "Of course I do, you idiot," she said, and we fell together into a very enjoyable embrace, which was spoiled by a lump digging into my left side. Abby looked at me strangely, until I removed the tape recorder from my inside jacket pocket.

"Did you have that on the whole time they were telling you about their evil scheme?" my wife asked, amazed at my deviousness.

"Naturally," I said. "If I got shot, I wanted you to hear about how I wasn't interested in sleeping with Stephanie."

"You know," she said, "while you were out, I finished reading your script."

"No kidding."

"No, no kidding," said my wife.

"*And?*"

"And, it's very good." Ah, the moment I live for.

Mahoney didn't want to stay for dinner, so I had twice as much fettuccine Alfredo as I should have, but that didn't seem very important at the time. I spent most of dinner gazing at my wife and children, and wondering how I could have been stupid enough to put my life on the line for a measly ten grand.

That said, I still had the five thousand words to write on Legs and how he hadn't actually been murdered, but had instead killed his brother and stolen his toupee, committing crimes against both society and good taste. After the kids went to bed, which was quite late, I started writing.

I won't bore you with all five thousand words (and besides, you should pick up a copy of *Snapdragon* and read all about it), but it began:

By Aaron Tucker

Everyone was agreed on one thing: Louis Gibson was an asshole.

The problem is: the use of the word "was" in that last sentence is premature. The fact is, Louis Gibson is still an asshole, a living, breathing one, and he is in all likelihood enjoying himself immensely on an exclusive nude beach as you read this, spending some of the thirteen million dollars he stole from private citizens right before he killed his own brother and robbed him of his toupee.

See? He really is an asshole.

I went on to explain the whole sick, twisted tale, in the most journalistic of terms. Included were interviews with Stephanie and Legs, Cherie Braxton, Louise, Junior and Jason, Mason Abrams (although he was quoted as "police sources" only) and Madeline Crosby. I left out Estéban Suarez, because it occurred to me he'd think the whole piece was about him. I wrote well into the night, then emailed the whole piece to Lydia at *Snapdragon* and waited.

The next morning, which was Sunday, I slept in for a change. When I woke up, after ten, the house was in full swing. Abby had made waffles for the kids, as she does every Sunday morning, and the dog had already been walked, after the rug in my office was cleaned up of Warren's nocturnal activities. Leah was already at Melissa's house and Ethan was deep into the latest episode of *Butt Ugly Martians*, a cartoon show aimed directly between his eyes.

From behind, I embraced my wife, who was still at the stove, and she turned to kiss me, still happy that I wasn't, in truth, dead. I looked at the stove, where she was making pancakes.

"Are those for me?" I asked.

Abby nodded. "I thought you might like a special breakfast after you worked so hard on this story."

"I am hopelessly in love with you," I said.

"Don't be," she answered. "Be hopefully in love with me." I got myself a plate and she actually flipped two pancakes onto it for me. I got the syrup and what passes for butter in my house (some concoction made with yogurt, it doesn't taste half bad) from the refrigerator, then sat down and took a bite.

"Mmmmm," I appreciated. "You make a mean pancake, my love."

"I'm sorry," she said. "I'll try to make a kinder one next time."

"Someday I must pay for you to take a course in receiving a compliment," I suggested. "You know what I mean. These are terrific."

"Thank you."

"You have a secret ingredient, don't you? There's something in here even the International House of Pancakes hasn't thought of yet, isn't there?"

"That, my friend, is none of your business." Just to be funny, she said it "busy-ness."

I stopped in mid-forkful. That was it. The way the word "business" was pronounced—I knew I'd heard it before. I stood up and kissed Abby again.

"What's that all about?" she asked. "Sit down and eat before they get cold."

I did, because they were really good pancakes. "I have to go out right after breakfast," I said. "Do we need anything?"

"Milk," she said.

"Perfect," I answered.

A half hour later, I was walking through the front door of the Kwik 'N EZ. I strode in, went directly to the refrigerated cases where the milk is kept, and sought out the no-growth-hormone one-percent. Knowing the way the Kwik 'N EZ operates, I reached far back onto the shelf to get a newer gallon, and sure enough, came up with one whose expiration date was six days after the one at the front of the shelf.

Feeling chipper, I also picked up a Nestle Crunch bar for Leah, a package of Oreos for Ethan, and a copy of *Rolling Stone* for myself. Abigail couldn't possibly want anything they sold at the Kwik 'N EZ, so I got her a pack of Devil Dogs.

Mr. Rebinow was at the counter, but tried to pass me off to his associate, a younger man with blond highlights and a baseball cap bearing the logo of no team I'd ever encountered. I shook my head when he came over to take my order.

"No," I said. "Only Mr. Rebinow can help me." The young man looked confused, and turned to Mr. Rebinow. There was no one else in the store. Rebinow shrugged, and walked over to the cash register.

"Go check the stock on the Ring Dings," he told the younger

man. "I think we're low." The younger man seemed about to dispute that claim, but saw the look on his boss' face, and decided to do exactly as he was told.

"I see you've given up on the stink bombs," I said, pointing to the spot on the counter where the offending items used to dwell.

He decided to play indifferent. "Too many complaints from the parents," he said. "My sales in milk and bread started suffering. It wasn't worth it. Now, what do you want?"

"It was you," I said. "You were the one who was making the phone calls, and you were the one who threw the rock through my front window."

"You're crazy." But he was already sweating.

"No, I'm not. You said the same thing on the phone that you said that day in the store. Except in the store, you said, 'that's their bus-i-ness,' three syllables, and on the phone you said, 'it's none of your bus-i-ness,' the same way. I always remember things like that, and you're the only person I know who pronounces the word like that."

Mr. Rebinow stared at me for close to a half minute. In his eyes, you could see him consider any number of possible responses, and discard them all. Again, he decided that nonchalance was the way to go.

"So?" he asked. "You ruined my business for two days, and I broke a window. So what?"

"What I did falls into the area of a prank, and what you did falls into the area of terroristic threats, destruction of property and, if I want to get nasty, attempted assault. Another five feet to the left, and you'd have beaned me with that rock."

"Oh, bullshit," he said. "I waited for the lights to go out before I threw the rock."

I pulled the tape recorder out of my jacket pocket, and he

turned a little green. He didn't know I hadn't turned it on.

"Now I've got you on tape confessing to the act, Rebinow. So it's time for us to start talking about how to solve this problem."

Mr. Rebinow's eyes darted back and forth a few times from the cassette recorder to my eyes, to the counter, to the front door, to the window. He had no idea how to respond, and being too cool for his own good wasn't working. So he started to cry.

"I'm sorry," he said. "It's just... I was so mad when the cops wouldn't do anything to you, and I just wanted to scare you. And then, when I was going to stop, you started coming in here again, and I thought you knew I'd been doing it."

"We can work it out," I said, inadvertently quoting the Beatles. "We can reach an agreement that satisfies everybody and we don't have to involve the police at all."

"How?" he asked, eyes wide.

"The first thing we're going to do," I said, "is get in touch with a sign painter."

EPILOGUE

Lydia from *Snapdragon* called me Monday morning, and told me the editors all liked what I'd written, which was a relief. The next issue of the magazine had a picture of Legs on its cover, with a detachable toupee, and a line indicating the International Symbol for "no" through his face. The headline read: "Louis Gibson Isn't Dead, But He Is An A**hole." There's nothing like the discretion of the American free press.

Of course, all the daily papers and the broadcast media got the story first. I talked to Mason Abrams on Sunday, thanked him for his help, and filled him in on what I'd discovered. I duped a copy of the cassette with Legs and Stephanie's confession, and FedEx'ed it to him on Monday, for Tuesday delivery.

By Wednesday, Fax McCloskey's daily bulletin was announcing the good news/bad news scenario Fax had to report: "We know who killed Louis Gibson—nobody. We know who killed Lester Gibson, but, um, they kind of got away."

Naturally, the press coverage was tremendous, but Fax had failed to mention that *Snapdragon* Magazine had broken the story, so nobody reported on it until Lydia started calling the major news outlets and telling them her reporter had done the reporting. My phone started ringing Wednesday night, and didn't stop again until Saturday.

Once things started to calm down, I attended a special ceremony at the convenience store. It had taken almost two weeks, but a new, red, blue and yellow sign proclaiming "Quick And Easy" was being hoisted above the front door. Mr. Rebinow, thrilled that he'd gotten off so cheap, beamed at me and offered me a free cup of coffee, which I declined. I did, however, accept a free Diet Coke.

Barry Dutton asked me once or twice about the window, but I told him we were better off forgetting about such things, since the damage had been repaired, and the threatening phone calls, amazingly enough, had stopped. Barry sounded a bit skeptical on the phone, but he had enough to worry about, and turned his mind to other matters, like how to keep Detective Westbrook in his office and away from the lunchtime buffet at All-You-Can-Eat.

Confronted by her mother after the Board of Education meeting, Susan Mystroft was forced to admit her crimes publicly and face the music. Among the punishments discussed was a one-week suspension from school, but Anne Mignano quite logically noted that time off from school was what Susan had been aiming for to begin with, so that would be considered a reward, rather than a punishment.

It was decided, at Anne's suggestion, that Susan be made to show up for school a half-hour earlier than everyone else, and stay for a half-hour detention every day for two weeks. This Solomon-like decision was praised far and wide, by everyone except Susan, who wasn't the least bit pleased, and Faith Feldstein, who still didn't believe a girl had thrown a stink bomb, so a conspiracy surely was afoot. She resigned from the Board of Education in protest, but virtually no one noticed. Oliver Stone was reportedly interested in the movie rights briefly, but moved on to something else.

Punishment for Stephanie and Legs was not so easy to enforce. There were rumors they were domiciled in the Cayman Islands, but an investigation by the FBI turned up nothing. Later, whispers surfaced that Stephanie had gotten fed up with Legs and thrown him off a yacht in shark-infested waters, but those couldn't be substantiated, either.

Louise Gibson died three months later after a blood vessel burst in her nose. Medical science couldn't explain it, but there were numerous explanations for the two million dollars found in seventeen different certificates of deposit in Louise's name after she died. They were, eventually, confiscated by the Federal Government, which will probably use them to pay for bribes that will cover up the next scandal. The world's not perfect, you know.

Jason Gibson continued at the Pringley School, his tuition paid by a blind trust, until graduation. He was accepted at Harvard, but chose to go to Rutgers instead. There was definite potential in that boy.

Louis Junior graduated from Georgetown and took a job working for People for American Values. Strangely, that organization folded its tents six months later, citing diminished donations, and as of this writing, Louis Gibson Jr. is looking for work in government or finance.

Life at my house slowly settled back into a routine. Ethan continued to walk Warren first thing every morning, even when the weather turned colder. Leah never failed to take the dog out after school, and Abby always gave him a long walk after dinner. Our routine was unalterably adjusted to accommodate Warren.

To cut down on the number of odiferous incidents that occurred during the night, I fell into the habit of giving him a walk just before bed. But Warren continued to favor my carpet over the curb, and the smell in my office became unbearable.

So, on an unusually warm November afternoon, I was moving all my office furniture so I could pull up the rug. Preston Burke had offered to do the work, but he was busy repairing the water damage in the kitchen ceiling, and I didn't want him to be distracted. So I took an afternoon off to get down to hardwood floors in my office.

I was pulling up the rug in the corner just to the left of my desk, where the bookcase generally stands, and thinking that in retrospect, it all began with the lizard, when the phone rang. The caller ID provided no return number, but it did note that the call was coming from California, so I gave up the opportunity to pull up tackless installation strips for a moment or two, and answered it.

"Hello?"

"I'm trying to reach Aaron Tucker."

"You've succeeded."

"Aaron. This is Glenn Waterman of Beverly Hills Films. We read your script, *The Minivan Rolls for Thee*, and we really liked it."

"Who is this, really?"

Waterman laughed. "That's the kind of humor we found so wonderful in the script," he said. "We'd like you to come out here for a few days so we can discuss it, with an eye toward an option."

"You're paying for my airfare, car, and hotel?" I asked.

"Yes," chuckled Waterman. "We're very excited about the script. We'll happily pick up the tab."

My mind reeled. The kids get home at two-thirty every day. Ethan is starting wrestling practice on Monday night, and Leah has basketball on Thursdays, gymnastics on Tuesdays, and Junior Girl Scouts every other Sunday. Who the hell would cover for me during my absence? There was no way I could just up and leave. It wouldn't do to pursue my long-shot career goal and mess up my family life in the pursuit.

I told Waterman I'd get back to him (he probably thought I was holding out for money) and walked into the kitchen, where Abby was trying to stay out of Preston's way while making chicken fajitas.

"Who was that?" asked Abby. Burke came down off the ladder and wandered out the front door, probably to get something out of his truck.

"A production company in L.A. They want me to go out there and discuss an option."

Abby, her face at once astounded and elated, turned to look at me, and gave me one of the hugs that keep one coming back for more. "Aaron!"

"Wait a second," I said. "There's no guarantee anything will happen, even if I go. I'd have to be out there for four days, at least. There'd be nobody here when the kids got home. You'd have to get them out in the morning, which means you'd get into your office late. There are after-school activities and schedules, and you know how Ethan is about changes in his routine. . . "

My wife, paragon that she is, laughed at me. She put a finger to my lips and gave me a look that would cause Will *and* Grace to reconsider their respective lifestyles.

"Come on," she said. "I'll help you pack."

We went upstairs.

Three weeks later, she helped me pack.

ACKNOWLEDGMENTS

Before anyone in my home town starts tuning up, yes, there *was* a stink bomb incident in one of our schools a couple of years ago, and yes, it did give me the idea. But as I recall it, nobody was especially upset, there was never any public uproar about it, the principal's job was certainly never on the line, and to be completely and totally honest, I don't know if the culprit(s) was/were ever caught, and if so, I definitely never found out who they might have been. So don't read more into it than that.

To those who went to high school with me: no, that's not you in the book. You may *think* it's you, but it's not. Herein are composite characters from that time of my life, other times in my life and, for that matter, now, but no one person is based on one other person. Most of them—honestly—are entirely made up. Sorry to disappoint, but that's why this book is in the "fiction" section of your bookstore.

And for the last time committed to print: no, I'm not Aaron Tucker. For one thing, he's about an inch and a half shorter than I am, and (I hope) better looking. And my wife is not Abby, my son is not Ethan, and my daughter is not Leah. Yes, I sometimes base characters on people I know, but this ain't no documentary—the characters are designed to suit the story.

Now to the important stuff: thanks to those who have written and emailed me (jeff@aarontucker.com) about *For Whom the Minivan Rolls*. I really do appreciate your kind words, even that one guy who suggested that when the movie is made, everybody should be played by Joseph Fiennes. I don't think Joe would make a good Abigail, but there's no accounting for taste.

Thank you to Libby Hill, who bought 20 (!) copies of *Minivan* and spread them around the Midwest. And thanks to friends and family who came to the book launch party (thank you,

Penny's Restaurant!) and introduced me to the lovely world of signing books.

Thanks, again, to Bruce Bortz, who perseveres when all signs indicate he shouldn't, and I'm glad.

A special thank you to the DorothyL crowd, whose many wonderful members have taken me to their hearts and encouraged me. When I wrote *Minivan*, I had no idea there was such a thing as a "cozy," so I've been well educated by the online mystery community. Special thanks to Meg Chittenden, Mindy Starns Clark (for showing me the ropes at every convention I've ever attended), and our intrepid moderator, Diane Kovacs.

An enormous special thanks to my web design genius, Judy Kolva, without whom Aaron would be homeless on the Internet.

And of course, my eternal gratitude to my family: Evie, Josh, and my incomparable wife Jessica. Without you, there is no point.

—Jeffrey Cohen
October, 2003

PRAISE FOR JEFFREY COHEN AND
A FAREWELL TO LEGS

"I declare Jeffrey Cohen 'King of the Zingers.' His Aaron Tucker character doesn't know when to stop . . . and that's the good news. *Legs* definitely has legs."
—**TIM COCKEY, BESTSELLING AUTHOR OF SUCH MYSTERIES AS *MURDER IN THE HEARSE DEGREE***

"A warm welcome back to Aaron Tucker! With his second novel, Jeffrey Cohen delivers another intriguing plot, more laughs, and the characters readers of *For Whom the Minivan Rolls* will happily recall. Like Spenser, Elvis Cole, and Stephanie Plum, Aaron Tucker is evolving beyond being a character—he's becoming a brand!"
—**MICHAEL LEVINE, RENOWNED HOLLYWOOD PUBLICIST AND BESTSELLING AUTHOR**

"A delightful, breezy mystery, staking a claim just as firmly in the world of realistic, human emotion as it does in the grand tradition of the classic whodunit. A fun ride, indeed."
—**DREW Z. GREENBERG, WRITER, "SMALLVILLE," "BUFFY THE VAMPIRE SLAYER"**

"Aaron Tucker has Groucho's wit, Harpo's sweetness, and Chico's talent for well-meaning screw-ups. *A Farewell to Legs* is shot through with wit that snaps and sparkles (but never wounds), not only in the dialogue where you expect it, but in the narrative, keeping the pace crackling and lively. I laughed aloud repeatedly. I mentally noted lines to steal and drop into my conversation, hoping to pass them off as my own (I should be so lucky). Read this book now while you still can. It's so much fun, it will surely be illegal soon."
—**P. CASEY MORGAN, DEVELOPMENT DIRECTOR, KWSG, NPR AFFILIATE, TULSA, OK**

"*A Farewell to Legs* is a marvelous ride from a New Jersey high school reunion to the solution of a politician's demise in Washington DC. Cohen writes a funny and touching novel that will keep you guessing to the end. His portrayal of the 'normal American family' is one of the best I've ever read in a mystery novel. Give yourself a double treat . . . read *For Whom the Minivan Rolls* (his first book) and *A Farewell to Legs*!"
—**BONNIE CLAESON, CO-OWNER, BLACK ORCHID BOOKSTORE, NEW YORK, NY**

"Jeffrey Cohen is a funny man, and behind the wisecracks there's a clever and engaging mystery. The pun also rises."
—**DANIEL STASHOWER, AUTHOR, HARRY HOUDINI MYSTERY SERIES**

"When I reviewed *For Whom the Minivan Rolls* on DL, I asked if there really are true-life dads like the fictional Aaron Tucker. Now, can you believe a dad who lets his family get a dog?! *A Farewell to Legs* is an excellent next book in the Aaron Tucker series. The title pun was almost more than I could handle without choking. The mysteries (there are several) range from the outrageous to the more outrageous. I found the solution to the stink bomb problem especially amusing. And Aaron's declaration to Abby on the subject of Ms. Cleavage should be included in the repertoire of all happily married people, or those who desire to be happily married. Read this. You'll like it."
—**DorothyL Moderator Diane K. Kovacs, aka Harriet Vane**

"Reluctant sleuth and writer Aaron Tucker is back and still trying not to get involved in murder investigations. This time, he goes to his high school reunion, only to find the best looking woman from his class determined to get what she wants from him. As Aaron is hopelessly in love with his wife, he is not at all disappointed that Stephanie Jacobs Gibson wants him to find out who murdered her husband. Stephanie pulls some strings to get Aaron hired by *Snapdragon* magazine to do some investigative reporting on the case . . . All is told with a lot of humor, and. . . enough zingers and funny lines for my taste. I'm looking forward to the next in the series."
—**Deadly Pleasures Magazine (Maggie Mason)**

"In *A Farewell to Legs*, Cohen hasn't lost his magic touch for snappy, believable dialogue, and for perfectly capturing all the nuances of family life in suburbia. Aaron Tucker and his family could be your neighbors, if you're lucky enough to have particularly delightful neighbors. Once again, there are laughs on almost every page, but the humor is never forced and the characters are never over the top. (A certain best-selling author of humorous mysteries could take lessons from Jeffrey Cohen.) Best of all, the humor doesn't overshadow the mystery—Cohen doesn't sacrifice plot or suspense while making us laugh. Those who read *For Whom the Minivan Rolls* won't need any encouragement to pick up *A Farewell to Legs*. Those who missed Cohen's inaugural effort are in for a real treat when they meet Aaron Tucker, his friends, and his family in this latest entry in the series. And after reading *A Farewell to Legs*, everyone will be eager for Aaron's next adventure!"
—**Reviewing the Evidence (Susan Anderson)**

"The best thing about Cohen's books is Aaron Tucker himself. A non-stop wisecracker who refuses to take anything seriously, Aaron is the type of everyman whom readers can relate to and commiserate with. He's our best friend, our neighbor, or even our husband. Unlike many of the tough-talking, hardheaded detectives that perpetuate fiction today, Aaron is someone we could easily know or be. It's also refreshing to have our hero be a stay-at- home dad whose wife makes more money than he does and who doesn't seem to think that cleaning up after dinner is beneath him. The lightheartedness of the book is also a joy. While many mystery books often leave us frightened of the way the world is today, Cohen's books leave us with a smile and a feeling of gratefulness for what we have. Not only is there a chuckle on every page, but there's a smile or a tongue-in-cheek observation in every paragraph. Cohen has definitely created a goldmine with his Aaron Tucker mysteries. With each book, he'll gain more loyal readers like this one. We can only hope that his hero stays around for a long time and that his creator graces us with many more books to come."

—BEST REVIEWS (ANGELA McQUAY)

"I enjoyed *A Farewell to Legs* more than I expected to . . . The best parts of this book, which was a very pleasant surprise, and the best parts of its predecessor in the series, are the pieces dealing with Aaron Tucker's home life—dealing with his kids on a daily basis, and what middle-class life is really like these days. The shlub-married-to-a-goddess wears thin after a while, but Abby calls him on it in this book, and does a good job of it. There is less detail in *Legs* about life with a child who has Asperger's Syndrome than there was in *Minivan*, but still enough so that the reader knows that Ethan is even more of a challenge than a 'normal' early adolescent male child might be. And, on his daughter, who's so close to a neighbor's child, Cohen has this kind of relationship down pat, and writes the hell out of it. *Minivan* is good. *Legs* is better."

—REVIEWING THE EVIDENCE (P.J. COLDREN)

"Aaron Tucker is an immensely likable guy, loving husband, devoted father, and not a super detective, but hey, he gets the job done. Jeff Cohen's portrayal of Aaron's son, a pre-teen with Asperger's Syndrome, is at times hilarious, at others poignant, and in every case accurate. Having some experience with this in my own family, I really appreciate the way Jeff is able to enlighten the public about this subject by weaving it into his story. He knows whereof he speaks. I hope Aaron will have many more adventures. Keep it coming, Jeff. We need the laughs."

—SHIRLEY WETZEL, MYSTERY MAGAZINE ONLINE,
RICE UNIVERSITY LIBRARIAN, AND AVID MYSTERY READER

"It's not often that I gloat, but I recently got an ARC of *A Farewell to Legs*, and read it before most everyone. It's another very entertaining read from Jeff Cohen. This man is definitely not suffering from a sophomore slump.

Jeff writes in one of my favorite sub-genres, the realistic suburban mys-, tery, with a stay-at-home dad and a family as well as a mystery to solve. *Legs* deals with a sleazy right-wing politician who is murdered in his mistress' bed. The wife went to HS with Aaron Tucker and asks him to investigate as part of a freelance magazine assignment that she arranges. Add to the mix threatening notes, a stink bomb crisis at the school, and a new dog in the house, and you have a great mystery and a great time figuring out whodunit. *A Farewell to Legs* is another witty winner from Jeff Cohen—a wry, yet dead-on, look at suburban life combined with a mystery full of unexpected twists. Definitely pick up a copy of your own when it comes out in November."

—**JEFFREY MARKS, AUTHOR OF THE US GRANT MYSTERIES,
AND NON-FICTION BOOKS ABOUT MYSTERY WRITERS**

"Cohen's wit sparkles from every page, some lines provoking mere smiles while others are laugh-out-loud funny. Wonderful humor, terrific writing, and an intriguing mystery—what more can a discerning reader ask for? Highly recommended."

—**GLORIA FEIT, 4MYSTERYADDICTS**

"Where but in an Aaron Tucker mystery would you find a dangerous pet lizard, several potent stink bombs, a guy with a kitchen knife sticking out of his chest, and a primer on how to register your screenplay with the Library of Congress? Jeff Cohen's quirky voice happily returns for a second go-round in *A Farewell to Legs*, with Aaron once again assuming the role of free-lance writer/reluctant sleuth. (By the way, there's no truth to the rumor that Abby, Aaron's beloved wife, is really the murderer.)"

—**KEN WALZ, TELEVISION PRODUCER**

"Jeffrey Cohen is the Jerry Seinfeld of mystery writing. Warm, witty and often wise, *A Farewell to Legs* is great entertainment."

—**MARGARET "MEG" CHITTENDEN, AUTHOR,
*DEAD MEN DON'T DANCE, DYING TO SEE YOU,
HOW TO WRITE YOUR NOVEL, AND A WHOLE SLEW OF OTHER BOOKS***

"The last time I reviewed a book by Jeff Cohen, I got carried away with hyperbole—or so I've been told. This time around, I'm going to be circumspect. I'm simply going to say: *A Farewell to Legs* is a delightful mystery romp set among the flora and fauna of suburban New Jersey. My new motto is: calm, cool and collected. Even when I'm crazy about a book! This second novel in Cohen's comically-inspired series expands on the zaniness of the first (*For Whom the Minivan Rolls*) where Aaron Tucker, stay-at-home dad and freelance writer extraordinaire, managed to solve the Madlyn Beckwirth murder. In *Legs*, the oddities of life among the not-so-rich and not-so-famous are again wittily exposed, and the lucky reader is led on another merry chase.

"Using humor as his weapon, Jeff Cohen slices and dices through the pomposities of modern "burb" life. He's quick to point out lunacy, often in laugh-out-loud dialogue, where he finds it. And boy, does he find it! The author is obviously having a great time guiding us through the wacky world of suburbia. Jeff Cohen has done what more seasoned writers have always attempted to do. He has created not only a terrific set of characters, but a specific world for them to live in; a world fully formed, fully fashioned and very appealing. Here, the strength of Tucker's enviable home life, the hub of all his activities, shines brightly through the murder and mayhem. (His continuing romance with wife Abby is particularly delightful.)

"Without preaching or moralizing, Jeff Cohen draws an engaging picture of a centered man, bemused by life. No sap. No clichés. No icky sentiment. Even when he is sent unwillingly on an errand to pick up a little dog from a shelter—a situation where it is almost impossible to avoid sentiment—Tucker's observations never lose their saltiness. Certainly, he is no fool—he knows that real dangers exist—yet his comfortably warped view of the world always helps carry the day. Reading this second book in what I hope will be a long-lived series was like revisiting a good friend. There is strength, comfort and hilarity (not a bad combination!) in Jeffrey Cohen's creation. And therein lies the main attraction of the series. Do yourselves a huge favor and get your hands on the Aaron Tucker books. And buy extras for your friends! Trust me, you will endear yourselves to them. Not to mention, Jeffrey Cohen."

—MYSTERY INK, YVETTE BANEK

"I just finished Jeffrey Cohen's delightful *A Farewell to Legs* and I still have a big grin on my face. What a super book! Once again, Cohen's wit, pacing, and engaging style have combined to create a winning mystery. Truly, this was the funniest—and most fun—book I've read since, well, since his last one! As in his previous book, *For Whom the Minivan Rolls*, Cohen takes the reader along with the witty and humble freelancer/at-home dad/sleuth Aaron Tucker, as Aaron dons his journalist hat and solves yet another 'unsolvable' mystery. The plot has just enough twists and turns to keep the reader guessing, with a surprising and satisfying conclusion. Of course, there are plenty of smiles, chuckles, and guffaws along the way. At the heart of the book is the relationship between Aaron and his wife Abby, a realistic and all-too-rare portrayal of a happy marriage. Throw in two interesting kids and an accident-prone dog, and what comes out is a family that the reader wants to spend time with and get to know even better. If I could buy stock in a person, I'd pick up a few hundred shares of Jeffrey Cohen. I predict nothing but great things for this series and for this author!"

"A very enjoyable. fast-paced romp, with mystery and humor in equal measure, *A Farewell to Legs* is up to the high standard set by *Minivan*."

"A very enjoyable, interesting, and entertaining mystery. The plot is complex enough to keep you guessing. The family situations presented in Aaron's day-to-day life are so identifiable. The humor injected by the author makes this book different from a lot of mysteries. Most folks will love it."

"If you're wondering what sort of protagonist Aaron Tucker is, think William Powell in *The Thin Man*, but with a modern-day twist: soccer dad, married to a career woman, with children. Aaron Tucker is not your ordinary soccer dad. He's out there solving murders while juggling kids in school, marriage, and job. This book was filled with plenty of humor. I'm definitely looking forward to his next outing."

"Prepare to chuckle! Jeffrey Cohen's second Aaron Tucker mystery is packed with humor, realism, and exciting twists. A FAREWELL TO LEGS, a riotously funny cozy, may be my introduction to Aaron Tucker, but I feel as if I have known him for half of my life. I'd never heard of Jeffrey Cohen before, but I felt right at home with this book and now I am anxious to catch up with his adventures in FOR WHOM THE MINIVAN ROLLS. Using wit, Jeffrey manages to portray Aaron and his wife, Abby, as any couple should be. Sarcasm may fill their dialogue at times, but their love for one another is undeniable. I only wish Jeffrey Cohen could write faster, as I don't think I could ever tire of his characters."

"Take equal parts Mel Brooks, Groucho Marx, and Woody Allen. Sweeten with enlightened sexual politics. Mix well with the completely original mind of Jeffrey Cohen. And laugh yourself silly over *A Farewell to Legs*. Aaron Tucker is a delightful, twenty-first century twist on the usual amateur gumshoe, and the lunatic doings of his friends and foes make for sheer reading pleasure."

ABOUT THE AUTHOR

Jeffrey Cohen has been a full-time freelance writer/reporter for 16 years, and has written more than 20 feature-length screenplays. His work has been published in *The New York Times, TV Guide,* and *Entertainment Weekly,* among many others, and his screenplays have been optioned by Jim Henson Productions, CBS, and Gross-Weston Productions, among others. His Aaron Tucker series has been optioned for film and television by Michael Sullivan Productions.

A graduate of Rutgers, he lives in New Jersey, with his wife and two children.

A Farewell to Legs is his second novel, a follow-up to Aaron Tucker's debut in *For Whom The Minivan Rolls.*